Through A Glass Darkly

Peggy Merritt

ISBN: 0615701124
ISBN-13: 978-0615701127

Treehaus Press
PO Box 91865
Austin, TX 78709

cover photo of the Marshall County Historical
Society in Marysville, Kansas: Regan Brown

CHAPTER 1

The lady at the Pony Express Museum was right, Briana decided as she steered Red Baby east on Center Street. There were plenty of historic sites to observe as she traveled on the old red-bricked surface. She glimpsed ornate Victorian homes down the tree-shaded side streets; some, according to the museum brochures, were open for tours. Briana knew she wouldn't have time to stop today, but Marysville wasn't that far from Topeka. Maybe she could come back.

Just ahead on the right loomed a tall, red building with a huge tower reaching toward the sky. From out of nowhere, Briana felt a shudder race through her body. She reflexively braked, causing the driver behind her to honk his horn. The closer she got to the structure, the more her heart pounded. She pulled over to the curb about a half block away, hoping the reaction would pass, then closed her eyes and leaned forward onto the steering wheel.

Was she sick? No, she had felt fine at the Pony Express barn. What was going on? Maybe she should have eaten breakfast? She raised her head and looked at the old building again; as she did, she felt as if she had been struck a physical blow. This building was frightening her to the point of terror, and she began to tremble as chills engulfed her body. Perspiration broke out at the same time. Each breath became a desperate gasp for air.

What is wrong with me? she wondered as she closed her eyes once more, blocking out everything while asking God for help.

She needed to reason this out and come up with a logical explanation for what was happening. Raising her eyes to the sinister building, she felt the cold grip of fear invade her again. *Okay, it's the building,* she concluded. She had never seen it before, so why was she having this strange sensation, this pain, this terror? Why would a building frighten her so much that she could do nothing but sit rigid in her seat, afraid even to drive away? It was like a nightmare, and she couldn't wake up. She'd had nightmares as a child, but not even her parents could pinpoint what set them off. She had outgrown them, and she knew she wasn't asleep now.

Briana knew what she had to do. She had to confront the big building and lay this ghastly feeling aside. She could do it. Good grief! It was broad daylight in a lazy little town in Kansas. What could possibly hurt her? Shakily she stepped out of the car, then hesitated. *Go on,* she prodded herself. *You have to do it!* She closed the car door, leaving her keys and purse, not even giving a thought to locking it. She had to get closer.

Maybe she had seen a building like this when she was a child and her parents would remember. But why would it scare her? She knew one thing for sure—there was no possible way she could have seen this building before. She had never traveled east of the Rockies.

She was close enough now to read the sign out front. It was now a museum, but for eighty-seven years it had been the Marshall County courthouse. The word JUSTICE was etched in huge letters above the entrance. She gazed up once more to the towering heights. The roof was slate, with the tower capped in copper.

She was shaking again. Déjà vu was not something Briana could accept as a Christian—she rejected any belief in past-life experiences. But what was this feeling? She wasn't a fanciful person who indulged in emotional drama. Who had time for that while carrying a full course load and working to pay the tuition? Even during law school, she had worked a few hours a week to avoid huge loans.

Yet this trembling fear was beyond her comprehension. She turned to escape to her car and drive away from this emotional scene, but somehow she couldn't make herself leave. Squaring her shoulders, she spun to face the building one more time. Just two steps later, tears began trickling down her cheeks as she broke down again. She felt lost and vulnerable.

"I don't have to stand here and be frightened. I don't have to tell anyone about this, either," she muttered to herself. Retracing her steps to the refuge of Red Baby, she left town and picked up Highway 99 at Frankfort, following it south to Interstate 70.

With iron control, she forced herself to concentrate on the road. She was tired from her journey and apprehensive about the new job. Perhaps that was the real reason for all this nonsense. She would get a motel first, then eat. She hadn't eaten any real food all day—only some stale cookies. Maybe dinner should come first. Even this simple process of planning helped her feel more in control. She needed to call her parents and let them know she had arrived. She wouldn't worry them with her experience in Marysville.

Physically, Briana still felt wounded and bruised. Her emotions were playing havoc with her conscious reasoning. Tears were just seconds away and all the diversionary thinking in the world wasn't helping.

Signs advertising motels and restaurants led her to turn off Interstate 70 onto Wanamaker Road in Topeka, where a truck stop called The Roost appeared on the right. She wheeled Red Baby into the parking lot and went in for dinner.

A friendly waitress seated her at a corner booth and told her about their food bar. It was the best food she'd ever eaten, or maybe she was just starving. Briana was very tired, yet she had driven fewer miles that day than the others. She could see a motel across the street and decided to spend the night there. Picking up her check, she went up to the cash register to pay for her meal, but the redheaded hostess behind the counter said, "Miss, your bill has been paid."

"Paid? How can that be? I don't know anyone here. I'm from California."

The hostess snapped her gum and flashed a broad smile. "Here's a note for you."

The note was written on a white paper napkin and said, "God be with you, Angel." The rest of the surface was covered with names. Tears welled up in Briana's eyes as she turned to look for the truckers, but found none.

"They left earlier," the hostess said as she leaned forward over the counter with a smile. "Friends of yours?"

"Good friends," she replied, suddenly feeling welcome in her new town.

That evening after her shower, she called her folks and told them what they wanted to hear. Her trip was fine, no car trouble, and Topeka looked like a nice town. She did not mention her flat tire, the events with the truckers, or the strange emotions that had flooded her in Marysville. If she didn't talk about it, perhaps she could convince herself that it had never happened.

CHAPTER 2

At 8:30 the next morning, Briana parked Red Baby on the street outside the fourteen-story Santa Fe Railroad office building. Trying not to be nervous, she looked at the letter in her hand, which instructed her to check in with Mr. Volke in room 240 at 9:00 a.m. She had chosen to wear a full, flowered skirt. Her sleeveless black shell picked up the black background of the skirt, and when she added her wine-colored jacket that matched some of the floral patterns, it made a striking ensemble; not too formal, not too casual.

Ricardo Volke welcomed her and thanked her for checking in. He said, "Officially, you'll start Monday." He took her up to the fifth floor where she would be working.

"This is Shelly Wyatt," he said, introducing Briana to a peppy-looking blonde girl at the reception desk.

Before he could even complete the introduction, Shelly popped out of her chair and came around the desk to pump Briana's hand. Mr. Volke cleared his throat authoritatively, but Shelly began telling Briana how glad she was to meet her, and how Briana was just going to love Topeka. "We've been counting the days until your arrival! Frank is anxious to meet you in person. I guess you guys talked a lot on the phone!" Briana was smiling, trying to follow Shelly's fast speech.

Then Mr. Volke grumbled, "Miss Wyatt, will you please be quiet?"

"Only until you leave," Shelly retorted, as she winked at Briana and blew a kiss to Mr. Volke. Briana had to chuckle. Mr. Volke's face flushed as he straightened his shoulders, trying to regain his reserve. He guided Briana to an inner office to meet the rest of the crew, including Frank Bartlett, her telephone contact.

Frank starting out by complimenting her outfit effusively. "We aren't used to California elegance like yours around here!" His open admiration embarrassed Briana to the point of blushing. Mr. Volke didn't miss a second of her discomfort, no doubt thinking it was justified because she had chuckled at him. His tone was gruff as he explained, "You'll be working directly with Kyle Cramer until he has surgery. He's having tests run today, but I can show you the priority case he's working on."

Mr. Volke opened his mouth to continue, but Frank came around the metal desk and opened a door to an adjoining office.

"Your desk will be in this office," Frank said. "You'll be assisting Kyle until you pass the Kansas bar, then you'll probably be assigned an executive office somewhere. Kyle is in pretty bad shape. They know he will have to have surgery, but they haven't scheduled him yet. We'll know today when he calls the doctor."

Mr. Volke was nodding while Frank explained. He turned to Briana and said, "Guess I'll leave you in Frank's capable hands." With a flash of bad humor he added, "Watch the 'hands' part, okay?" He laughed knowingly and nudged Frank with his elbow.

Briana smiled stiffly at the unprofessional pun as she sensed already that this whole atmosphere was going to be slanted for the new Quota Queen. She had fought that enough when she was hired as a special agent for the Santa Fe Railroad in San Francisco. The good old boys, who had years of seniority, loved to set her up with things they thought she'd fail to handle. True, the company had been forced to include some women in the department, but she had proved herself there and was confident she could do it here.

Frank gave her a quick tour of the building, introducing her to people she would be dealing with on her new job. "You'll probably be doing some research on the Marshall County case," he explained. "The railroad is terminating service on a spur line up there, and the farmers are having a fit. They hired a hotshot lawyer to do battle for them, so it could get messy. At any rate, Kyle will need some legwork done, and with a set of legs like yours you'll put a whole new meaning to the phrase!" He patted her back and laughed, leaning in close to her face. Briana must have reflected her displeasure because he curtailed his laughter and quickly said, "Don't mind me. I'm just so glad you're finally here. You are just beautiful!"

"I'm sure you say that to all the new lawyers!" Briana's voice was icy, and Frank knew right then he had blown it. Trying to make amends, he said, "I have reservations for us for dinner at the Plantation House, Saturday night. I'd like to welcome you to the Midwest."

"Frank, I want to be up front with you so you don't feel like you're being rejected on a personal level, but I just don't date co-workers. That has always been my practice and I don't intend to change for anyone. We talked about this on the phone, if you recall."

She felt a twinge of guilt because she had actually contemplated dating him. He had seemed so friendly in their long-distance conversations. She could tell he was displeased, but he shrugged his shoulders and said, "You'll probably change your mind when you know me better." With that, he delivered her back to Shelly Wyatt with instructions that Shelly help get her settled.

Shelly, with a twinkle in her eye, informed Briana that it was break time and promptly guided her to a small lunchroom equipped with coffee maker, vending machines, and a microwave oven. There were four tables with brightly colored plastic and chrome chairs, and the view from the large windows gave Briana an opportunity to look out over her new city. She was surprised to see the Capitol Building standing so close, its green dome towering above all other buildings.

"Bet Topeka seems like a hick town after living in California," Shelly said as she inserted money into the soda machine.

"I think I'll like it. I wasn't all that sold on bumper-to-bumper cars and heel-to-toe people, anyway. The air was full of smog, too. I'm going to enjoy waking up in the morning and seeing blue skies and sunshine. But I'll miss the mountain views."

"Wait till winter hits before you brag on our weather. You'll be in for a real thrill when the blizzards begin. What kind of pop do you want? My treat!" Briana assumed that "pop" was the Midwestern term for soda. She decided that she liked her outgoing co-worker as they got acquainted while sipping their drinks.

Shelly wiped the moisture from her Coke can with a paper napkin, then glanced up at Briana. "Frank is a nice guy, she began," then paused. "You shouldn't get involved too fast, but of course, it's none of my business. You can do as you please." The longer she talked, the faster she talked and finally Briana burst into peals of laughter.

"What you're saying in plain English is—he's a jerk!"

They were both roaring with laughter when Frank came through the door.

"So who's minding the store?" Shelly asked. "I told you we were going to take a break."

"Kyle came in, so I thought I'd just join you in welcoming our new attorney. I see you have a drink, but I could get you some of those cookies in the machine? They're pretty good. Fresh, too."

"Thank you, Frank, but I'd like to meet Kyle now and see what he needs me to do." Briana stood up and smoothed down her colorful skirt. The gesture was not missed by Frank, which made Shelly laugh out loud once more.

"What's so funny?" Frank asked, looking from one to the other.

"Nothing, Frank! Take Briana back to the office while I step out to the ladies' room." She pitched her can into the recycle barrel and left.

"We don't have to hurry back. Sit with me while I have my break, okay?" Frank was smiling so sweetly that Briana almost wavered. But remembering her talk with Shelly, she decided to leave Frank on his own.

This isn't going very well, Briana thought as she left the break room. She suspected she had been hired on the merit of her gender, not her genuine strengths. And already she had possibly aggravated two of the men at her new office. She could have easily stayed a few minutes with him, yet she couldn't justify socializing in the lunchroom when she should be discussing her new job with Kyle.

Kyle Cramer rose to greet her when Shelly ushered Briana into his large office. He had to be at least six-foot-seven, towering over Briana by nearly a foot. He seemed quite robust for someone in such bad health. His blue eyes were sharp and friendly; his handshake firm and secure.

"Happy to meet you, Miss Sheldon. I'm thrilled to welcome you to our team. I was very pleased at the company's choice on this position," he said. "Perhaps you've heard that this job was slated for a woman and that's the lone reason you were selected. That's not true. There were four male candidates who did not measure up to your expertise. Have a seat and I'll brief you on the case you need to start with." He pulled a black leather chair closer to his desk and Briana sat down.

"I was hoping my tests would prove that I wouldn't need to have surgery. That's not the case. In fact, I'm scheduled for surgery Monday at 8 a.m., and the doctors wouldn't hear my plea to put it off. I'm confident they know best, of course!"

"How long will you be in the hospital?" Briana asked.

"Possibly two weeks, depending on what they find. It eases my mind knowing you'll be here to keep my desk clear of backlog."

Briana wondered if that was why he was having heart problems. People no doubt came to him at all hours of the day and night, and over the years it had taken its toll. She made a mental note to keep some time to take care of herself. Once she found a place to live, she'd have to find a nearby karate school. Or perhaps she should look for one near the office.

Kyle told her about the spur line that was being closed up north, then went over some minor issues that would need to be dealt with immediately.

"I'll leave you to do some research for me. There is a preliminary meeting being called for next Friday at the Merchants Bank building here in town. Shelly has the details and will get you there for that. I'll go over my notes with you in a minute. Their lawyer already has documents from the railroad specifying why it's necessary to shut down the spur and also the date of closure. The farmers aren't pleased about this, but we're losing money. The Santa Fe officials get nervous when they lose money."

"Does this kind of thing happen very often?" Briana asked.

"It's more common nowadays with modern technology," Kyle said. "We try to help the people affected find alternate routes or other methods of transportation for their products. I might warn you that their lawyer, Tyler Rainger, is the son-in-law of the man who is fighting the closure. Dolan Roswald and the rest of his dynasty run Marshall County. Marysville has had a Roswald in a city office since the town was founded. But then, you probably don't even know where the town is located."

He opened his mouth to continue, then looked at her and asked, "Are you okay?"

This was bizarre, Briana thought. She had planned on blocking that town out of her mind forever, and here she was taking on a case from there and becoming involved with the family who ran it!

"I'm fine," she answered. "I actually do know where it is. I came down that way when I arrived. Kansas has some quaint little towns." She was thinking that Marysville wasn't one of them, and the mere thought of it sent her mind scurrying to block the memory.

After the meeting with Kyle, Shelly helped Briana get settled and worked with her the rest of the morning, familiarizing Briana with briefs and reports about the spur line.

Over lunch, Shelly asked Briana where she was going to live.

"I really want to rent a house. I've lived in apartments all the time I've been away from home, so now I want to plant flowers, mow my lawn, and sit out on a big front porch with a glass of iced tea and watch the grass grow!"

"Have you looked at any ads since you've been here? I can tell you what areas are the best. Also, you shouldn't go looking at night by yourself. Our town is pretty safe, but—well, I guess you know the dangers of the big city better than me!" Briana decided this was not the time to tell Shelly about the job in Richmond or about the drug bust.

"I might just rent an apartment until I find the right house," she said. "I don't want to be pressured into taking a house just to get out of the motel. Also, I can wait until I find the perfect house before I have my stuff shipped. It's amazing all the junk I managed to collect, even living in an apartment. I miss that stuff already."

Shelly laughed and agreed how important stuff was to the average girl.

"Why don't you stay with me until the right house comes along?" Shelly raised her hand and added, "I know we've just met, but I feel we are going to be good friends. I would love it. Don't give me your answer now. Just come over and have dinner with me tonight and I'll fix my famous spaghetti and meatballs."

Briana couldn't help but feel a warm friendship for this openly spontaneous girl, who looked as kooky as she acted. Her hair was a mass of contrasts, teased and spiked then sprayed stiff with something that looked like lacquer. She was slightly plump, looking heavier because of the gathered material in her dress. Her eyes were her greatest feature. They were soft green with a dark ring around the iris, and very expressive. Yes, they were going to be good friends.

CHAPTER 3

Shelly welcomed Briana into her bright, cheery apartment that evening and gave her a quick tour. The front room was large and roomy, and a sliding glass door off the adjacent dining room led to a small patio. The kitchen was tiny, but the two bedrooms were average size. On the wall of the guest bedroom Shelly had tacked up a huge sign saying "Bri's new pad!" in big pink letters. It almost brought tears to Briana's eyes.

"Shelly, are you sure about this? You don't know anything about me. I could be a real slob!"

Shelly laughed, "I'm not Miss Perfect by a long shot, but we can work on the place on the weekends. Of course, you'll have dates and I'll just stay home and do all the work like Cinderella!" She was pouting and looked totally rejected, which made Briana explode with laughter.

"Like I have a string of men in my life! I don't even know anyone here and I'm pretty picky about who I date. I'll plan on helping you clean, if that's okay!"

"I'm so glad you're here!" Shelly's arms went around Briana in a big bear hug. "You can be my sister! I've always wanted one. Shoot, as few relatives as I have, I'd be glad for anyone!"

Briana raised one eyebrow and said, "Thanks—I think!" She added, "I promise not to stay any longer than necessary, and we'll make some rules first so I won't cause you any problems."

"First we have to eat!" Shelly said. "I have the table set in the dining room because you're company tonight, but that will change. From now on, we'll eat in the kitchen like family. Do you cook?"

"Sure. I've been on my own for a while and Mom made sure I could cook before I left home. Of course she's the best, but I do have a few good meals I can fix. Nothing too fancy, though." Briana opened a paper sack she had left by her purse before they toured the apartment. "I brought a bottle of wine to go with the spaghetti."

"Oh, how perfect! Let me get the tossed salad out of the refrigerator, and we'll be ready to eat. The bread is in the oven. Want to grab it for me? The pot holders are there by the sink."

The meal was superb, and Shelly kept Briana laughing with funny stories and jokes. She was like a breath of fresh air.

"So tell me about this spur line conflict," Briana said. "What will I need to know before the meeting next Friday? I know you probably don't want to talk work on your evenings off, but I'd like to know some of the personal side of this. Mr. Rainger is related to this Roswald man who's contesting the closure? A son-in-law, I think was what Kyle said."

Shelly closed her eyes and swooned. "He's the dreamiest dish I've ever seen. He's just a year older than me, thirty-one. Tall, dark-brown hair, and those gray eyes—well all I can say is I wish he were mine!"

Briana laughed. "I doubt if his wife would share. But thirty-one is pretty young to have the reputation of being a hotshot lawyer, isn't it?"

Shelly pondered this for only a second then said, "First of all, his wife died and second, you just wait until you meet him and you'll sense a certain something special about him. He's very smart, but also a good man. I don't really know him all that well, but Tom works with him at their law firm here in town."

Shelly's eyes widened a bit as she exclaimed, "But you don't know about Tom, either!"

Briana smiled. "You're going to tell me, right?"

Shelly looked doubtful and said, "I might."

"Tell me! Tell me!" Briana hurried her. "You've been keeping secrets. Is this a clandestine love affair?"

"Actually, we met at our church singles group. We attended the same high school, but never met because he was a couple of grades ahead of me. Anyway, we had a lot in common so we started dating. If I can't have Tyler Rainger, I guess I could settle for Tom."

"Shelly, that's a horrible thing to say! How would you like to know you're second best?"

Shelly looked pensive for a second then said sadly, "I've always been second best. All my life."

Briana sensed acute pain coming from her new friend and gleaned a bit of insight into why this girl was so vivacious. She had been hurt, deeply hurt, at some point in her life. Briana thought of her ex-fiancé Jim and remembered afresh what hurt and betrayal felt like.

"So you met Mr. Rainger through Tom? How does Tom get along with him? Are they friends or rival lawyers?"

"Tom is Tyler's assistant. Kind of what Frank is to Kyle, only Tom is taking night school courses to become an attorney. Frank is good at what he does, but nowhere near Tom's caliber of brilliance. Of course, Tom has the experience of working with the best!"

"If Tyler Rainger is the best, how will the Santa Fe ever win?"

Shelly laughed. "He isn't God, you know! It's the Santa Fe's spur. They can close their own spur line or do whatever they can to sell it off. The farmers are pretty hot about it all, and since Tyler has a farm in that area, and is related to the Roswalds, he would be their first choice of legal assistance."

"If this Tyler has a farm up near Marys...ville..." Brianna stumbled over the mere name of the place! "Why does he practice law in Topeka?"

Shelly began picking up the dirty dishes while she answered Briana's question.

"Because there's more business here. And of course he'll probably go into politics before long, according to Tom. Anyway, he owns his own plane, so he can fly home in just over a half hour. He has a couple who live there fulltime as housekeeper and foreman."

Briana collected some of the dishes and followed Shelly to the kitchen. "How do you know so much about him?"

"I ask questions, silly. How else do you get information you need?"

"You mentioned your church. What denomination is it?"

"It's a great church, but not one of those big, stuffy kinds," Shelly said. "It's a large church building with just us common parishioners in it. We are more the down-to-earth, 'Praise the Lord' sort of people."

Briana began to laugh. "If ever I were curious about a church, a statement like that would definitely catch my interest! Guess I'll have to go with you and check it out. My family is Presbyterian."

"Well, we certainly won't hold that against you," Shelly promised as she loaded the dishwasher. "In fact, Tyler and one of the Roswald women came to church on Easter. Tom said she's stalking Tyler now that he's free. It must really be tough to be that popular!"

The word "stalking" made Briana think of her experiences, first with Jim when she broke off their engagement, then later with the drug dealers who had crossed her path. It had been difficult, but the infamous Tyler probably didn't feel that way about the women vying for his attention.

"I bet he just takes it in stride," Briana said. "Being popular isn't really his fault, I suppose. Imagine how he feels being sought after for his looks and position, not for himself. Maybe he hates it."

Shelly shrugged her shoulders. "Tom says he's such an honest person that people in general are drawn to him. He has a sense of compassion for mankind. Me, I'm more interested in his passion for my kind!"

Briana burst out laughing. "Whoa there, tiger woman. Remember Tom! Is this relationship serious?"

Shelly turned, plate in hand, and sobered instantly. "Oh Bri, I'm afraid to care. I've been hurt and disappointed before and I'm not going to let it happen again. Tom was married shortly after he graduated from high school, and his marriage failed bigtime. He's gun-shy like me. We're 'just friends' right now." They both laughed at that.

Briana said, "That was what Frank said we'd be—just friends! I do feel bad that he read more into our phone conversations than I intended. I hope we can work well together, but I told him I wouldn't date him. He's behaved like a perfect gentleman lately. Is there a chance he and his wife will patch things up?"

Shelly shook her head. "She took the girls and moved to New York. I think she has someone else living with them back there. Frank is rather secretive about it and that's okay. He deserves better and he loves the girls. I pray for him every day."

Briana enjoyed the chance to spend the evening with her new friend and learn more about the people and community around her. Before turning in for the night, the women arranged to go to church Sunday.

After the service, with the Sunday ads in hand, Briana began a serious search for a house to rent. Shelly took the wheel of Red Baby and they cruised around some of the areas where the listings were located.

"People are going to think I'm a spy," Shelly teased. "A hot little red Firebird with 007 for a license plate should definitely turn a few heads. I bet this car could tell some secrets!"

Briana laughed at how close Shelly was to the truth. "Red Baby is not a car, she's a friend. We've been through a lot together! I've been teased about her ever since I got the license plate. It seemed fitting when I was a railroad agent. I guess, I should get a new one, now that I'm in a new profession."

"Don't change it!" Shelly said. "A blonde James Bond—wow! It fits you."

"Coming through Donner Pass on my way out of California, some truckers thought they could have some fun with my plates and me." Shelly turned briefly and caught Briana's expression. "It appears it didn't bother you very much," Shelly said.

"As a woman driving such a sporty car, I expected to get noticed, but the plates were just the icing on the cake." Briana chuckled recalling her father's frustration. "I could hear the trucker's chatter on my CB," she continued. "The guys were getting a little out of hand."

"What were they saying?" Shelly asked.

"It was hard to understand them at first. They sounded like Festus on the old *Gunsmoke* reruns." That made Shelly giggle.

"One of them saw me as he passed and got on the radio telling the whole trucking fleet that '007' was headed east. He even gave out the mile post where I was, and he told the whole world about my Red Baby and the 'sexy blonde' at the wheel."

Shelly turned for a second. "Well, go on!"

"He told anyone listening that 007 was traveling east on 80. I had reached over to turn off the CB when a man came on the air and told them they could be talking about his daughter. He suggested they change the subject and leave the girl alone."

"Wow! Did they really?"

"Yes, they did. In fact, they kind of took me under their wings. I had a flat tire in Wyoming and truckers stopped to help me."

Shelly began to laugh. "Oh man, I should be so lucky!" She pulled up in front of the next rental on their list.

"These houses sound great in the paper," Briana said as she crossed off the last ad, "but most of them are dumps." She was feeling discouraged.

"The Lord will find you the perfect house when the time's right—trust me!" Shelly responded brightly. "Trust Him!"

Monday at the office was busy. Briana went over Kyle's reports and briefs about Santa Fe's stand on closing the spur. A notice of closure had been filed with the Interstate Commerce Commission on May 14. It stated that due to declining profits and the astronomical expense for general upkeep, plus repairs on bridges that needed to be done and two bridges due to be replaced, the Santa Fe Railroad would close the Blue Valley spur line in Marshall County, Kansas.

The figures were there and the notice was precise and legal. Briana had other notes Kyle had made about a cost analysis as well as salvage prices on the rails. There was good money in salvage, she discovered. Another option was trying to sell the spur to a shortline railroad company, or perhaps a group of farmers. The county government might be interested.

At 10 a.m. Shelly reported that Kyle had come through the surgery and would be in recovery for many hours. "His wife, Sherri, said his full recovery depends on him and a long recuperation time, which means he'll probably be off work all summer. Guess it was a good thing they did the surgery when they did!"

Relieved that Kyle's surgery had gone well, Briana focused on the many facets of her new job. She reviewed a report on an accident at one of their crossings where the plaintiff contended the railroad signal hadn't worked. A landowner was claiming that hazardous waste from a tanker car had been spilled on his property. Railroad signal wires had been stolen right off the poles and the thieves were caught with the stolen wire rolled up in their truck. They claimed, of course, that someone else put the wire in the locked camper shell on their pickup. Clearly, there was plenty of work for her to do.

Frank had decided to start their friendship anew, which made the office more comfortable. He would be a good friend to have, Briana reflected, and she had to accept part of the blame for the misunderstanding of their telephone conversations when she was in California. She hadn't meant to imply they would date, though she had thought about it. But that was only if he were her dream man. He wasn't, and it didn't matter. She was going to be too busy for a social life.

Briana moved into Kyle's office temporarily, which was more convenient and, because of the caseloads, more efficient. The week progressed so fast that it wasn't until Thursday that Briana began to get nervous about the next day's 10 a.m. meeting about the spur.

CHAPTER 4

In honor of the first meeting with the infamous Tyler Rainger, Briana took special care with her attire that morning. She donned a business suit in a navy gabardine material with straight skirt and navy heels. She tried three blouses and finally settled on a soft pink chiffon that left her collarbones exposed. A small gold cross lay gently on her tanned throat. Her gold button earrings added the final touch.

Looking in the mirror, she critiqued her appearance. Her skirt fell just above her knees, as was the fashion. But she worried that her long legs made the skirt seem too short. She had always been coltish; then as a teen it seemed her legs kept growing till she reached her final height of five-foot-eight. How she had longed to be petite like her mom!

Her jacket fit well when standing straight, but when she moved, it pulled taut across her breasts. Her thick hair, if left down, made her look too young and immature so she coiled it up in a bun at the back of her head. A few tendrils had already worked free and hung down by her ears.

Briana was dreading this meeting like the plague. Her co-workers had warned her that Tyler Rainger was a very competitive lawyer, out to make a name for himself. With his striking good looks, he charmed his way through the female judges and jurors when he was in court. Briana wondered if they were envious—it sounded like sour grapes to her. She would make up her own mind.

Briana turned away from the mirror and collected her navy purse, which matched her heels. They had been an extravagant purchase, but hopefully it would give her the confidence she so badly needed. As she reached for her burgundy split-leather briefcase, she once again checked the mirror. Perhaps she should have braided her hair? A few more strands were threatening to come loose.

She found herself wondering what the young lawyer would look for in an adversary. Would he just ignore the importance of this preliminary meeting, dismissing her as a woman too new to know anything? This was her chance, and she didn't intend to give this hotshot lawyer the opportunity to look down on her. She felt prepared and confident that she could make the company proud of her. Personally, she dreaded meeting Rainger at all. If only she had been told nothing about him! Shelly could have waited to expound on his attributes as a man.

The bright blue eyes that looked back at Briana from the mirror showed a hint of interest she would be hard-pressed to disguise. Her full lips pursed for a second, then smiled back at her nonsense. She was making too much of all this. Perhaps he wouldn't even show up, sending a staff assistant to do the preliminaries.

Later, when the elevator door opened on the sixth floor of the Merchants Bank building, Briana stepped out looking self-assured, but a bit breathless. Shelly was waiting for her in the hall, along with other secretaries and assistants. An older gentleman opened the big oak conference room door and waited for the group to file into the chamber.

"Well, Shelly, what have you done to your hair this time?" began a young man standing next to them.

"Shut up, Tom!" Shelly was always doing things to her hair, according to the office chatter. Today it was blonde, as it had been for two weeks, but Shelly had moussed it to a stiff texture and pulled it up and out into a mass of disarray. The black roots were still visible.

"Bri, this is Tom Johnston, one of Mr. Rainger's assistants. Tom, Briana Sheldon." They shook hands and Briana noticed the usual male interest in her looks. She smiled in response, yet wished he had shown some awe of her position and reputation. Of course, she had neither, so she had better be content with what she got. As the group began to find places at the large mahogany conference table, Briana and Shelly found themselves sitting right in front of the door. Shelly began to get out her steno tablet while Briana sat her leather case on the floor between them. The room was filled with the light-hearted banter of people who had worked together before.

As Briana reached down to pull out her papers, Shelly started to help, knocking them from Briana's hand to fan out in the middle of the doorway.

"I'll get them," Briana whispered, hoping it all went unnoticed. She squatted down on her heels while collecting the truant papers and had all but the last one in her hands, when before her, almost touching her hand, appeared two shiny black shoes. Briana recognized expensive shoes—she had a brother who dreamed of owning just such a pair. Her gaze lifted to the two black pant legs that became visible as a hand at her elbow raised her easily to meet the most beautiful gray eyes she had ever seen.

"Miss Sheldon, I presume?" the deep voice asked. His lips turned up at the edge at her dumbfounded expression. She stuck out her hand to shake his, only to find papers in it. He reached past her to pull out her chair, escorting her back to her seat.

"What a pitiful way to meet one's adversary," Briana thought with red-faced chagrin. From her position when he entered the room, she knew he had seen an ample portion of her stocking-clad legs. She tugged at her skirt even now. Briana was aware that he took a place at the end of the big table, but she avoided any eye contact. Shelly was right. He was a very handsome man, but probably knew it and expected every woman to grovel at his feet. Her face flamed at the memory of the escapade that allowed him to find her waiting in exactly that position.

Silence fell in the room and the conference began. Briana was impressed with the way the meeting flowed. Santa Fe made an excellent presentation as to why the spur line was closing. However, when Tyler Rainger finished his rebuttal she could understand more clearly how this would affect the farmers. This would not be an easy settlement.

Over lunch that afternoon, Briana tried to hide her feelings from Shelly about the attractive attorney. "Well, what did you think of Tyler?" Shelly asked while they waited for their salads to be served.

"He is good-looking like you said—rather cool, but precise in his dealings. I don't think he respects me as an opponent yet, so I'll have to prove myself and be brilliant!" Briana remembered his probing gray eyes and how her heart had raced at their close encounter. She was not going to share that with anyone. How unfortunate that Kyle had to be hospitalized right now, forcing Briana to be involved with this Marysville case and Tyler Rainger.

Back at the office, she tried not to dwell on the meeting. Shelly had stayed behind to collect the petitions and documents presented by the farmers. That gave Briana time to think about her opinion of their opponent, and to be honest with herself. She had felt Tyler's gaze each time it rested on her. It was intense and unnerving and Briana purposely did not meet it, but she had glanced at him while he was speaking to others and she felt she could watch him unobserved.

Mercy, what charisma! The others at the meeting hung on his every word as he stated the farmers' side of the case, and even Briana felt their fear of the closing. Tyler made it clear that his farmers depended on the spur for their livelihood. They had flourished and made the railroad profitable in the past. Just because some farms had gone through bankruptcy did not mean the railroad should assume the rest would. He presented a good defense with figures and statements.

Briana hoped her report on the railroad's side of it sounded as good. She also had charts and figures, and even the worst businessman in the room could understand that a railroad as big as the Santa Fe would not dream of keeping a spur or station that wasn't profitable. The facts told the story.

Back in the office, Shelly explained to Briana about the upcoming meeting in Kansas City with the officials from the Interstate Commerce Commission. It was a routine hearing and the ICC would be setting one up with the farmers in Marysville, also in a week or two. Briana would be expected to attend both.

She could handle the Kansas City meeting with no problem, but Marysville was a whole different matter. Briana didn't see any way she could enter the town and not see that building. Her stomach churned just thinking about it. Other people would be there and she would have to explain her strange reaction. Maybe say she was ill. What could she say? The sheer terror of this had haunted her for days and she had slept so badly that

Shelly asked if her bed was uncomfortable. Briana explained that she was used to a waterbed, which wasn't a lie. Well, just a little one.

Tuesday of the following week, just three days before the Kansas City meeting, Shelly transferred a call to Briana announcing only that Mr. Rainger was on the line. Then his low, already familiar voice was explaining that since the four of them—Briana, Shelly, Tom, and he—would be going to the Kansas City meeting, he would be willing to drive if that suited her.

Briana was at a loss for words. Was this proper? Two opposing sides traveling together to one common meeting? What should she say? What would Kyle have said? Kyle would probably think like a man, realizing it would save gas and be more efficient. Since Briana had no idea where to find the ICC office, she would surely be a nervous wreck. She decided to be just as gracious as she imagined Kyle would have been. "Thank you very much, Mr. Rainger. Shall we meet at your office?"

"Tom and I will pick you and Shelly up at 8 a.m. in front of your building. This meeting is only a formality, so don't be nervous. It won't take long, either. I'll see you Friday."

The phone clicked in Briana's ear, and she felt a quickening in her body. This thoughtful man did not have to put her at ease, or was he doing this as a ploy to get her off guard? Once again she wished Kyle were here to go in her place, but Kyle would be going home from the hospital about the time of the meeting. He was a very sick man who needed prayers, not worries about work. Briana had him on her daily prayer list along with her folks and the boys, and her school friend Lisa and her family. Shelly was pretty close to the top of the list, too. What a blessing she was.

At about five minutes to eight that Friday morning, Shelly and Briana were waiting on the walk in front of the modern Santa Fe building. When Tyler's shiny, navy-blue Mercedes pulled up to the curb, both Tyler and Tom got out to open the back doors for them.

"There's room in the trunk if you want to stow some of your gear," Tom offered. Briana walked around to the trunk and removed her suit jacket, laying it on top of the men's coats. She had been worried about it being wrinkled by the time she arrived at the meeting.

Tom closed the trunk as Briana entered the car from the street side. Tyler held the door for her, but her heel turned slightly as she stepped into the vehicle, prompting him to catch her elbow. She was so very much aware of him and she hated that feeling. His touch was like an electric shock though her body. She was sure he felt nothing and was careful to hide her reaction. She should have gone with her first instinct and rejected his offer of the ride. But by the time they had reached the turnpike entrance, they were all chatting like old friends, and she felt some of her tension subside.

Tom turned out to be almost as nutty as Shelly, only not in appearance. He looked like the traditional businessman but had a great sense of humor. Shelly had colored her hair again, which was the first subject discussed when the car was in motion. "How do you like your ever-changing roommate?" Tom asked, turning to look at Briana.

"She's great, but she isn't ever-changing," Briana challenged.

They laughed and Tyler said, "She was blonde last time I saw her."

"She had dark hair a month ago!" Tom added, turning to wink at Shelly.

"All right, you guys! You talk like I'm not even here. I don't have to sit here and take this abuse. Tyler just pull over and I'll get out and walk!" Shelly was pretending to be upset but blew it by giggling.

"You love it, Tom," she continued. "Come on, admit it."

"Well, it has done wonders for my image," Tom said. "I was never one to date very much, with school and work keeping me busy, but now I'm seen everywhere with a new girl every week or so. One day a blonde, the next a redhead. All the women chase me now cause they think I'm so popular."

"Yeah, right," Shelly responded in utter disgust. They all laughed.

"What I want to know, Tom, is how you find her in a crowd? I'd have a tough time remembering which gal I brought," Tyler said.

"What is this, Pick on Shelly day?" Shelly demanded, trying to pout, but smiling. "You've only seen me a couple of times, yet here you are criticizing me for being unique." This she directed to Tyler, who was laughing in spite of the jab.

Tom broke in and clarified it all. "You're beyond unique, Shelly. Bizarre is closer." He reached between the soft leather bucket seats and patted her knee. "I used to have problems locating her, Ty. One time she was lost for a half hour at Worlds of Fun. She hid herself from me in broad daylight. Of course, I was looking for a blonde. Any blonde would have done!"

"Watch it, guy. You are skating on thin ice!" Shelly playfully slapped his hand off her knee.

Tyler's laughing eyes met Briana's for a second in the rearview mirror. His broad smile displayed white, even teeth and Briana's smile faded slightly as her heart pounded in her ears. Even when his expressive eyes returned to the highway, she continued to look at him. The gray color was enhanced by his tanned skin and perfect features. His eyebrows were moderately thick and his dark brown hair tended to be unruly. It was longer than most businessmen would wear, but she doubted if he really cared what fashion dictated.

Just then he glanced again at the mirror and met her searching gaze so she looked away quickly, becoming intent on the view from the window. Again, as it had been in the conference room, she felt his eyes each time they rested on her.

Tom began asking her questions about California and her family and Shelly told them about Briana's shiny new car. "She calls it Red Baby and her plates read BRI 007!"

"So we have Ms. James Bond on board today, ladies and gentlemen," Tom said. "We hope you will enjoy the trip and have lots to tell your grandchildren!" They all laughed, even Briana.

She touched lightly on her trip from California. She didn't share any details, and she definitely didn't mention Marysville.

CHAPTER 5

It was a pleasant ride to Kansas City. Tyler had the radio on low, so even during lulls in the conversation they could all relax to music.

The meeting progressed rapidly, just as Tyler had predicted, and the committee scheduled the next meeting for the following week in Marysville. It would allow the farmers and Tyler to state their objections over the closing, and Briana would have to attend.

She shut her eyes for a moment as a picture of that big red building invaded her thoughts. Somehow she would have to come to terms with that while she was up there. Whatever this horrible feeling was, she could not allow it to keep returning and taking control of her.

The foursome decided to stop on the way home at the turnpike service plaza for a late lunch at a handy Burger King. Briana thought the area looked similar to the truck stops she had frequented on her route east. They ordered hamburgers, causing a small argument to break out when the girls insisted on paying for the men's meals, since they were playing chauffeur.

They were almost finished eating when a tall man came around the corner of the divider and walked up to their table. When Briana glanced up, her face lit up with recognition and the others turned to see why.

"Howdy, Angel. How's tricks?" It was Don Stillman, her trucker friend from Laramie.

Tyler stiffened briefly, but Briana stood up and threw her arms around the big man.

"I've been a good girl, Don. Can't be otherwise anymore. Have you been hanging around in any shadows at the truck stops lately?"

"Hey, things are pretty quiet since you left. The boys all miss you."

At this point Briana realized she should introduce her friends, but when she turned to do so, she met Tyler's icy glare. Instead, she turned back to Don.

"Some of the boys bought my first dinner in Topeka, but I didn't see them. When I went to pay for my meal, the hostess said it had been paid by a whole table of truckers, and that made me feel welcome in a hurry."

Don's glance dropped to Tyler. Noting Tyler's interest, he asked, "Just who are you?"

Briana opened her mouth to do introductions when Tyler answered coldly, "My name is Tyler Rainger. How is it you know Miss Sheldon?" The whole atmosphere became alive with friction.

"None of your business, actually." Don answered rudely, in response to Tyler's frozen expression. "What are your intentions with Angel?"

Tyler sat straighter in his seat and probably would have stood up, except Don was too close.

"None of your business," Tyler retorted in a terse, guarded tone.

Briana couldn't decide whether to laugh or smack both men for their macho posturing. Then the big trucker's laughter boomed out across the room. Other truck drivers strolled over until a small crowd gathered. Briana resumed her seat next to Shelly and listened to all the friendly greetings. A couple of the men even reached across Tyler's shoulder to shake her hand.

"We'd better move along," Don said as he put his crumpled hat back on his head. "Remember, Jesus loves you and so do I. We'll be seeing you, and if you ever need help—just get on the CB and give us a holler."

He glanced down toward the others at the table and said, "You are in the presence of one special lady. Don't ever forget that!" With that he gave Briana a loving smile and left. The other men followed, waving until they were out of sight.

"Wow!" Shelly exclaimed as she looked from the truckers to Briana, then to Tyler and Tom as they became engrossed in stacking their cups and papers onto the tray to be discarded. Briana sucked the last of her drink through the plastic straw and glanced up in time to catch an exchange of looks between Tom and Tyler. At one point, Tyler directed his stony look at

Briana, but she made no attempt to explain what had just occurred.

Finally when Tyler could stand it no more, he asked in a his clipped voice, "So, you are one special lady, are you?"

She met his penetrating look and shrugged. "I guess so."

Briana could hardly control the laughter bubbling up inside her. She couldn't imagine what her new friends thought about all that. She'd tell Shelly later, but she'd let Tyler think what he wanted.

As they walked out into the parking lot a group of truckers by the big rigs yelled, "Have a good one, Angel!" and gave her the thumbs-up sign. Briana thought Tyler growled something under his breath but couldn't be sure. The rest of the short ride back to Topeka was very quiet. Shelly continued to give her friend questioning glances; Tom started a couple of conversations, but when Tyler seemed unresponsive he too lapsed into silence. A few times Briana met Tyler's eyes in the rearview mirror and each time looked away. She shouldn't have to explain why there was concern about her safety, she thought. She would find a more opportune time to tell Shelly the whole story. A smile played across her lips as she remembered seeing her trucking friends again. When Briana emerged from the Mercedes in front of the Santa Fe building, she politely thanked Tyler for the transportation. Shelly collected their belongings from the trunk with Tom's help, and the two women ran lightly up the wide marble steps and into the building. Shelly remembered something to tell Tom, so turned and retraced her steps.

Minutes later, as Briana got out the notes from her briefcase, Shelly burst into the office. Closing the big door, she leaned back against it and doubled over with laughter. Briana couldn't imagine what had happened to cause this.

"When I went back to talk to Tom, Tyler had just said, in his cool, correct tone, 'I wonder just how *special* she is?' He said, 'Seems like Ms. Lawyer has a past. The whole darn trucking fleet knows her!' Then they saw me and he shut up. Oh, Briana, it was so funny! Tom asked me if I knew anything about it, but I said no. Are you going to tell me or let me die of curiosity? You told me there were some truckers talking about you on their CBs, but you didn't tell me you'd met them! How did they recognize you?"

"Tonight over dinner I'll go into detail, I promise," Briana said. Shaking her head in disgust she added, "Men! You can't live with them—you can't live without them!"

Shelly snagged a few tissues and went to a small mirror on the wall to repair her makeup. "So what did you think of Tom?" she asked, turning slightly to see Briana's reflection in the mirror.

"You need to stick with him. I'm not totally impressed with your Mr. Rainger, but maybe you see something in him that I don't."

"But isn't he handsome?" Shelly persisted.

"A handsome face sometimes can hide an ugly heart." Briana spoke with conviction, remembering Jim.

He perhaps had spoiled her forever on men. He had been good-looking, personable, and clever, yet also deceitful and cruel.

"I, for one, think Tyler is great, but you're right about sticking with Tom." Shelly giggled and pitched the used tissues into the wastepaper basket like a basketball.

"I think Tyler likes you, that's why he was making such a scene." With that surprising statement, Shelly exited the room.

CHAPTER 6

Later that evening as the girls lounged in the front room with iced tea and cookies, Briana began her tale. Her mind had been working on it since they left work and she was, once again, only going to tell only a portion of the incident. She didn't know Shelly well enough to discuss her broken engagement. That was still a very private, sore subject. Nor would she mention San Francisco.

"Okay, Bri. Why are you so 'special' to these truck drivers? There have to be a jillion truckers on the road every day. How is it that you know them? You told me about the CB chatter, but you didn't see them. If we'd been in your car today and they'd seen your plate I would have understood them recognizing you. But how did they know you when we were in Tyler's car?"

"You're right, but these truckers are not the same guys."

"Good grief! Tyler was right. You must have met them somewhere and somehow you knew them really well."

Briana smiled. "I'll tell you and you can decide. Remember when I told you about the truckers giving me a hard time on my trip to Topeka?"

Shelly said, "Sure, but another trucker told them to quit. Wasn't that the end of it?"

Briana smiled at Shelly's eagerness to hear the story, then tried to think where to start. "My parents were worried about my long drive back here, so Dad marked my route on the map and gave me the normal fatherly advice.

"The fact that I'd been on my own for a few years didn't matter. Being in the same state was one thing, but going across country was a whole different story. My family waved goodbye as Red Baby and I headed up the pass. Mom's homemade cookies and a sack of worms from my brothers were on the front seat and...."

"Worms?" Shelly made a face.

"Candy worms, silly. I love them."

Shelly shrugged her shoulders. "Okay, just get on with the truckers."

"Wendover, Nevada was my first night's stop," Briana remembered. "I have to explain the setting so you can understand how the truckers entered my life." Briana's mind also raced forward to a big red building, but she wouldn't share that with anyone.

"I stopped at Wendover the first night," Briana began, remembering how glad she was that her father had suggested that. "I was tired and needed some gas. I filled my tank and checked into the hotel, then went through the casino to the restaurant at the back of the building. A lot of the customers went for a big buffet on one side of the room, but I decided to just order a hamburger and a salad from the menu. After the meal, I wandered through the casino and put one quarter into the slot machine."

Inwardly, she had wondered if this was the way Jim had started. He was the only man she had ever loved. They had their lives planned and the wedding date was set. She had overlooked his compulsive gambling, thinking that when they were married it would all change. But she hadn't realized he was also hooked on women.

"Earth to Bri! Hello, I'm waiting!" Shelly said.

Pushing away those memories, Briana said, "I-80 was my route the next day. I've never seen land so flat. The Great Salt Lake Desert was surrounded on all sides by snow-capped mountains and the lake itself stretched north as far as I could see. Beside the highway people had written graffiti with stones, bottles, or whatever they could find." Briana could see Shelly getting impatient again, so she went back to her story.

"My friends Lisa and Wendell's home wasn't all that far, but I knew if I went on, I would disturb their whole household arriving so late. Anyway, Dad had suggested I make my next overnight stop at Laramie. By that time I was ready." She recalled how Laramie was nestled below the Medicine Bow mountain range, with the Laramie River winding across the flat valley.

"The motel was clean and close to the highway. The big truck stop next door had a café, so for once I went against Dad's advice. Casinos and truck stops were a taboo, at least, for me."

"What an adventure!" Shelly agreed.

"You have no idea," Briana laughed. "Are you sure you want to know all of this?"

Shelly said, "You can't possibly stop now!"

"Well, I was really hungry, so I stashed my gear and went over to the restaurant. It was dusk when I left the motel, so I decided to drive the short distance. As I pulled Red Baby into a parking place, her beams illuminated a man dodging behind a semi. My training as a railroad agent instantly kicked in, and I watched to see where he went. After a couple of minutes I decided that it was possible he was just a trucker checking his rig and I could have misread his movements. Not everyone who acts suspicious is a criminal.

"I went into the restaurant and chose a booth by the window. The place was full of truckers. I had a delicious dinner and the waitress was chatty.

"Before long, I heard her story. This waitress had a sick boy and tests had suggested he might have leukemia. I told the mother I would pray for her son. Tears welled up in the mother's eyes and she gave me a hug. The men at the nearby table began to joke about sharing hugs until the waitress turned and they saw her tears. They got real quiet.

"It was dark when I came out of the truck stop and crossed the parking lot toward my car. I recalled the guy I had seen earlier in the parking lot and decided I must have been wrong about his intentions. Everything looked normal.

"I was almost to Red Baby when I heard a scuffle. I stopped abruptly and listened. I heard gruff voices that were raised for only a second, then silenced. A truck was parked about thirty feet from me. I couldn't see anything, but I suspected the voices had come from the opposite side. I crouched down and crawled under the trailer. If it were just some truckers' horseplay, I definitely didn't want to be seen, but my instincts told me that it was something criminal.

"I could see two men, but the shadows of the rigs partially hid them. In the dim light, I saw a flash of steel in the hand of the shorter man. He wore dark coveralls, like mechanics wear, and I could see it was a knife, not a wrench, in his hand. The trucker was fishing in his pocket, and a chain glittered as he extracted the wallet connected to it.

"'Hurry up!' the man with the knife growled, looking around.

"I slipped my service revolver out of my purse, then peered out to assess the situation. I stayed as close to the rig as possible and inched my way forward, using the shadows for cover. The man was concentrating on the trucker's wallet and the cash inside, so I was able to move closer. Then the trucker caught sight of me and his glance alerted the thief. At the same instant I leveled my gun and shouted, 'Drop your weapon!' My voice seemed to roar in my ears, but the sharpness of it and the surprise factor worked wonders, giving the trucker a chance to overpower the thief. As the knife hit the blacktop, I moved forward, kicking it away. 'Drop to the pavement!' The other people started to rush over. I guess they heard all the commotion."

"Good grief," Shelly groaned.

"As the first men arrived, one produced a plastic tie and used it to tie the thief's wrists. I checked the restraint, then turned to the big guy who was the target and asked if he was okay.

"'Yes, ma'am. I sure appreciated ya steppin' in like ya did. I'm hoping this here guy is the one who's been making a career out of robbing us. Guess the cops will tell us. They been on his tail, before, but he's been darn smart.'"

Shelly shivered. "Bri, you're crazy! You could have been killed!"

"I've had training for this kind of confrontation and I used it back in San Francisco when I was a special agent for the Santa Fe Railroad. That was my job while I was working on my law degree."

"So you were a special agent for the railroad? Is that like a being a cop? How long did you work there?" Shelly asked.

"Special agents conduct criminal investigations committed on railroad property. I worked out of the Richmond office in California for three years. I had some situations there that prepared me."

Briana noticed Shelly's serious expression as her new friend asked, "That sounds like such an exciting, but scary job. But I guess it was a blessing you had that experience so you could jump into action in Wyoming.

Is the guy locked up now? Does he know who you are? I would have been so terrified!"

"All in a day's work!" quipped Briana to calm her friend. "The trucker who introduced himself to me, Don, told me how several drivers had been victimized by this thief and no one could catch him."

"So did the cops come, or did the truckers take care of him themselves?"

"Shelly have you been reading mystery novels?" Briana laughed, remembering the handshakes, hugs, and smiles from the crowd. "Someone had called 911 and pretty soon the police arrived. I went back and picked up my purse back from where I'd left it under the tractor trailer, knowing I would need ID and my permit for carrying a firearm."

Shelly could stand it no longer, "How boring this lawyer stuff is going to be! You'll crave the excitement and fame, you know you will."

"Excitement isn't always a good thing," Briana responded with a smile. "I went with the officer and Don Stillman to police headquarters to give an account of the crime and details for the report. Manny Crow, the thief, had been holding up truckers for six months. He even killed one man in Arizona when the trucker tried to defend himself."

"Wow, betcha Tyler will be shocked when he hears about this!"

"Shelly, you are sworn to secrecy right now and don't even consider telling Tom. I don't want to get a reputation here as a pistol-packin' mama. I already worry that they think I was only hired to fulfill some quota. This is just between us. Okay?"

"Yeah, us and the whole trucking industry! Are you sure I couldn't just—?"

"No!" Briana hoped that Shelly would keep her confidence because someday Briana might tell her other secrets, like about Richmond and maybe even about Jim. But right now, their relationship was too new. Briana felt she could trust Shelly, but there were some secrets she was simply not ready to divulge. Secrets like a scary red building in a small Kansas town. Just thinking about that made a wave of fear wash over her and she fought to take control once more. Not even her logic could keep that terror away.

CHAPTER 7

Briana was relieved when there was no call from the Rainger office about sharing a ride to Marysville. She had expected Shelly to go with her but the meeting fell on the same day as a dental appointment, so Frank suggested that he go instead. Briana declined his offer. She had visited with Kyle about what to expect and decided it would be routine, similar to the Kansas City meeting. Everyone so far had been laying the groundwork and getting their petitions and complaints out on the table. Kyle was feeling pretty good, but when Shelly talked to his wife, she found out he would be laid up for quite a while. The girls visited him at home twice and Frank stopped by a few times as well. Briana held to her decision not to bother Kyle during his recovery, so her call was the first business call and he was pleased to feel needed again.

She would be going to Marysville alone. Perhaps that would be best if she were going to slay the dragon that terrified her. Yes, it had been divine intervention that made it all work out this way, she thought as she retraced her route to the Marshall County area.

Briana was exactly on time when she stepped out of Red Baby and walked toward the modern courthouse. Tyler Rainger's Mercedes wasn't in sight so perhaps he had sent an assistant rather than coming himself, she thought. However, he was the first person she saw when ushered into the conference room. Just as he turned toward the door, an older gentleman who had been at the Kansas City meeting greeted her and offered her the chair beside him.

During the proceedings, Briana chose to take notes rather than look around, which made her appear studious and kept her from looking at Tyler. She was having problems concentrating anyway. How dare he judge her? So what if she had known all those truckers? So what if she had a boyfriend in every town or ten ex-husbands stashed away in California? Who did he think he was? She flashed him her favorite dirty look only to find him smiling at her. Or was it at her? Maybe someone was behind her. She wouldn't look.

When the meeting was over, Briana hurried to her car and had just started to pull out when she saw Tyler in her rearview mirror getting into a big red Dodge truck. Mud caked the fenders and there were bales of hay in the bed. Then she remembered he had a farm close by. He must have flown his plane up from Topeka and was staying at the farm.

She wondered what his farm would be like. Modern, no doubt, probably large. Would it be a working farm or a place to entertain? Would he need the spur line also? He had so completely taken over her thoughts that she came upon her castle before she realized it. Castle? Why had she referred to it as a castle?

She parked Red Baby closer than the last time and willed herself to gaze up at the large structure. Her mind was in control as she studied the historic courthouse. The word JUSTICE stood out above the entrance while the copper towers glowed in the sun, contrasted against the dark slate roof.

As she scanned the building, she relaxed her concentration for a moment and felt the fear creeping back. She fought it once more, but it was no use. She began to cry and tremble like before. Once again she clenched the steering wheel and rested her forehead on her hands. Something terrible had happened here and she was feeling as if it had happened to her. That was impossible, of course, but Briana knew whatever happened here had caused terror for someone.

God, help me to understand why I am affected by this old building and what I am supposed to do about it, she prayed. *You know I don't believe in déjà vu and I don't scare easily, but I'm scared now.*

She started her car and drove carefully away, consciously avoiding a glimpse of the building in her mirrors.

Briana felt exhausted. Her strength was gone and she realized she was in no condition to return to Topeka that night, so she decided to stay in Marysville. She remembered seeing a motel a few blocks from the courthouse and headed there. After checking in at the office, she found her room and decided to take a nap.

The queen-size bed was comfortable and she fell into a deep sleep almost immediately.

She awoke about 7 p.m., feeling stiff and crumpled. She felt better after bathing in the white-tiled bathroom and decided to go next door for dinner. When she returned to the room, she called Shelly and told her she was staying overnight. Shelly was curious about the meeting, but Briana convinced her all had gone well.

Briana scanned a local newspaper while the TV droned in the background. It was a chatty paper and Briana wondered if there would be mention of the Roswalds or the Raingers in it. The only thing she found was a reference to a Historical Society meeting at Stone House. It didn't elaborate on what or where that was, but encouraged people to come and hear Lavida Roswald's talk on the Roswald ancestors who had founded Blue Valley.

Since Briana had napped earlier, she didn't expect to fall asleep quickly. Around midnight, though, she was awakened by the sound of vehicles screeching to a stop outside her room. She could hear loud voices and yelling.

Alarmed, she reached in her handbag for her service revolver. Fists were banging on her door as she switched on the lamp next to her bed. The male voices were angry, but Briana imagined they had the wrong room.

"Get away from my door or I'll call the police," she shouted above the obscene language.

Suddenly the wooden door jam splintered and the whole door fell flat into the room, followed by about six big men. The ones in front stopped short when they saw the young woman sitting cross-legged in the center of the bed. Of course, it wasn't the sight of her that stopped them as much as the steely blue revolver in her steady hands.

"Get out of my room!" she barked, keeping her weapon steady.

The first man in the group was huge. He had a protruding beer belly, scraggly beard, and a worn cowboy hat that was shapeless from sweat and hard use. His tight Wranglers hardly covered his hips, leaving a stretch of his ample gut exposed below his T-shirt hem.

Briana could smell liquor and knew this was a bad situation. She glanced quickly at the other men who were through the door and wondered how many were still outside. Some were wearing farmer's caps with seed logos on the front panel. Seeing that, she decided they were probably the town bubbas, well tanked and clearly out of hand.

The first man tried to tell the ones behind him that she had a gun, but they were pushing and shoving, forcing him farther into the room.

Briana couldn't even guess how many men were in her room. She saw dirty cowboy boots and leather belts with wide, worn buckles. Some men had open whisky bottles, some cans of beer.

"You'd better change your mind about closing that railroad line, little lady, or you're gonna to regret it!" This was yelled from the back of the group in a hateful tone. It was the first inclination that they really were after her and not just looking for trouble because of the booze.

"Get out!" she ordered, looking right in the eyes of the big guy in front.

"Grab her, Tiny, and let's have some fun," bellowed someone from the rear as the men in front were pushed forward even more.

The explosion that followed was deafening and the big guy looked down at the frayed carpet and wood chips between his feet.

"Holy —" He didn't have time to continue; he just looked down the barrel of the weapon pointed at his face. Utter silence fell after the echo of the shot faded.

Tiny was trembling. He had dropped his beer can to one side, and Briana noticed a strange expression on his face as he grabbed for the front of his jeans. A wet stain became visible and a puddle collected on the carpet close to the bullet hole. The good ole boy had wet his pants!

The crowd of attackers was gone when other lodgers began to arrive, dragging the reluctant motel attendant with them.

"I—I called—I called the cops," he stammered. "Are you okay?"

Briana still sat cross-legged in bed, but had lowered her gun across her ankles. The white nylon slip that she had been sleeping in seemed to be very thin in front of the crowd, so she pulled up the lightweight bedspread to cover herself.

When the police arrived, they asked her to come with them to police headquarters to give a statement.

This was getting to be a common occurrence. After dressing in the bathroom, she grabbed her purse and went out the door.

"I'll follow you," she told the policeman.

"I don't think so, ma'am. Your car has had a bit of vandalism. You can ride with me."

She ran over to Red Baby and saw that her tires had been slashed. Anger and frustration washed over her as she wondered how she would find replacements for her tires in a small town on a Saturday. But of more immediate concern, Briana once again, as in Laramie, had to tell the police who she was, why she had a gun, and where to call to verify it all.

It was 4 a.m. before she was free to go. As she left the police station, she discovered that somehow, someone had put four new tires on her little car and put her briefcase in the front seat, ready for her to leave town. One of the young officers escorted her to her car and told her to drive safely. No handshaking or thanks. No congratulations for scaring off the drunken crowd or even the slightest apology for being harassed in their sleepy little town. Just "Here's your keys and bye."

So she did the only thing she could think to do. She left. As Briana drove off in the starry night, the thought of this old historic town was like an albatross hanging around her neck. Perhaps she would never have to come back. In fact, she'd make sure she didn't.

CHAPTER 8

When Briana arrived home, Shelly was still asleep, so she quietly let herself into the apartment and went to bed. Sleep was fitful, and she had another nightmare about that old red building. When she awoke in a frenzy, she was tangled up in her bedding and damp with perspiration.

The next thing that woke her was the phone. She waited for Shelly to answer it, but it kept ringing. She finally got up, hurried next door to Shelly's room, and picked up the little pastel receiver.

"Hello," she said, sleepily glancing at the digital clock radio on the bedside stand. It was 11:05. Where was Shelly?

The voice on the other end of the line asked, "Are you okay?" It was Tyler. The husky sound of his voice sent shivers up her spine.

She wanted to resent his question. She longed to say "Of course!" or "Just because I'm a woman doesn't mean I can't take care of myself!" But in reality, she was so shocked to hear his voice all she could answer was a simple "Yes."

"I'm still up here at the farm, but when I heard what happened I had to call and check on you."

"I was asleep. I'm afraid I'm still groggy. But thank you for calling."

She had almost hung up when he added, "You won the admiration of a lot of people by not pressing charges. The guys just got a little drunk and unruly, but they aren't really bad."

"Not really bad? A little unruly? Where were you when the door caved in?"

"One of them was Dolan's boy."

"So who is Dolan? Was he the jerk they called Tiny?" She was racking her brain trying to remember where she'd heard that name.

"Dolan Roswald is the man who organized the group to contest the spur line closing. My father-in-law, actually. My late wife, Deb, was his daughter. You don't know about any of this and it doesn't matter except to tell you that he appreciates what you did. He also replaced your tires, and if you've noticed, they're the top of the line. The best."

"I'm sorry now that I didn't press charges," Briana snapped. "And if I had had any idea some big shot's kid was involved, I would have filed in a second!"

Here again she considered hanging up but he quickly told her, "It isn't too late." He added, "You seem to have an authority problem."

"This Roswald bunch has no authority over me or my company. Perhaps you will tell them that for me." Her blood was boiling now, but before she ended the call she declared, "I will not be bullied, even if it is by rich kids and their friends!"

Before the receiver could crash down Tyler said, "For being such a 'special lady,' you don't have much compassion, do you?"

That was it. Bang! went the phone and she hoped it hurt his ear.

Shelly came bouncing in the front door as Briana came flying out of the bedroom. "So you're awake!" Shelly began, then noticed the look on Briana's face. "What's wrong?"

"I'm going to take a shower, and by then I might be able to talk about it. Who does that man think he is?"

"Who? What's going on?" Shelly sat her groceries down on the kitchen counter and followed Briana into her bedroom.

"I can't wait until you've had your shower. Tell me now!"

Briana sank down on the end of the rumpled bed. "I'm so mad! Really, really mad," she began, fighting tears.

"I can see that! At who? Why? What happened?"

"Tyler Rainger, for the who! Because he's trying to excuse what happened last night…."

Shelly's mouth flew open. "You were with Tyler last night?" She looked incredulous.

"No, I wasn't with Tyler last night!"

"But you said—" Shelly began.

"I was too busy entertaining half the good ole boys of Marysville in my motel room!"

"Oh my God," Shelly exclaimed as she looked up for Divine assistance. "You stayed all night at a Marysville motel with the local boys?" Shelly was trying to digest all this disjointed information, but finally gave up and started to laugh. "Wait until your trucking fleet hears about this!" She dropped to the carpeted floor and sitting cross-legged at Briana's feet, asked, "What were you doing with 'the boys' in your room, or do I want to know? How did Tyler get involved? Briana, I don't know if I can stand to let you move out. I've never had so much excitement in my whole life!"

Briana relaxed a little and joined Shelly in her laughter. After explaining about the break-in and tire slashing, Briana described the phone call from Tyler.

"He all but made the whole scenario my fault! He said Dolan Roswald's kid was involved, and because I didn't press charges, Roswald bought me the best tires to replace my slashed ones."

"Well, that was a good deal," Shelly decided.

"No, it wasn't! Briana countered. It's like a bribe. He knew I didn't press charges and this was a payoff. Tyler probably suggested it!"

"But Bri, what did you want them to do?"

"The boys should have been made to pay for the tires. They should have apologized to me or something." Briana had run out of steam now. What did she really want out of all this, and why did she get so mad at Tyler?

"What did Tyler say that irked you?" Shelly was sure she was missing something here.

"It wasn't what he said but how he said it. He made me feel cheap, like his reaction to me being called a special lady when those truckers dropped by our table. Like he thought I had enticed those punks to my room!"

"Oh Bri, Tyler isn't like that and I don't think for a minute he believed what he said about the truckers." Shelly rose and started for the door. "Get your shower and I'll fix you some breakfast—or lunch. At any rate, we'll eat. I hope the ice cream hasn't melted!"

As the warm water cascaded down over her body, Briana remembered the low voice that asked if she was okay. That was the problem. He should have supported her. He should have told her he was proud of her courage, but instead he made a dig about her being a special lady and supported her adversary. Of course, that man was his father-in-law and client!

That evening Tom and Shelly went to a movie. They invited Briana, but she had an appointment to see a house. It was the perfect house, with three bedrooms, a dining room, big kitchen, bath and half, a large front room with generous windows, and a garage. Best of all, it had a porch and cozy yard. Briana had driven by the house a few times before calling the realtor, but now that she had seen the interior, she knew it was perfect for her. It was in a good area, close to a shopping center, and the other homes were well kept. The rent was very reasonable compared to what it would have cost in California.

It would be the end of June before she could take possession, which would work out well because she would need to purchase some furniture and have her things shipped from home.

When she got back to the apartment she called her folks to tell them about her new house. "I wish you were here to help me decorate," she told her mom. "You always make home so cozy. By the way, did Dad ever get in touch with the Bureau of Vital Statistics to see about my birth records? Now that I'm a lawyer, I can see how important that kind of thing is."

"He talked like he had been in touch with one of the bureaus, or maybe he said he would call," her mother said. "I'll remind him."

Briana talked to her younger brother Mark, but Richard was out on a date. Her dad sounded tired or worried, so she didn't ask him about the records.

When she got off the phone, it was well past her usual dinnertime. Just as she started to prepare a light meal, the doorbell chimed and Briana called out from inside the door, "Who is it?"

"Char's Florist, ma'am. I have a delivery for Briana Sheldon."

Who would be sending her flowers? She took the long, slender box to the kitchen to open it. Inside was a single long-stemmed white rose and a bud vase for it. The card read: "I'm very sorry I woke you! Ty."

Briana had to laugh. It was a truce, and perhaps he wondered why she had been so upset. He blamed it on waking her up but of course, he probably knew better.

Sunday morning Tom came by to take the girls to church. The service was inspiring and Briana was impressed with the young pastor's message. She was scanning the congregation when she saw a familiar face. Tyler Rainger! He hadn't seen her, but she watched as he whispered softly to the striking young woman sitting next to him. The woman was facing Briana so Briana couldn't stare at them as much as she wanted to.

Shelly noticed the direction Briana was looking and whispered, "You aren't going to fight with him at church, are you?" Briana shook her head and looked toward the pulpit once more. Maybe she wouldn't even have to talk to him at all. She wondered if the rose was sent as a truce or a jest.

As the congregation left the sanctuary, the young pastor and his wife greeted them in the foyer. The church body as a whole was made up of friendly people who had accepted Briana into the fold like a true sister. Christians were like that, she knew.

Tom, Shelly, and Briana were visiting in the parking lot with another young couple when Tyler and his companion walked up to them. Tom saw them first and greeted them both. Shelly gave Tyler her super-duper smile that she claimed was for only the best-looking men. A faint smile tilted the corners of Briana's mouth as she witnessed Tyler's friend take offense to the smile. Then Briana glanced at Tyler and his amused eyes gleamed down on her.

"Shelly, Tom, you remember Deb's cousin Adrian Day. Adrian, this is Briana Sheldon, who recently moved to Topeka from California to start a career in law with the Santa Fe."

Tyler's introduction was not bad, Briana thought, considering she had slammed down the phone on him the day before. She suspected he could easily have said something derogatory.

"How do you do?" Briana said, extending her hand to the cousin. As she met the woman's unfriendly eyes, she retracted the hand and watched as the woman took her time looking at her figure, her face, and then her hair. This was not an introduction—it was an inspection. A clipped "hello" was all Adrian said before she turned and walked toward Tyler's Mercedes.

Tyler, however, reached out and caught Briana's hand in his. "It's very nice to meet you, Miss Sheldon," he said laughingly as he pumped her hand. "Hope we can be friends." His steel-gray eyes were alive with humor as they probed hers.

She opened her lips slightly to respond but her pulse was doing a strange drumbeat in her ears. Looking down at his hand, still closed over hers, she decided that was the cause, so she extracted her hand from his grip.

"What was that all about?" Tom asked when Tyler left to join the impatient woman by his car.

"We'll bring you up to date on the escapades of 'Angel' over lunch, but only if you are willing to take us to a fancy restaurant. Not McDonald's, either!" Tom was famous for his love of the golden arches.

"But, Shelly," he said opening the car doors for the girls, "a Big Mac is a meal in itself. I would even spring for fries since it's Sunday." Tom teased during the drive, until he pulled into the parking lot of a steakhouse that had a lovely salad bar and desserts.

Over their meal, the girls told Tom about Briana's ordeal in Marysville. Briana was pleased Shelly had kept her promise not to tell Tom what had happened on the phone with Tyler. Briana didn't want the differences she had with Tyler to cause problems with Tom and Shelly.

During the meal, Shelly asked Tom where Adrian lived. "Maybe she'll be your new neighbor, Bri," she added jokingly.

"Ask me if I care," Briana said flippantly, then laughed as Tom explained that her parents had a home at Lake Sherwood, but Adrian now had her own apartment.

"Melissa, Adrian's mother, is Dolan Roswald's sister. She's married to Carter Lancaster, who's a well-known psychiatrist at the Menninger Clinic. Of course, I might mention that Adrian and her mother don't get along very well, according to Tyler. I wonder if Adrian left Brenda with Dolan and Irene?"

"Who is Brenda?" Briana asked while she buttered her roll.

"That's Adrian's eight-year-old daughter," Shelly put in quickly. "She's a real brat!"

"Oh Shelly, she isn't that bad," Tom said. "It's always bad for a child when her parents split up." He turned to Briana and added, "They've been divorced about three years now. Adrian used to take Brenda over to Tyler and Deb's, which delighted them all until Debby became aware that Adrian had an eye for Tyler.

Deb was pregnant and very sick while her beautiful, sexy cousin was chasing her husband.

"I don't think Tyler was even aware of all that. I noticed, but didn't say anything until I found Deb crying one day in Tyler's office. Adrian and Debby had come into town together but Adrian had been very coy about what she had planned for the day. After Debby finished her doctor's appointment she dropped by the office to surprise Tyler by taking him out to lunch. He wasn't in and his secretary told her he had a luncheon engagement. Debby assumed he was out with Adrian and was crushed."

Briana felt Debby's pain acutely. Adrian was so chic and beautiful, how could a nauseated, pregnant wife compete?

"That's too bad," Briana whispered.

"But he wasn't out with the cousin. He had a business luncheon in Lawrence that day so he wasn't even in town. But Deb didn't find that out until he returned home to the farm that weekend. His secretary didn't even tell him Deb had been there and Deb couldn't bring herself to ask why Tyler hadn't called. Poor thing. She must have hated them both."

"But the secretary got fired anyway," Shelly volunteered.

"What happened to cause Debby's death?" Briana asked.

"She must have had a birth defect that had gone undetected all those years because she was fine one minute and gone the next," Tom said. "There was a hole in her heart or something. Tyler found her dead in the bathroom at their apartment when he got up one morning. The doctor said she had no doubt gotten up in the night, feeling sick or perhaps just to use the bathroom, and her heart just stopped functioning. Of course, the unborn child died also. Tyler was devastated and the whole Roswald family was in shock. The child would have been Dolan and Irene's first grandchild. Irene and Deb had a nursery all fixed up at the farm, with baby clothes in drawers even though the delivery was four months away. It was a tragedy, but now it looks like Ty might be ready to find someone else."

"I've never seen Tyler with anyone but Adrian," Shelly said.

"Do you think it's serious?" Briana asked, trying not to sound interested.

"No," Tom answered. "Tyler isn't interested in her but that doesn't stop her chasing him. Of course, never underestimate you women on the prowl. Look at me. I had my life in order and someone blew that all apart!" He was teasing Shelly and at that point, Briana decided that was the kind of love she wanted. He obviously loved Shelly unconditionally, and though Shelly didn't admit it, Briana was sure she felt the same way.

CHAPTER 9

Shelly pitched in and spent time in the evenings helping with painting and decorating the new house. Briana had not moved in yet, but her shipment from California would arrive any day. The people who owned the house had stored their possessions before leaving for an extended tour in their motor home. They told Briana they would be gone six to eight months, which suited Briana just fine. By then she would know if she wanted to buy or go back to apartment living.

The house was in good shape and the owners had offered to paint two rooms before they left. Briana said she could do the job herself, so they rented her the house with no deposit. The kitchen was a light pea-green color that just had to go. It reminded Briana of the paint from the office walls and old classrooms in California.

The bathroom was pink—bright pink! Shelly described it as Pepto-Bismol pink, which said it all.

Briana chose an ice blue that was very close to being white, it was so light, then picked out some border wallpaper for the trim. It was colonial blue and chocolate brown. She would buy a dark-brown bath set and towels before she moved in.

She changed the kitchen to a light, sunny yellow and planned on purchasing some white lace curtains for the windows. Yes, she could be happy here. The yard had an abundance of flowers in bloom. Iris, peonies, and daffodils provided a riot of color in the front beds, while the forsythia bushes were bursting with yellow blossoms and the apple tree behind the garage was a spray of delicate pink and white.

One evening after work, Tom stopped by to check the girls' progress and found them adding the wallpaper trim in the bathroom.

"Hey, anyone home?" he yelled through the front screen door.

"Come on in, Tom," Briana called.

"Yeah, come see the good work we've done!" Shelly added.

"I picked up some pizza and drinks," he announced, sticking his head in the bathroom door. "This sure looks better than pink!" he exclaimed, surveying the walls and new trim. The girls followed him out to the kitchen and checked the pizza as the tempting aroma wafted from the counter.

"What? No Big Macs?" Briana teased as she reached for the sack with the drinks, napkins, and straws.

"I know I'm spoiling you girls, but you're doing such a good job here I figured you deserved pizza tonight. The kitchen looks better, too," Tom added, glancing around at the fresh paint.

They had just lifted warm slices of pizza out of the box when a car pulled into the drive. Briana hurried to peek out the dining room window and saw a familiar dark Mercedes stopped in front of the garage. Tyler Rainger was stepping out from the vehicle. He crossed the front walk and was ringing the doorbell before she could even bring herself to move, then she only turned slightly as Tom yelled from behind her.

"Come on in, Ty!"

Tyler opened the front door and stepped into the spacious living room. Briana forced herself to meet him there, and tried to smile but she felt herself flush with embarrassment as Ty's eyes slowly took in her attire.

She had changed into very short, cut-off jeans that were easy to work in and old enough to be past caring about paint splatters. Her sleeveless, button-up pink blouse was also old and oversized so she had tied it up in front, exposing her tanned midriff. She was instantly self-conscious of all the bare skin.

Her long thick hair was pulled high in a ponytail, tendrils now hanging loose over her ears. She had no makeup on and a slice of pizza, minus one bite, dangled from her hand. She felt suddenly young and ill-matched to her unexpected guest, who was dressed as if he had just left the country club.

"There ought to be a law about you wearing anything other than a nun's habit!" he growled quietly, laughing at her expression. "And I'm not sure that would do the job!"

"At least that's better than a pillowcase over the head like my dad used to talk about," she retorted, abruptly turning back toward the kitchen. Briana heard him chuckling behind her and wondered what he would do if she turned and threw herself into his arms. The impulse had been there when he gazed at her. There was definitely some strange kind of chemistry between them and Briana suspected he was aware of it, too.

"Have some pizza, Ty," Tom offered when they entered the kitchen. Shelly poured some pop into a Styrofoam cup and sat it next to him at the table. Briana grabbed a napkin, opened it, and tucked it under his chin like a child.

"In case you drop a bite, or drool," she explained, laughing as he began to protest, but couldn't, around a mouthful of pizza.

"No respect!" he complained, wiping his mouth with the napkin.

They had a pleasant meal and as before, Shelly and Tom were a riot. Tyler had some business to discuss with Tom, which was the reason for his visit. When he was about to leave he asked them if they'd like to spend the Fourth of July at his farm.

"I don't have anything special planned other than relaxing around the pool and eating. I know you can handle the latter." He waved his hand over the empty pizza boxes.

"We could fly up Saturday morning and come back sometime on Monday. I have horses to ride and miles of country lanes to walk."

"The pool sounds the best. Just lying around while you wait on us hand and foot." This was Shelly, of course.

"That sounds great to me, too," Tom agreed. They all turned to Briana.

"Well, I don't know...." she began. "You don't have to include me in on your holiday plans. I have a house now...."

"But Bri, your stuff won't be here yet! You certainly don't want to stay trapped here in town all weekend when you could be basking in the sun by a pool?" Shelly wanted to go, that was obvious. She probably wouldn't go without her and, of course, it wouldn't be proper. At least, Briana hoped Shelly would think not. But would it be appropriate for the four of them to spend a weekend together? Should she and Tyler be socializing this way while being on opposing sides in a court dispute?

"My caretakers, Cecil and Bea Miller, will be there, also," Tyler added as if he could read her mind.

"It will be fun, Bri," Shelly encouraged. "Please say yes."

"Well if you're sure you want...this much company...." Then she looked up at Tyler and asked, "How are you fixed for nun's robes up there?"

He laughed outright and Briana caught the silent question in Shelly and Tom's eyes.

"Private joke," she explained.

As Briana tried to fall asleep later, she wondered again about her decision. She had vowed never to go to the Marysville area again, and here she was planning a weekend there. Perhaps being at the farm she wouldn't have an occasion to see the town of Marysville or that horrible building.

A few nights later, her mother called to tell her the date to expect her shipment. The railroad had arranged for the transfer of all her belongings and they would be delivered to her new house two days after the holiday. It was a good phone visit, but hearing about home and the family made Briana homesick. Her mom asked her about the new house and Briana went into details about the changes she'd made.

"I have two spare bedrooms for you guys when you come to visit in September. Of course, the boys might have to sleep on air mattresses since I only have the two beds, but I could let them stay at Shelly's. You'll just love her, Mom."

Then, on a sober note she asked, "Mom, do you ever have the feeling you've seen something before, yet there is no way you could have? Like déjà vu?"

"Yes, I've felt things like that, but I think everyone has. Remember when we went to the Grand Canyon, and we went through a small town where your dad stopped for gas? I had seen that gas station in my mind, and when it was there for real, I couldn't believe it. It was eerie! I don't know why it happens, but I know one thing for sure, I had never been there before."

After they had hung up and Briana was lying in bed, she thought of the conversation with her mother and wondered if this strange feeling was inherited—a weird trait of some kind. She felt better knowing it had happened to her mother and was glad her mom hadn't asked to hear her experience.

Saturday morning the men picked Briana and Shelly up at the apartment about eight. Tyler explained about the flight they would be taking and asked if either of them had flown before. Shelly had been on a 747 jet once when she went to see her dad in Dallas, but Briana had never been in an airplane.

"Does the thought of going up frighten you?" Tyler's eyes met hers briefly in the rearview mirror.

"No, I don't think so. I slept well last night and I don't do that if I'm worried about things. I'm confident that if you wanted to get rid of me you wouldn't use your plane, particularly with a crowd on board."

"Yes," he agreed, his eyes dancing with humor. "This plane is far too expensive for pest control."

Shelly squealed, "Bri, are you going to take that?"

"I'll get even," she promised. "I never forget!"

The plane was a white Piper Arrow with blue stripes. When Briana said it was cute, Tyler shook his head in disgust. The interior was smaller than the Mercedes, but very pleasant. It had blue upholstered seats that felt like recliners. Tom and Shelly sat in back so Briana could have the best view, but Briana suspected they were playing Cupid.

They all had separate headsets that were plugged into the console, and Tyler ran a series of checks to make sure each set worked and that each mouthpiece was the right distance from their mouths. The first thing

Briana heard was Tom asking if they could unplug Shelly's if she talked too much. Shelly chucked him on the shoulder while the rest of them laughed.

The seatbelts were fastened—shoulder harnesses in front, lap belts in back—and as the propeller started, Briana felt the powerful vibrations as the plane leapt to life. Tyler began a systematic pre-check of all instruments and gauges, then checked the windsock one last time before taxiing down the concrete runway.

"This is your last chance to bail out," he cautioned Briana, but she shook her head.

At the end of the runway Tyler checked the engine again, made radio contact with the terminal, and accelerated. The nose of the small craft lifted and they were airborne.

Briana watched the ground fall away and felt a thrill similar to a roller coaster, but in reverse. She felt free suddenly and wondered if it would feel like that when the Rapture came.

"We'll climb at a speed of 85 to 91 miles per hour and level off to cruise at about 125 miles per hour. It's approximately 70 nautical miles to my farm, which will only take about 45 minutes," Tyler announced. Briana turned to look at him as she spoke into her mike. "That sure beats a three-hour car ride!"

The view in all directions amazed her. The fields looked like a giant quilt with blocks in all different colors. The major roadways, like I-70, looked like long gray ribbons, making the small dirt roads look like threads. She saw patches of woods, rivers, and creeks blending with farms and small towns. Then Tuttle

Creek Reservoir, with the big dam holding back miles of water, came into view with recreation areas visible.

Tom said this ride was more pleasant then his last trip to the farm had been. "This little baby was bouncing like a rubber ball. Up and down, down and up, side to side...."

Shelly moaned. "Shut up, Tom you're making me sick!"

Briana turned to see if her friend was truly having problems, but Shelly winked and shook her head.

"We're about 2100 feet from the ground right now. The calm ride has a lot to do with the cool morning. Later in the day, the heat causes airs pockets and makes a bumpy ride," Tyler informed them. "The horizon is about a hundred miles away," he pointed out, then added, "We'll make a circle around Tuttle so you can get a better view."

The plane turned slightly, and Tyler told them it was only a ten-degree bank, but it seemed steeper. Briana couldn't even imagine how it would feel to streak through the sky in a jet fighter, rolling and flipping. Ugh! The cars on the roads below looked like ants on a trail. The tiny dots on the lake, Tyler explained, were boats.

"Well, what do you think about flying now?" Tyler asked as he glanced over at Briana.

"You could spoil me for life!"

"Is that a challenge?" he asked seriously.

Embarrassed, she felt the growing heat burn her cheeks and she shivered as if he had physically touched her. She turned to examine the view to avoid answering his question and shield her flushed face from his view.

They circled an area that was mostly hills and valleys. Just beyond that, the land flattened and crops could be seen for miles. The plane banked once more and Tyler pointed out Blue Valley, with Blue Springs winding its way through the area like a huge snake that slithered out of sight in one place, only to appear once more behind the next knoll.

"That's Blue Point Hill." Tyler directed her attention to a large hill as their altitude began to drop. "Roswald country," he said proudly.

Briana once more questioned the logic of accepting this invitation that brought her into their country. She had no idea the farms were so close, but listened intently when Tyler continued, "There on the lower eastern slope is Stone Haven. Can you see it among the big trees?"

Briana caught a glimpse of an old native-stone farmhouse, then spotted a beautiful Queen Anne home complete with corner towers, conical roof, and projecting gables. How lovely! A small road, connecting to the larger county road at the base of the hill, ascended to the stone house before winding past the Queen Anne home.

"Does the big mansion have a name, Tyler?" Shelly asked. "It looks like a storybook house!"

"It's called Blue Valley Manor. That's where Dolan's parents, Bevin and Gladys Roswald, live. They're in Europe on an extended vacation."

Tyler acted as if this were a common occurrence. Briana wondered what it would be like to be rich. She'd never know and it didn't matter, as wealth usually came with a price tag.

The meandering road went around the manor, circling the spacious green lawn and trimmed shrubs, then ran past the towering trees and began to climb in earnest up to the crest of the hill. A modern brick ranch-style house sat there proudly, overlooking the whole valley.

"What a fantastic view they must have up there," Briana thought. The panorama left her breathless. What a lovely place to live, and how wonderful to have family so near.

The plane was descending now and Tyler got busy with the landing procedure. A small paved airstrip became visible at the western base of Blue Point Hill; in the distance, pressed against the base of the hill, nestled a large earth-berm home. Briana caught a flash of blue in front of the home and realized it was an in-ground swimming pool. There wasn't time to see much more as they landed lightly and taxied to a small hangar. A van arrived at the same time the passengers disembarked and an older man walked toward the plane.

"This is Cecil Miller, my right-hand man and friend," Tyler announced, introducing the girls. "Cecil and his wife are my caretakers and have a mobile home on the east side of my house."

Tom greeted Cecil and said the crops looked pretty good from the air, then began a conversation about the growing season while Tyler extracted the weekend luggage from the compartment behind the rear seat of the plane. Cecil loaded the bags into the van and drove them around the base of the hill and up a small incline to Tyler's lovely home.

"Okay, Ty, what do we call your house?" Shelly questioned, straining to see the partially underground dwelling.

"I call it home," Tyler answered. "The names on the old houses are okay, but not for me. Dolan's rancher up on the point is just the Roswald house. They aren't into the historical stuff, either. When Deb and I considered building after Dolan gave us this tract of land for a wedding present, we decided to build for our comfort and style of life."

"It's lovely here," Briana murmured, looking out across the fertile valley.

"My horse barn is beyond the airstrip and the rest of the farm is combined. Dolan runs cattle and has crops also, so you can see it's a huge operation. I keep mostly to myself, but between Cecil and I, we have a pretty good stable with some fair-looking mares." Ty turned briefly to Cecil and asked, "What do you think? Is Abby going to drop that foal while we're here?"

"Quit rushing things, Ty. Nature takes just so long to make a baby, whether it be human or horse. We'll have a colt when it's time and not before."

"You sound like an expectant father for sure," Tom added.

Briana wondered if all this banter about the mare brought back memories of Debby with their child dead in her womb. Was this subject hurting Tyler? She cast him a furtive glance, but he was looking ahead at the house and appeared lost in his thoughts.

Cecil let the party out by the front patio. The building was shaped like a horseshoe, with the pool and surrounding patio occupying the center. Scattered around the pool were lounge chairs and other patio furniture, welcoming either conversation or solitary relaxation. The entrance to the house was through a large enclosed patio, with upholstered country-style furniture on a carpeted floor. Storm windows around the outer walls were wide open, giving it an air of openness like the area poolside. Briana imagined it would be a comfortable place to sit even when the weather was cool. The heat from the southern sun would radiate warmth into the room through the glass windows.

When they entered the house, they stepped into a wide hall that continued east and west into the other wings. The outer walls on the patio side of this hall were all glass, with striking curtains pulled open in two sections. On the far side of the foyer, directly in front of the entrance, was a sunken living room. Briana stepped through the wide archway and gasped at the remarkable architecture. She took in the native stone fireplace that dominated one wall, then gazed up to the sixteen-foot cathedral ceiling with windowed gable ends that allowed sunlight to streak across the open beams.

Briana turned to tell Tyler how lovely it was, but he was talking to Cecil's wife, Bea, who stepped forward to show the girls to their rooms.

As the men turned to leave through the east wing, they waved and said they wouldn't be long. They had farm business to deal with, but Bea would get them settled. The housekeeper led them in the opposite direction along the same ceramic-tiled hall with the patio still visible on the one side.

"As you can see, the house has a simple layout," Mrs. Miller began. "The living room takes up most of the center. Tyler's office is next on the west side and then the bedroom wing." She opened Tyler's office and gave them a glimpse inside. Briana could see a big mahogany desk, but that was all before the door was pulled shut.

"The main hall follows the contour of the court with windows and sliding glass doors looking out to the patio and pool," Mrs. Miller explained as they continued. Two bedrooms were off another hall near the office, along with a large bathroom, beautifully decorated with tile. The last bedroom would be Tom's, Bea informed them.

"I've put you girls in the next room, which will be closer to the patio and has a window view of the courtyard. The king-size bed should be comfy, but you'll probably be so tired after using the pool all weekend you'll sleep like logs!"

They left their luggage on the big bed and followed Bea Miller to the next room, which was the master bedroom. The hall ended just beyond a sliding glass door that opened onto the enclosed patio area. The bedroom door was also a sliding glass door covered with thick, wine-colored drapes.

"Deb and Tyler used to enjoy the moonlight reflecting off the pool and they seldom pulled the drapes at night—at least in the summertime. They were so happy."

Loving one another in the moonlight, Briana instantly thought. How romantic!

"If you want to settle in, you can, or come with me now and I'll show you the east wing."

The girls chose to follow Bea. They retraced their steps back to the center foyer and continued to the east side of the front room, where they found a large formal dining room. Next to that was the modern kitchen and a utility room that led to a three-car garage at the end of that wing. Briana felt comfortable here and found Bea Miller warm and friendly. Tyler's home was truly lovely.

"Whenever you get ready, feel free to join the men at the pool. It's getting pretty warm outside, so you may want to go for a swim before lunch." Bea headed back to the kitchen, humming a tune as she went.

Briana and Shelly changed quickly but the pool was empty when they arrived at the patio. Laying their towels and cover-ups on lounges, they entered the pool and were splashing about in the cool, sparkling water when the men appeared minutes later. Briana tried not to look at Tyler as he dove off the side into the area below the diving board. She turned and swam to the opposite side.

"This is just great, Tyler!" Shelly called from the far end, then dipped under the surface and swam toward the center of the pool. Tom strode out on the diving board and bounced a few times, then yelled

"Geronimo!" and jumped, holding his knees and splashing half the pool on impact.

Tyler was swimming the length of the pool, but stopped short as the water sprayed over him. He was about ten feet from Briana.

"Tom really can dive," he explained, "but he gets more attention with a cannonball!" He closed the gap between them and treaded water a few feet away.

Briana's gaze took in his muscled shoulders and damp, glistening hair. The water made his hair appear black rather than brown, and the length of it begged her hands to push it back off his forehead.

"Do you dive?" he was asking, forcing her to take her mind off his curls.

"I've done some," she answered in a breathless voice, allowing the crystal water to cover more of her shoulders. "This is really a wonderful place you have here, and what an ideal place to entertain us city folks."

"Thank you, Bri. We always enjoyed having guests, but recently I haven't entertained quite as often. If you haven't already put on sunscreen, though, I should warn you not to underestimate the strength of the rays. You don't want to get burned. Of course, you know about sunburn from California, but the sun probably doesn't feel as intense here as it really is. Being blonde, you probably burn quickly."

She was having problems breathing as his eyes roamed over her shoulders. "I'm not really a blonde," she admitted.

"Oh! Only your hairdresser knows for sure?" he joked, repeating the hair color ad from TV.

"I lightened it when I was in college and just got used to it. I've been thinking about going natural before it turns gray." She pulled her long hair forward to squeeze out the water and was glad she had fastened it in an elastic band to minimize the tangles.

Before Tyler could respond, Shelly arrived in a frenzy of splashes. Chasing after her was Tom, cutting through the water like an Olympic athlete. Briana welcomed the distraction from the conversation with the very distracting Mr. Rainger.

CHAPTER 10

It was close to noon when they left the pool. Tyler had been called to the phone earlier and had not come back. Bea told them lunch would be ready in the kitchen at the breakfast bar whenever they were ready. She also explained that she might not be there because their little dog was about to have her pups.

When the group collected in the kitchen they found bread, cold cuts, fresh fruit, chips, and salads waiting. Briana was the last to arrive and felt self-conscious walking into the kitchen alone. She had first dressed in jeans and a long-sleeve shirt, but that was too warm, so she changed to white shorts and a mint-green, sleeveless T-shirt. To keep her damp hair neat, she had quickly braided it.

"Sorry, I'm late," she said when she saw their plates full and iced tea glasses in hand.

"That's okay. We were just famished and knew you'd forgive us if we waited for you like one pig for another." They all chuckled at Shelly's excuse.

"Are you calling me a pig?" Briana bristled playfully.

"If the trough fits, wear it." They all had to laugh at that.

Tyler ushered Tom and Shelly with their food to the shaded area of the patio, saying over his shoulder that he'd save a chair for Briana. "Bea will be right back if you need help," he added.

"I have never had problems feeding my face," she joked, "and this looks scrumptious!" When she finally walked out onto the patio, plate and drink in hand, she realized that the only available place to sit was a lounge across from Ty.

She sat her food and glass on the low table beside the lounge that Shelly and Tom were also using for their drinks. Swinging her long legs up in front of her, she leaned back and then reached for her plate.

When she glanced up to see why the buzz of conversation had halted, she met Ty's eyes. As always, her heart did a somersault.

"I couldn't get my hair to dry," she blurted out in confusion. "I think I'll cut it short before long."

"Your hair is beautiful. Don't cut it!" Tyler's voice seemed to hypnotize her. She tried to look away, but his eyes had captivated hers and she just couldn't draw them away. Her fork, with a piece of sweet cantaloupe on it, was suspended somewhere between plate and mouth.

When Ty's glance dropped briefly to her partially open lips and then back to her eyes, her whole body felt the onslaught of emotion. She could feel a sudden fire sear through her body, setting her aflame as everything around her receded and the air between them became alive. Briana wasn't paying attention and her fork tilted, allowing the small piece of cool melon to fall, landing on her tanned, exposed thighs. Ty's eyes followed the mishap and she could almost feel the caress on her legs.

"Come on, Bri, let's raid the kitchen and get some of Mrs. Miller's chocolate cake!" Shelly jumped up and grabbed Briana's half-full plate, setting it on the low table while Briana retrieved the wayward melon piece and gladly followed her friend to the kitchen.

"Whew! What was all that about? I felt like we were watching a sensuous encounter of some sort. And you looked like you'd been turned to stone, except for your red face." Shelly was looking closely at Briana. "You felt it too, Bri. You know you did!"

Briana tried to downplay the heart-pounding incident. "He's very good-looking and is an excellent host. Don't read anything into that embarrassing scene. I could have died when that melon cube dropped. How will I ever face him?"

Just then, the men entered the kitchen with dirty plates and empty glasses. "Where is this great cake everybody was bragging about?" Tom asked, looking around.

"Over here, Tom," Shelly called, deftly cutting a towering slice of the cake. Tom moved closer with a waiting plate to help Shelly serve. Briana was left beside Ty and she couldn't even look at him.

"I'm sorry if I made you feel uncomfortable. Forgive me?" The husky sound of his whispered voice sent shivers up her spine.

"Want some cake, Ty?" Shelly waited patiently for his answer while he waited for Briana's. Briana turned and met his searching gaze but couldn't speak.

"Make it two, Shelly. Briana didn't eat enough lunch to keep a bird alive." He walked over and waited for the two servings, giving one to Briana.

Before they returned to the patio, Bea came in from the utility room, grinning.

"Come see what we have," she encouraged. "Spunky had a puppy and is ready to have the next one any minute. She's been acting strange all day and a short time before you arrived, she began panting. We've been taking her to our place each night so we'd be nearby if she went into labor."

A cardboard box lined with faded towels sat in the corner of the neatly tiled room and in it was a little white poodle, busy with her firstborn. Spunky, seeing Tyler, tried to get up, but another offspring was about to be born. Suddenly the small dark puppy slipped out of her and lay wiggling until the good little mother began its first bath.

Briana turned to Tyler with tears in her eyes. "How wonderful life is! God made each creature so unique, but mothers are all the same. See how proud she is! If she could speak, she would be bragging already!"

"She'll be a good mother," Tyler said his voice full of feelings that caught Briana's attention. "This is her first litter, but she's been practicing on the old mother cat and her kittens. We found Spunky babysitting Heidi's new kittens last week and figured there would be one big fight when Heidi came back to her box. We were fooled 'cause the cat crawled right in and curled up by the dog! Grandpa Cyrus would never have believed it, since he thought cats should only be in a barn. He had hunting dogs and, of course, being pedigreed, they were kept in the estate kennels that were tended by a hired man."

"Where did you get Spunky?" Tom asked as Ty reached down to pet the new mother.

"At the humane society shelter in Topeka. Deb wanted a housedog, so one day we went looking. This little ball of fur was in a cage crying so pitifully that Deb couldn't pass her up. She's been a good dog." Ty turned away abruptly and left the room.

Bea shook her head and said, "You'll have to forgive him, Briana. Sometimes the memories of his loss come crashing in unexpectedly. His wife was so young, so vibrant. What a tragedy!"

As they stood feeling a bit uncomfortable, another puppy arrived and broke the tension. Three puppies seemed to be it.

"How old was his wife when she died?" Briana asked.

Mrs. Miller, in a hesitant voice, counted the years. "She had just turned twenty-one and of course Tyler had double grief because she was pregnant. They had only been at the farm for a few months and they were just kids. Her folks deeded them the property and Tyler had it built as their love nest. Tyler was eight or nine years older than Deb, but it didn't matter and the family felt it was a good match."

"How did they meet?" Shelly asked. Was "Tyler a local boy?"

"No, he came from back East and had some money from his family, I think. He had been in the Marines, then went to college. That's where he met Deb. Dolan and Irene were not real pleased when she brought him home. Of course, she was their daughter and their firstborn, so what could they say when she got married and didn't finish college? The family took Tyler in like he was their own son."

CHAPTER 11

The women returned to the patio and found the guys finishing their cake. They had brought out the girl's servings also, along with the cool pitcher of iced tea. Tyler got up and poured each of them a drink.

"We should have known they'd be feeding their faces again," Shelly teased as she took her glass.

"But we didn't have any cake!" Tom complained, shoving another bite into his mouth.

This felt comfortable now, relaxing and visiting about everyday things. Briana could look at Ty and not get flustered, and he seemed comfortable also.

"I thought you girls would like to see Stone Haven this afternoon and probably the manor as well," Tyler said. "I called to see if Irene would have time to do a tour, but she said she had one thing to check on and then she'd give me a call."

Briana told them about reading the article about Stone Haven in the Marysville paper, and then asked who Lavida Roswald was.

"She's Dolan's grandmother," Tyler explained. "Cyrus, the one with the dogs, was her husband and they lived in Stone Haven until Cyrus died. Gladys and Bevin invited her to move in with them at the manor, but she refused, so they built an annex."

"So what's an annex?" Shelly wanted to know.

"A glorified hallway," Tom broke in, laughing, then added, "Its actual purpose is to connect Stone Haven to the manor, but they have a regular picture gallery in there."

The phone rang and Tyler answered it on the cordless phone by the lounger. After a brief conversation, he hung up and said the tour was set for three that afternoon.

They drove over in the van that Cecil had used that morning when he picked them up, but Tyler was at the wheel this time. As the county road curved around the hill to the east, the big Queen Anne manor came into view, the old stone house sitting quietly in its shadow. They looked larger now than from the plane and Briana marveled at the manicured lawn and the abundance of flowers.

The walkway to Stone Haven's front door was made of huge flat stones that were slightly irregular, and no doubt had been there since the house was built. A larger single stone, directly in front of the door, was used as a doorstep and showed footstep indentions from years of wear. Above the door was a squared stone with STONE HAVEN 1880 carved into it.

Tyler knocked on the thick oak door and it was quickly opened by a small, trim woman in her early forties. She wore a period costume with a floor-length cotton dress, high collar, long sleeves, and long white apron. A frontier-style prairie bonnet covered most of her hair, and she wore high-topped shoes fastened with buttons instead of laces.

Before the woman could greet them properly, a child came running out from the interior of the house, also in costume. Well, almost, Briana thought with a smile. The bonnet the little girl wore was tilted to one side with the ties hanging loose, and her long hair had begun to fall around her face in disarray. The long pinafore she wore was more like an apron, tied around the waist with ruffles over the shoulders, but when she turned, Briana could see that underneath the little girl was wearing plaid shorts and a matching shirt with sneakers on her feet.

"Welcome," the little girl said politely, before bowing gracefully and then throwing herself into Tyler's arms. Everyone smiled and Irene began the tour properly.

"Welcome to Stone Haven! I'm Irene Roswald and this is my assistant and niece, Brenda Day. We are pleased you cared to come to Stone Haven and hope you are ready to step back into the 1880s with us this afternoon."

Tyler introduced his guests while Briana wondered if this child was Adrian's daughter.

Stepping into the house truly felt like entering another era. There was no entry hall; the big door opened right into the parlor. The walls were very thick and had been finished with oak panels. The decor was that of the 1880s with kerosene lamps, period pieces of furniture, and braided rugs on the oak floors. Irene explained that the rugs were made at Stone Haven around the turn of the century.

"The door and door jambs are not original," Irene said. "They burned in a fire years ago, caused by this old stove in here." She pointed to a potbelly stove in the corner. "That's the culprit! It dropped a cinder onto the rug during the night and the room became an inferno. Elijah, Sarah, and their two sons saved the place. Cyrus was about eight and his brother six."

Brenda was whispering to Tyler and they looked at Briana when she glanced in their direction. The child smiled and turned back to Tyler.

"Now I'll tell you about the people who started the Roswald clan here in Marshall County." Irene began her discourse wistfully, as if she was reliving it, even though she was not a blood relative.

"It was 1870 when fifteen-year-old Jebidiah Roswald came west to seek his fortune. We don't know much about him, but we suspect he had hidden out in a wagon train or perhaps was a hired hand of some sort to people of means.

"Martha was another story, however. The diary she kept about her trip west, which we still have although it's badly faded, told it all. She started west with her Aunt Frances and Uncle Emil. She didn't say exactly how she came to be with them or where her parents were, but she was poor and her aunt and uncle needed someone to help with the children. Frances was pregnant and sickly. They already had four children under ten years of age."

"The poor woman!" Shelly said.

"They were with a wagon train that left Independence, Missouri, headed for Oregon, until a sickness began. To protect the rest of the people, they were asked to leave. The younger children and their mother died first. Martha talked about caring for them, fearing for her own life and being so tired she could hardly move. Of course, they had to keep going.

"She mourned over one of the little boys who was her favorite and prayed God would spare him, then had to bury him herself because his father was too sick. She soon was on her own and every day thanked God for sparing her."

Irene smiled and said, "Years later Martha wrote that she had thanked Him expecting each day that she would succumb to the plague, but she never did. She said we all must keep 'prayed up' even today. Isn't that amazing?"

"So she traveled by herself, then?" Briana questioned.

"Emil prepared her for what had to be done before he died. She knew which star to follow, so she just kept going, looking for civilization of any kind. She found Marysville and when she told her tale they made a heroine out of her. In 1879, at age seventeen, she met and married Jebidiah Roswald."

"Seventeen?" Shelly squeaked. "Now I really feel like an old maid!"

Everyone laughed when Brenda asked Irene, "What's an old maid?" When Irene explained, Brenda said her mother was an old maid too.

"No, Princess," Tyler began. "Your mother, Adrian, was married. An old maid has never been married."

"But she isn't married now," the child insisted.

"Everyone is aware of that," Irene commented, a little sharply. She continued, "Jeb and Martha settled on this piece of land and built a sod house. She had her first child by herself at age eighteen. When they could afford it, Jeb started building Stone Haven."

Briana looked around at the interior once more. The windows were small, allowing only a limited amount of light into the room, and the thick walls meant the windows were deeply recessed. The sheer curtains at the windows were a pale pink, which matched the padded cushion on an old maple rocking chair in the corner. What charm! What a step up from a sod house!

Irene led them into a hall and showed them a small room next to the parlor. It had been either a small bedroom or perhaps a sewing room. Now it was decorated and furnished as a bedroom, with an old wooden bed and primitive dresser and chair. The quilt on the bed was hand-sewn: faded, but spectacular. A smaller braided rug lay on the floor next to the bed.

Back in the hall, Irene led the party toward the rear of the house into a large dining room with a big fireplace. The bare wooden floors were polished to a fine sheen under the handmade wooden table and chairs, and an antique hutch displayed old china and pewter cups. A steep stairway at one side of this room led upstairs to Lavida's quarters.

Irene explained to them that Lavida was Cyrus Roswald's widow and mother of Bevin Roswald, who was Dolan's father. Because the ground-floor ceilings were so high, the sturdy steps seemed endless. A landing at the top turned at an angle and three more steps led to Lavida's living room, which looked like it was caught in a time warp from the 1970s. The shag carpet on the floor was orange and the avocado-green tweed sofa was worn and frayed. There was a bed pillow at one end, as if she had napped there while watching TV.

Briana was surprised by the contrast. She had expected the whole house to be done up in original decor. A blond coffee table, in stark contrast with the rest of the house, was strewn with religious magazines, and a stack of Bibles stood on an end table under a cheap lamp. The TV set was small and sat on top of a dresser right in front of the sofa. Irene led them through two bedrooms toward the front of the house. One of the rooms was restored with a four-poster bed and handmade quilt. An ancient spinning wheel sat in the corner; although it was dusty now, it was obvious that it had been much used at one time.

"How old is…er…Mrs. Roswald?" Briana asked, peering briefly into the next cluttered room.

"She's eighty-five. You can call her Lavida if you want. If she doesn't want you to, she will let you know!" Irene laughed and might have added more, but Brenda broke in.

"She gets real crabby sometimes. Mom says it's her age, but I think she likes it!"

"Brenda, do you want to leave?" Irene spoke quietly, but her threat was quickly recognized.

"No," she whispered, dodging behind Tyler.

"We were all sure Lavida would want to live with Gladys and Bevin in the manor, but of course, that didn't happen. She has her life here and I'm sure she misses Cyrus. We're afraid she'll fall on all these stairs, but so far she's been lucky. She says they keep her young."

As they retraced their steps down to the dining room, Briana was glad Lavida wasn't at home. Somehow Briana felt she wouldn't want the tour to include her private quarters.

Back on the main floor they entered the small kitchen, which had wooden wall panels like the rest of the house. It was decorated in the old style except for a microwave oven Briana noticed under a luncheon cloth on the counter.

Shelly and Tom were not very interested in all of this—at least not as much as Briana was—so they dawdled on the tour, which had put Briana and Tyler together as they entered each room.

"Ty, this is marvelous," Briana said. "I followed the California and Oregon trails all the way from the West Coast and marveled at the bravery and stamina of the pioneers. Thank you for letting me see what it was like living on the plains years ago! How spoiled we are with our modern conveniences like power, plumbing, and running water."

"Wait until we show you the pictures of the sod house Jeb and Martha lived in when they first got married."

"Perhaps they were so in love it didn't matter?"

"Is that the kind of love you're waiting for, Bri?" His voice, richly masculine, sent shivers up her spine.

"Yes, doesn't everyone want that?" She met his penetrating gaze in an attempt to let him know he had no effect on her at all.

"Some people settle for less," he answered, leaning slightly toward her in the narrow hall.

Irene's voice invaded their small world. "Now we'll go over to the annex." She led them into a large hall that connected the stone house to the big Queen Anne home on the west side.

"This is a gallery of old pictures dating from 1870 to the present time. These older ones are tintypes, but you can see they are still very clear." She pointed to the first group, which showed the old sod house with grass growing on the roof. The couple standing in front looked elderly, yet Irene said they were newly married.

"How old was Martha here?" Briana asked, looking closely at the image,

"She was seventeen," Irene said. "Don't they look old?"

Tyler pointed to an earlier picture of the Queen Anne house. The name on it was Blue Valley Manor.

Briana's eyes strayed back to the sod house, and she thought about Ty's question. Was it love or convenience for them?

"Here's our house!" Brenda pointed proudly at the photo of the brick home.

"Yes, here is our house," Irene said. "We wanted to be on the crest of Blue Point. Dolan and I were tired of historical homes. We just wanted a ranch style, all one floor with plenty of space and no steps to climb! We planned to have a big family so designed it accordingly."

"So do you live here year around?" Briana asked the child. Brenda hung onto Tyler's hand and acted shy all of a sudden.

"Adrian lets her spend the summers with us," Irene said. "It's better than being cooped up in an apartment in Topeka." Briana heard a tinge of disgust, or maybe cynicism, in her voice.

"I used to spend my weekends with Deb when I was little," Brenda admitted softly. "She died."

"Brenda, never mind," Irene said sharply.

The little girl looked bewildered and hurt, and she turned to Briana and mouthed, "But she did!" Briana nodded and took the child's hand in hers.

She looked at a modern color photo, slightly larger than the others and in a walnut frame that set it apart. It was a lovely home. Briana had seen it hugging the top of the hill with big trees gracing the wide sloping yard, surrounded by a white picket fence. The outbuildings were metal utility barns in colors that matched the beige color trim on the house. Most of the house was brown brick, with bright blue shutters and front door. An aerial shot showed part of the huge farm. The fields of green crops separated Stone Haven, on the lower slope of the hill, from the Queen Anne manor home on the summit.

"When Ty and Debby got married, Dolan gave them the West Farm," Irene said. "They had a plan in mind for a partial underground home, and Dolan about had a fit!"

Ty sighed and admitted softly, "You've got that right! But when he saw the plans he came around. Just barely!"

"It's lovely. You'd never know it was partially underground," Briana said.

"It's cool in the summer and stays warm in the midst of a Kansas blizzard. We have a solar panel system to help with heating," Ty added.

From the one window in the gallery, Irene pointed out the orchard that had been used for over a century. "They had apples and cherries in Jeb and Martha's day, but we've added to that. See the stone fence around the back property? In one of the papers here, it said there were 160 rods of stone fencing and 75 rails. They didn't use boards or hedges in those days. They raised wheat and Indian corn, Irish potatoes and later oats. They also made their own butter and had gallons of molasses."

"Tell her about the mules, Aunt Irene," Brenda prodded.

"Yes, they had mules to work the land. They were mentioned in one of the papers, also."

From the window, Brenda saw a playmate coming to the house. "Here comes Penny, I've got to go. See ya!" And with that she was gone.

"Penny is our twelve-year-old daughter," Irene explained. "The girls are very close."

Irene walked on and opened a large door, entering the foyer of the Queen Anne mansion. Tyler ushered Shelly, Tom, and Briana into the three-story entrance hall.

"Welcome to a new century of architecture," Irene said. "This home was built in 1925 when Cyrus and Lavida married. Of course, only the best grades of building materials available were used."

Briana heard the stress on "best" and wondered if it was a given fact of life for the Roswald family. Cyrus' dogs were pedigreed (the best, she was sure) and now the materials, too, were the best. Irene didn't seem to be bragging and probably Briana would not have picked up on it if Ty hadn't once emphasized that her new tires were the best.

Briana's eyes were drawn to a shimmering chandelier hanging from the ornate ceiling. Its prisms sparkled in the light streaming through the small windows on the landing. So beautiful, she thought, as her gaze followed the curved oak paneled staircase down to the newel post at the base.

Suddenly, like a physical blow, she felt the terror she had felt in Marysville. She raised her hands to her eyes and started to step back, only to collide with Tom.

She moaned, "No! Oh no!"

"Bri, are you all right?" Tom caught her elbow to steady her.

"Bri, you're white as a sheet!" Shelly exclaimed.

Briana was trembling so hard she thought she would fall. "I'm waiting," she said in a strange voice that didn't sound like her own. "I'm waiting," she repeated again as tears coursed down her cheeks.

Tyler put his arm around her and asked, "Are you sick? Briana, why are you waiting?"

She wasn't waiting. She was losing her mind! *Calm down and pull yourself together,* she thought frantically.

With her eyes closed, the strange feeling began receding. *God, please tell me what's going on. I can't keep this up. There is no logic to what is happening.* She became aware of Ty's arm and turned toward him. *He'd protect me. No. I have to get some help. Professional help.*

With her eyes closed, she tried to think what similarity there was between this building and the big red building in town. She had to look again. She was trained to take in details and recall it all later—skills she had used for years on her rounds at the rail yards.

Briana squared her shoulders briefly and opened her eyes. Tyler's concerned face floated into focus.

"I think we need to get you home. You've been out in the sun too much today, and you're not used to our humidity here in Kansas. We'll come back another time. Okay?"

"I'm waiting" slipped out of her mouth once more and she felt tears flowing again.

She turned and slowly scanned the whole entryway once more, holding tight to Tyler's hand as she did so. Then she forced her eyes to rest on the curved staircase.

It was starting again. It was the staircase! *God, please help me.* Her mind screamed silently. *I rebuke Satan in the name of Jesus! I reject this.* She let her mind work on this little by little, and she leaned almost totally on Ty. He turned her around and guided her out the big oak front door and into the warm breeze of the afternoon.

"Thanks, Irene," he called back over his shoulder. "We'll finish this another time. I think this young lady needs some rest."

Shelly and Tom thanked her also and then Shelly made an attempt to cheer Briana up.

"Bri, you're going to be okay. Do you feel better now that we're outside?"

Bri didn't answer. She was in a state of shock. Tyler helped her into the front passenger seat and fastened her seat belt. His face was just inches from hers, but there was no response. She was oblivious to her surroundings.

Resting her head on the back of the seat, Briana couldn't take her mind off the terror she had felt on the staircase. What could it mean? What must everyone think?

"I'm so sorry," she whispered. "I've ruined everyone's day."

"Don't worry," Shelly assured her. "Tom and I were ready for a swim anyway. But I agree with Tyler, you need to lie down for a while. Do you do this kind of thing often?" Shelly was blunt as only Shelly could be, and silence hung in the car's interior.

When Briana laughed shortly, the tension was released. "No, I don't, Shelly. I wish I could account for this in some way. I seemed to panic. It's like I become someone else." She glanced at Tyler behind the wheel and met his serious, searching gaze.

"You'll be fine. Two aspirins and a nap will have you fit as a fiddle." He didn't sound convinced, but his bravado boosted her morale.

CHAPTER 12

It was five that afternoon when Briana conjured up enough courage to rouse herself from the king-size bed she would share with Shelly all weekend.

She had slept fitfully, tossing and dreaming, then waking up afraid. She concluded that she probably needed a psychologist to help her deal with this problem. Or perhaps she could talk to the pastor at her new church. That sounded like a better idea and he could help not only by listening, but would pray for her, too. She needed lots of prayers! What would she tell him? How could she verbalize the terror without sounding like a complete idiot?

She finally got up and went to the bathroom to wash her face with a cool, damp cloth. A pale, solemn face stared back at her from the mirror. She was frightened! Were these the feelings people had when they were possessed or had past-life experiences? That was evil. Wasn't it? *Oh God, help!*

She found Tyler in his office and hesitated at the door. Sensing her presence, he looked up.

Hi, sleepyhead," he teased. "Tom and Shelly went for a drive, but they'll be back in time for dinner. Do you want something to drink or a snack?"

"Can we talk? I really need to explain…." Her voice faltered and she looked down at her clenched hands.

"Let's go out by the pool in the shade and you can tell me everything. I'll get us some iced tea." When she hesitated, he added, "Better yet, I'll get the tea and you put the ice in the glasses."

Briana knew he was doing all this to make her feel more at home. It did. She loved his home. Slowly she glanced around the office, wondering what would set her off next. First a building, then a staircase. It just didn't make any sense.

They settled on lounges, sharing the low glass table for their drinks. Briana remembered the intense yet silent exchange that had shared earlier on this patio. Everything was so intense now. Was it caused by the changes happening in her life, by her move, her new job?

"So explain to me what you felt at the manor." Tyler shifted his position slightly and gave her his full attention.

"I don't know if I can. I'm afraid. Really afraid." Her voice was barely a whisper.

"Go slow. If you don't want to finish, just stop. I really feel if we get it out and look at it, we'll find a very logical reason. I'd like to help you if I can." His last words comforted her.

She began nervously. "Today wasn't the first time that happened. I stopped in Marysville on my way to

Topeka, intending to get lunch, but got scared instead. I was driving down a street and before me was a huge brick building and I felt like a force of some kind had dealt me a blow. I couldn't drive, I could hardly breathe, so I made myself get out of the car and approach the structure to prove I wasn't scared. But I was! I cried and felt panic like I did today. It was like something bad had happened there. Do you think I have psychic powers like the people who witness a crime in a dream, then go with the police and help locate a body?"

"You have never had this happen before? Not in California or here in Topeka?"

"Never. I was sure I must have seen something like that building somewhere else as a child and I even asked my mom about déjà vu experiences. She said everyone has them at some time."

Tyler set his glass back down and inquired, "What did she say when you told her about your happening?"

"I didn't tell her about that exactly," Briana answered hesitantly. "She was worried enough about my move to Kansas without complicating it with—with happenings! Strange happenings!"

"So did you say anything in front of the building? Today you said 'I'm waiting.' Have you ever seen stairs like those before?"

"Only in the movies. What a beautiful home," she sighed, but her mind was not on the dwelling—only the staircase.

Tyler watched her expressions as she sipped her tea, then said, "So, tell me about your home. About your family and friends."

Briana hesitated at first, then gave statistics: one mom, one dad, and two brothers. She recounted her strong family ties with her loved ones and a normal middle-class life. She told Ty all about Richard and Mark, her friend Lisa who had moved to Cheyenne, and some of her other friends. She added information about school and her work in Richmond as a railroad special agent. She shared her joy about her promotion and her sadness to move so far away.

"So, what about the guy you left behind?" Ty questioned.

"No 'guy' was left behind," she countered quickly. Ty's probing eyes saw her uneasiness.

"What is the matter with California men now days? Seriously though, have you ever been married? Had children? Done drugs? Don't give me that look!" he laughed. "I also want to know if your parents always lived in California? If you might have a twin somewhere?"

"No, I'm the oldest, then Richard and Mark. Why?"

"Sometimes one twin feels things the other is experiencing, particularly traumatic incidents. I might do some checking, if you don't mind? Now about my other questions. What about your love life?"

Briana blushed and refused to meet his eyes. As awkward as it was to share the past with a new acquaintance, it was doubly so to share in such a clinical and one-sided manner.

"I've never been married or had children. I was engaged once." She paused then added, "We didn't get married."

Ty laughed his boyish chuckle that Briana was beginning to like so well and said, "Even I figured out that much. Are you going to talk to me, so I can help you?"

"I am talking to you." She knew this was fruitless so added, "I was engaged once and we were so happy. At least, I was until I found he was addicted to gambling and had a thing for my best friend. She was going to be my maid of honor."

"And so that soured you on men forever?" Briana had thought that herself, until she met Tyler. Of course, he had Adrian. She stared away rather than answer the question.

Ty sighed and got to his feet. "Let's take a swim before dinner. There's partial shade on one side of the pool, so you'll be okay. You need to forget about what happened and enjoy the rest of the day. We have all day tomorrow to talk about this and see what we can sort out. Okay? Now go get your suit on and I'll meet you in the pool."

He reached out and caught her hand, pulling her slowly up from her lounge. The feel of his firm grip shouldn't affect her at all, but it did. She liked him touching her. Briana looked down at the bronze fingers grasping her, then pulled away. She didn't have time to be attracted to Tyler or anyone at this point. She needed to get her life in order, not add to the confusion!

When she returned to the patio area, Ty was already in the pool. His tanned shoulders glistened in the water as he swam over to the edge just below her.

"The water's great! Are you coming in or do you need help?" A strong hand closed around her slender ankle.

"I can manage," she answered, putting her other foot on his head and dunking him briefly. Before he could retaliate, she dove with hardly a splash into the deep end. The water felt cool and refreshing as it swirled around her body. She was glad she had worn her red one-piece suit so she could dive and feel confident that everything would stay in place.

Surfacing, she saw a lightweight beach ball spiraling through the air and landing squarely in front of her with a splash. She pitched it back in Tyler's direction and dove under the water again, only to find Tyler diving to divert her. They came up laughing and Briana pulled her long wet hair to one side and squeezed it.

"Looks like I've lost my band," she said, feeling through the loose tendrils.

He was treading water close to her and he reached out to extract the band from the back of her tangled hair. "Here it is. Do you want to put it back on?"

"I guess not, since the damage is done. If it were short I wouldn't have this problem."

"Are you fishing for another compliment?" he teased, as he raised his eyebrows slightly.

When she flipped over in the water and struck out for the air mattress a few yards away, she kicked water all over him as an answer. Briana pulled herself partially onto the air mattress with her arms over the top to hold her. She treaded water, expecting Ty to dump her or at least pull her down, but he surprised her by surfacing on the other side of her float and leaning onto the mattress with her.

"You're ornery!" he accused. "Must be from your brothers ganging up on you as a little girl."

She couldn't understand how his mere physical presence caused her heart to do strange things. She had loved Jim so fully that she planned to marry him, yet he'd never had this strong of an effect on her.

"I'm not ornery. A maiden has to protect her image!"

"I thought maidens were always protecting their virtue!"

She had intended to answer, but his face was just inches from hers. The laugh lines by his lips and eyes caught her attention. He was too handsome and too nice. She would have to be very careful.

He reached out toward her face and lifted a wet strand of her long hair that had affixed itself to her cheek. The brief touch of his fingers made her burn with the desire for him to kiss her. She was feeling things she hadn't felt for a long time. Briana had felt like this with Jim in the beginning and had vowed never to let things go that far again. Why was she the one who always had to pay the price? Her eyes clouded with tears and she laid her head between her arms on the mattress, hiding the wetness from Tyler.

"Ready or not, here we come!" A voice broke the spell as two major splashes announced the arrival of Tom and Shelly.

When Shelly surfaced she informed them that Bea would serve dinner at 6:30.

"I'd better go get dressed, then," Briana said, pushing away from the float.

"Give me ten minutes to swim and I'll come, too," Shelly said. "I might even skip dinner. This feels so good!"

"You, miss dinner?" Briana laughed as she toweled off near the lounge. She raised the towel to her hair, turning slightly as she did so.

Holding the towel to her face, she caught Tyler's glance. She stuck her tongue out at him in a childish gesture. She enjoyed the surprised look in his eyes, followed by his booming laughter.

After dinner, Tom and Shelly announced that there was a good movie on TV. Tyler's satellite dish brought in all the stations available by cable in Topeka, so there were other options if they couldn't agree on the original suggestion. Tyler asked Briana if she wanted to watch the show; if not, he needed to get some information from her for his investigation. They left Tom and Shelly to enjoy the movie and set up in his office.

That evening it was all business. Briana had come to terms with the superficial attraction between them and decided that Tyler was playing the excellent host and was probably not averse to flirting with young women. He was most likely just now ready to begin dating again after the tragic loss of his wife and unborn baby, although she was sure he still mourned her. Then, of course, there was Adrian.

Briana wasn't sure she wanted Tyler to waste time on her problem. She regretted telling him about the old building in Marysville. If she had kept that to herself, she could have easily glossed over the staircase at the manor.

There wasn't much information to share, but she touched on the details of her job in California and her role in a the drug bust connected to a suspicious railroad shipment. "The contents were marked FRAGILE," she said. "The billing label said it was antique pottery for a museum in New York. Later, when we called in a team of dogs we found something different. It was a large shipment of drugs."

"But you just don't call in dogs to check all the boxcars, do you?"

"This wasn't in a boxcar. It was a semi-tractor trailer on a piggyback car, and you're right—we don't call for help as a rule. But the seal had been cut, and when I opened the door to investigate I heard a noise. It was a terrible night, with fog so thick my flashlight was only effective for a short distance. Since I couldn't decide what I'd heard, I cautiously stepped inside and waited."

Tyler leaned forward in his chair.

"Then I heard it again and dove for cover, switching off my light as I went. It was human, I decided, so I called out, 'Special Agent Sheldon!' and ordered them out with their hands up. It was so quiet that I began to think I had imagined the whole thing. Just as I began to inch myself toward the crates I'd seen, I heard a man's voice. He was speaking a foreign language. I waited and finally the voice cried 'Help me!' This is where I tell you that with my extensive training and skills, it didn't faze me."

"Yeah, right," Tyler said.

Briana's smile faded as she continued, "I ordered the man to show himself and I put some light on the area. In the beam of my flashlight I could see a spill of what looked like oil about five feet from me, so I crawled over to check it out. It wasn't oil; it was blood. A lot of blood.

"At that point, I called for immediate backup and crawled slowly forward. Suddenly an arm dropped out from the crate next to me." She watched Tyler's face, then admitted, "Now that scared me. I heard a man's voice, but couldn't understand him, he spoke so rapidly. I decided he was speaking Italian. I told him to speak English, and he finally said, 'I'm bleeding.' At that I called in once more and requested an ambulance. Of course, I had to help him. If all that blood had come from him he would be too weak to attack me. He was lucky to still be alive.

"I asked him if he was alone, and he said, 'Yes,' so I went forward and found him crumpled on the rough flooring. He seemed to have lost consciousness, but I could see his chest and the blood was pumping profusely out of the gaping hole in it. I had a sick feeling he'd been shot in the back at close range. I also suspected that internally he was in bad shape. I saw a shirt on the floor nearby and used it as a compress to slow the flow of blood. When he came to the next time and found me working on him, he made an effort to stay alert because he said he had a story to tell."

Briana hesitated, then added, "It seems there had been a falling out over some territory in San Francisco, and a guy named Tony had shot him. Some other person—Vinnie—had ordered the hit. His English was so poor that I was hard pressed to understand it, but when he said there were drugs present I knew we were both in grave danger. I had no idea how this man had gotten into the carrier with a wound that critical. The infamous Tony could have been lurking in the dark ready to shoot me as well. They wouldn't hesitate to get rid of me if their cargo was in jeopardy. "

"All that and you let a building and a staircase freak you out?" Tyler exclaimed.

"It wasn't all that bad. But I decided it was time for some extra help. I began praying Psalms 16, 'Keep me safe, O God, for in you I take refuge!' I'm not sure the dying man understood this, but it certainly helped keep me calmer.

"It seemed an eternity before help arrived. They loaded up the victim, and when I told them about the drugs, everything got wild. It was a long night. Usually I was home by eight in the morning, but I had to go downtown and give my statement, and somehow the press was tipped off. The police precinct filled with reporters and my picture was on the front page of the paper that evening."

"A celebrity! I'm impressed. You're going to find office work rather dull, I fear. So, did the victim live?"

Briana shook her head, "He was DOA, but they found a scrap of paper in one of his shoes with all kind of information about the drug deals. I'd say he knew he was in trouble long before he was shot. His note implicated some very well-known businessmen in the Bay area."

"Hey! I remember that. It was on national news," Tyler said. "I was traveling somewhere when it was announced."

"After the first news coverage the cops put a gag order out to keep my name out of the case. But even so, I had been receiving some threatening phone calls, even with an unlisted number."

"Why?"

"Well, no one knows for sure, but the detective handling the case thought that the criminals suspected the dead man had confided in me that foggy night. The fact that he was still alive when I found him put the fear of God in them. I suspect it will be years before all the connections are discovered and the criminals are convicted."

"How did they get your phone number?"

"I guess if you're powerful enough you have access to the phone company and can get unlisted phone numbers." Briana's mind trailed off to the reason she first got an unlisted number. Jim had been persistent when she had first broken off the engagement and would call, pleading for her to come back to him. That was in the beginning, when he was trying to convince her how innocent he was.

"If I survived all that, you would never expect me to freak out over a building or a staircase. I'm not fanciful, nor do I hallucinate, but I am very fearful now, not knowing what could set me off again. There has to be some common denominator. Are you sure this isn't some mental thing? If I were older, maybe senility?"

He laughed. "I shouldn't laugh because this is very serious to you. And you scared us all, to be quite frank."

The telephone rang and Ty reached for it. Briana felt she should leave him in private, but his hand motioned her to stay.

"Tyler speaking," he answered pausing for the response.

"Hi, Brenda!" He winked at Briana. He listened then said, "Yes, you can come swimming tomorrow after church. Do you want to come for lunch, too?" Another pause.

"Good evening, Dolan." Tyler sat up straighter in his swivel chair. "Yes, she's fine now," he glanced over at Briana. "We don't really know what happened. Some flashback or something."

"What time will it start?" he asked, then said, "Let me get back to you in a few minutes. We'll see what the rest of the party wants to do. Sure, thanks." He replaced the receiver.

"The Roswalds are having a barbecue tomorrow evening with fireworks, hog on the spit, and all the trimmings, and they wanted to know if we would like to join them. Would you like to do that?"

Briana smiled briefly. She knew that whatever they had planned would be the best.

"Should I be socializing with the Roswalds?" she asked aloud.

"It won't make any difference. In fact, it might help you understand why they are fighting this railroad closure so much. We won't talk business, if that's what you are worried about. There will be a crowd, as usual, but you'll have a good time. However, it's up to you. Do you feel like a crowd?"

"Why aren't they doing this party on the Fourth?"

"There are usually family members from Topeka who drive up so they have always had an annual Fourth of July barbecue on Sunday. Want to go?"

"I guess, if Tom and Shelly want to." Briana felt trapped. She didn't want to meet Dolan Roswald, and she certainly was not eager to meet the son who had invaded her motel room with his buddies.

Naturally, Shelly and Tom thought it would be great.

"You have to have fireworks on the Fourth!" Shelly explained at dinner.

"How about on the third?" Tom questioned.

"Then, too, silly!"

Briana wandered out of the living room and into the kitchen for a drink of water. Bea was finishing the dishes, so Briana grabbed a tea towel and dried the pans that wouldn't fit in the dishwasher.

"Now you don't have to work while you are up visiting, child. I can do it," Bea protested.

"I used to help Mom with the dishes. My two brothers said that was woman's work. You should have heard the fight when Dad informed them if they intended to eat, they would do dishes!" Briana could still hear their squawks, and laughed at the memory.

"They did help, but when they really had to pitch in was when I moved out. They deserved it," she chuckled, remembering them trying to get her to stay in Sacramento. Of course, her job was in the Bay area and she had her own dishes to wash.

"How are the puppies?" Briana asked as she hung up the damp towel.

"Come see them. We have one male and two females—they are so cute! Look like little fur balls, as wide as they are tall. Spunky is doing well, but I think she would give up this motherhood business to have the run of the house again. Babies can cramp one's style. She used to follow Ty everywhere, especially after we lost Deb. They kept her in town with them and would bring her home on the weekends. Deb would stay here during the week sometimes and Spunky would sleep at the foot of her bed."

The proud poodle was nursing her brood when they went to check on them. The mama cat Heidi stayed nearby, observing the procedure.

"Heidi was lying in the box with the pups this morning when Spunky went outside. These are not your normal pets! Spunky just laid down outside the box and waited until the cat felt like moving."

"Here, you are!" Tyler exclaimed as he stepped into the utility room. "Thought I had lost you for sure."

Briana was aware that Bea Miller glanced first at him, then at her. She mustn't read anything into Tyler's joking, Briana thought.

"I need to go down to the barn and check on Abby. Want to ride along?" Briana had been curious about his horses and knew Abigail was due to have her colt anytime.

"Sure."

He grabbed a cowboy hat off a peg in the utility room, then led her out through the garage to a four-wheel-drive Dodge pickup—the same one she had seen him drive in Marysville. They traveled down the drive to the county road, past the airstrip and hangar, then climbed to a plateau where a couple of modern barns stood.

"I brought you the front route, so you'd be impressed. We'll go home the back way, which is faster but bumpier. Have you ever been around horses?"

"No, I haven't. I'm really a city girl in every sense of the word except for this desire to live on a farm. It's crazy, but our family always talked about buying land in the country and having a farm. Of course, none of us knew anything about farming and Dad had a good job with the telephone company, so he couldn't justify a career change with a family to feed. By the time he could think about it seriously, we teenagers didn't want to be uprooted. Life is full of dreams that don't materialize." She had started this subject on a light note, but somehow sadness crept in. A glimpse of the dreams she and Jim had shared with a relationship of love and trust. A naive woman with blinders on. Then the hurt and humiliation, anger and frustration. Then finally recrimination and disgust.

"Are you all right?" came Tyler's low voice. The truck had stopped and the engine was turned off. She had been reliving things that by now should be put to rest, and must work at getting on with life. She nodded her head and jumped lightly out of the truck.

Inside the barn, Ty guided her down the center aisle to a dimly lit area. The barn smelled of horses and hay and the concrete floor was swept free of debris in this area. A few horses came forward in their stalls to peer out, and Ty patted each of them on their heads, calling them by name.

"So you heard me coming, did you, Abby girl?" he called out to the beautiful black mare who was straining her long, sleek neck out over the half door of her stall. Ty opened the door and stepped inside, checking her condition and talking softly to her.

"It won't be long now, girl," he promised, patting her back as he returned to the aisle, shutting the door.

Briana noticed the horse responding to his every touch and Abby's eyes following him while he dipped into a bin and got her a handful of grain. After Abby finished eating, Tyler rinsed his hands in a low sink in the hall.

Briana stroked Abby's shiny neck when he returned. "She's lovely, Ty!"

"So are you," he murmured against the back of her hair. Briana turned to find herself trapped, her back against the stall with Ty's hands on either side. He brushed his lips against hers in a feathery kiss.

"What are you doing?" she asked to hide her confusion and to give her heart a chance to stop pounding in her ears.

"I'm kissing you," he answered, his tone deep and sensual.

"That was a kiss?" She met his eyes in the dim light and added, "I think it was a full-fledged attempt of sexual harassment!"

"So you admit it felt sexual?" he countered, inches from her lips.

"Who is hearing this case?" she challenged playfully, her back still against the wall. "I would like to enter a plea of not guilty, your Honor," he said and they both laughed. Briana made an attempt to push him away as she said, "Perhaps we could plea bargain?"

Ty's hands moved from the wooden barrier to Briana's shoulders and he murmured, "Judge, I don't think my colleague realizes the magnitude of this case." Briana's dimples were flashing, so Ty bent his head to kiss the one on the right.

"Fellow councilor, Ms. Sheldon, ma'am, why don't you drop this case? You don't have one chance of winning!" He wrapped his long arms around her, pulling her close to his chest.

"Your Honor, I object," she began breathlessly, but the rest was lost as Ty's mouth claimed hers in a kiss that sent passion coursing through her body. Briana had never been kissed like that in her life. She put her arms around his body to pull him closer as the kiss slowly deepened. When at last he raised his head he took her head in his hands and studied her expression.

"I rest my case, your Honor! She coerced me into this by tempting me with her beautiful eyes." He planted a gentle kiss on each eyelid. "And her adorable dimples," kissing each, "and her sexy lips that seem to send out signals to my body. I'm glad the Judge is here to chaperone us, or I would carry you back in the hay and have my way with you."

Briana's voice was shaky as she whispered, "Is this more sexual harassment? You could be cited for contempt of court."

"As long as it's not your contempt, I don't care, but I'm not sure this is such a good idea," he began and her heart pained with the brief rejection.

He saw her confusion and lifted her chin to continue, "Because now I won't be able to stop. You've been driving me crazy ever since I walked into that boardroom and saw you crouched down on the floor picking up those papers. When you looked up, I knew you were going to change my life. Those beautiful electric-blue eyes just scared me half to death."

Briana felt a nudge from behind and suddenly the mare's head pushed between them. Ty began to chuckle as he released Briana to moved her away from the stall door. "Looks like my other girl is getting jealous!"

The interruption brought Briana back to sanity. The term he had used, "my other girl," scared her. True, she felt very drawn to Ty, but she was in no condition to enter into a relationship at this point. She glanced shyly up at him and disengaged herself from his hold.

"I...I think we should get back to the house," she began. "Tyler...." the words just hung in midair.

He released her totally then at the last minute caught her hand and raised it to his lips. "It's a little late for this 'I ... was' business but I won't pressure you." He dropped her hand and turned back toward Abby, handing the horse a sugar cube from his pocket.

CHAPTER 13

Shelly was in bed and almost asleep when Briana entered the bedroom.

"Hi," she mumbled into her pillow. "Tom and I fell asleep in front of the TV! Must be the exercise or the fresh air. Can't be old age."

"Ty and I went down to see his mare," Briana said. "Go on and sleep. We can talk in the morning." Shelly pulled her pillow into a different position and said no more. Briana, on the other hand, was wide awake—partly because of her nap, but also because of the scene at the barn and the attraction she felt for Tyler. She left the bedroom and walked through the house to the kitchen, where she poured herself a glass of water. She stepped out onto the enclosed patio and curled up in the corner of one of the overstuffed couches facing the pool.

The night was so clear that it made the moon and stars seem artificial. Crickets and locusts were chirping and every once in a while she'd see fireflies glittering in the night. Her mom would enjoy sitting here, she mused—and what a contrast from California! Briana missed her folks very much, but she and her mother always had a special closeness. So how would she tell her mom about her strange experience at the manor? How would she ever explain the sheer terror of it, the helpless, sinking feeling and the fear of it happening again? She sighed and set her glass down. Perhaps everyone was right and it was too much sun. But what about the red building in Marysville?

Briana snuggled a little deeper into the couch and tried to force her mind to switch channels. She was dreading the picnic and fireworks at the Roswald place. What should she wear to that? She had only packed a small bag and wondered if they would wear casual or dressier clothes. She decided to ask Bea in the morning.

Then her mind turned to Tyler. She smiled, remembering their playful discourse at the barn, then sighed when she relived his kiss. The flame of that kiss made her heart pound even now, sitting alone in the moonlight. What had started as a soft and gentle caress had burned almost out of control with passion—an explosive feeling with such velocity that all she could do was surrender. She should have put a stop to it, she realized now. She should have sidestepped his hands as they trapped her playfully against the stall door. He would have backed off, she felt sure.

But his kisses on her neck had made her pulse race and sent fire coursing through her whole body. She hadn't been mistaken in noticing that Tyler also looked startled. Perhaps he had expected her to pull away and play the role of the virtuous young maiden. She should have and would have, except— well, she hadn't given it a thought!

It was hours later when Briana awoke to someone calling her name. In the dim light, she became aware of Shelly shaking her gently and whispering her name.

"What are you doing out here?"

Briana started to sit up, then noticed a man's shirt spread over her.

"I don't think I ever went to bed," Briana began, removing the shirt slowly. "I guess I fell asleep."

Shelly sat down on a hassock in front of the couch, smiling as she watched Briana fold the shirt. "I thought perhaps you were in the master bedroom?"

"I hope you're kidding," Briana said as she held the badly folded shirt to her chest and stared at her friend.

"Of course I am, silly. But how did you come to be sleeping with his shirt?"

"I don't know. Am I awake or dreaming this?" Briana was only half serious with this question.

"I got up to use the bathroom and you weren't in bed. Your side hadn't been turned back and your clothes weren't in the closet. I peeked to see if you and Tyler were out on the patio or taking a nighttime swim. I wouldn't have disturbed you if that had been the case. You look like a foundling sleeping on a doorstep. Come on to bed. You've had a big day and from what Tom described, we're in for another one tomorrow. He said we could go to church in the morning if you want and then we'll have free time until the barbecue. I'm going to lounge by the pool."

"The pool is nice, isn't it? It's so—er—healthy!" Briana wondered if "healthy" was the right term after all the problems she'd had. Her friend sensed her confusion and smiled.

"Bri, you're going to be all right. There is a logical explanation for what happened to you. Tyler told Tom he knows a woman who had conducted searches for his firm before and she had access to computers that store all kinds of information. I know this is upsetting for you and you scared us too, but it will be okay. Trust me!"

Briana felt such a love for this girl. How fortunate she was to have a friend like her. Briana knew Shelly was worried, despite her bravado.

"I don't think I want to go to church at Marysville tomorrow." Briana laughed shortly and added, "Today, I mean!"

Shelly patted her friend's knee and smiled gently. "I understand your reluctance, and so will the men."

"It's not just the motel episode. I had that same feeling of fear like I did at the house when I was in front of a big building in Marysville. I just can't go back there—not even for church."

"Oh Bri, I'm so sorry this is happening. You're confused, and I'm reluctant. What a pair we make."

Briana looked puzzled, not following her comment.

"Tom proposed this evening."

"Oh Shelly, how wonderful! You said yes, didn't you?"

"That's where 'reluctant' comes in."

"But you love him!"

"But I'm not sure I want marriage. My dreams of married bliss were obliterated early in life. My folks split up when I was in grade school after years of battles and disappointments. We kids were caught in a tug-of-war that left each of us scarred for life. I don't know if I could trust a man enough to marry him. I want a marriage that will last forever, but men change and I would never put my children through the pain I've felt." Shelly's eyes were brimming with tears.

"I'm so sorry, Shelly, but Tom isn't your father and you're not your mother. Men and women both change during life, but the true kind of love lasts. My parents have been so happy all these years. Couples who are true partners grow together and strengthen their love each year. That might sound overly hopeful to you, though, with your family history. Do you have any idea what you're going to do?"

"I don't know. It's not fair to Tom when he's so wonderful." The tears began to flow in earnest.

Briana stood up and wrapped her arms around her friend. "Come on, let's go to bed. We're going to look like real messes by morning. Do some praying about this and don't think about your parents' failure. Just learn from it and go on."

The next morning the girls were late getting up. Briana entered the kitchen and found that Bea had cooked them a luscious breakfast.

"Tyler and Cecil got roused out of bed real early by Chad," Bea explained. "Seems something spooked the cattle down in the lower pasture and they tore out a whole section of fence, then took off. Cecil took the truck with his old horse in the trailer, Ty saddled Jet and headed cross country to meet up with Dolan."

"Does this happen often?" Briana asked, accepting a cup of coffee.

"It has been lately. The men think it's a cougar, but haven't found any tracks yet. The cattle will do fine for a night or two, then stampede and wipe out a different section of fence every time. Dolan thought at first it was the neighbor's dogs, but the boys camped out one night and Chad said it sure sounded like a cat. They sound almost like a woman screaming and can cover a lot of ground. Of course, the cattle just panic."

Shelly bounced into the kitchen and said, "We've definitely missed church. Guess we'll have to just lay around the pool today." She winked at Briana, then listened while Bea filled her in on the stampede.

"Tom was here earlier, ate a bite, and then went for a walk," Bea said. "He said he wouldn't be gone long."

"I hope he keeps his eyes open for running cattle," Shelly joked.

"I hope he doesn't call 'Here, kitty, kitty!'" Briana added, and Bea joined in on the laughter.

"Shame on you two," Bea reprimanded, then laughed again.

When Brenda appeared around eleven o'clock with a tote bag on her shoulder, she was noticeably disappointed that Tyler was gone. But after changing into her swimsuit, she enjoyed swimming with the girls and Tom. She showed them all her swimming accomplishments, but explained that she could only dive when Tyler was present.

Shelly got out of the pool to tan and Tom followed, helping spread the suntan lotion on her shoulders and back. Briana could see the love they shared and hoped for their sakes that they could work out their problems.

"Are you coming to the picnic tonight?" Brenda asked. "We're going to have a lot of fireworks!"

"Yes, we're all going to be there. Will there be many people?" Briana asked curiously.

"Yup. We always have a big crowd at all our parties."

Briana smiled at Brenda's pride. Perhaps she, too, would refer to this sort of thing as "the best" when she got older. It had to be a family trait.

After splashing around a while longer, Briana and Brenda finally got out of the water and spread their towels on the tiled area around the pool.

"I like your bikini," Brenda said while sprawled out next to Briana. "You have a mark there." The child pointed to the side of Briana's midriff where she had a birthmark about the size of a dime.

"That's a birthmark," Briana explained. "My mother used to tell me that God puts marks on special people and that made me feel good when I was a child. Of course, that's not true. One doesn't have to have a mark to be special. You are pretty special," she added to emphasize her point.

"My mom doesn't think I'm special. She says I'm a pain. But see this?" The little girl pulled at the side of her swimsuit until you could almost see her bellybutton. There on her stomach was a mark similar to Briana's.

"I think I'll remind my mom about my birthmark and tell her I'm special." Then she paused. "Maybe not. She'll say I'm not."

Brenda straightened out her suit and asked, "Do a lot of people have birthmarks?"

"I don't know. Probably everyone has some sort of mark or blemish. Even moles are common and freckles are like sprinkles of sunshine. That's also a quote from my mother."

"I wish your mom was here. She sounds cool."

"I sometimes wish she was here too because I miss her very much. She's in California where I grew up, with my brothers and my dad. They're all pretty cool, too."

Brenda smiled at Briana and then returned to the subject.

"I think birthmarks are different than freckles and stuff," the child decided with age-old wisdom.

Briana had to laugh at her seriousness. "We can say they are since we each have one," she said, then added, "But let's keep them a secret. Only you and I will know."

This made an instant bond between them, and though it was rather silly, even childish, on Briana's part, she enjoyed Brenda's reaction.

Tyler came out through the patio and greeted everyone. He looked so handsome that Briana couldn't help staring. Brenda jumped up and ran to him so he lifted her up on his shoulders.

"You're either getting too big for this or I'm getting weak," he joked, staggering and almost dropping her on purpose into the pool. "Are you going to show the nice people how you can dive?"

He put Brenda down and she quickly positioned herself on the side of the pool, ready to dive. Tyler corrected her stance, then said, "Go!"

Her dive was good for a novice and when she surfaced, Briana immediately complimented her.

Ty spent pool time with Brenda and the bond between them was very obvious.

Later, Briana went in the house to ask Bea about the dress code for a Roswald barbecue, then went to her room and changed out of her swimsuit into shorts and T-shirt for the rest of the afternoon.

CHAPTER 14

That evening about six, the van made its way up to the crest of Blue Point Hill. The view was breathtaking. Bea had packed a picnic hamper, and Cecil kept referring to a cake she was guarding from him.

"We missed the picnic last year," Bea explained. "Cec and I took time to visit our daughter who lives in Spokane, Washington. She has such a lovely family."

Briana had no time to hear any more about them because the van stopped and a middle-aged man walked forward to welcome them.

"Bri, Shelly, this is Dolan Roswald. Dolan, this is Briana Sheldon, whom you have been hearing about, and her friend and co-worker Shelly Wyatt." While Tyler was doing the introductions, Dolan extended his hand to greet them.

Briana just knew she would feel repulsed by this man and had spent most of the day wishing this moment would never come. Now that it had, it was surprisingly easy. Dolan was very good-looking and appeared to be in his early forties, with brown hair graying slightly at the temples. His trim body was muscular and well proportioned for his height, which was at least a couple of inches over six feet.

"I'm so glad you've come to our little get-together," he said, searching Briana's face with brown eyes that were friendly and very expressive. Briana thanked him for his hospitality and wondered whether she should mention his involvement in her car repair. Before she could, he commented that his wife had told him about Briana getting sick at the manor and said he was pleased that she had recovered.

If he only knew, she thought. Irene walked forward about that time, followed by a teenaged boy. He was introduced as Mark Roswald, and Briana instantly compared him to her own brother by the same name. They were even about the same age.

When they all moved to where the crowd had gathered, Tyler began introducing his guests. Adrian was there, wearing skin-tight shorts and a tube top that barely covered her. She ignored the introductions and walked away to talk to another couple. Tyler followed with his guests in tow and broke into their conversation to introduce them, but Adrian blew him a kiss and strode provocatively away.

The couple was introduced as Adrian's parents, Melissa and Carter Lancaster. They were friendly, polite, and a pleasant contrast to their daughter. After chatting for a few minutes, Briana learned that Melissa was

Dolan's older sister. The couple filled her in on their granddaughter Brenda's latest adventures.

When Briana had asked Bea about how guests might dress, she had told Briana that the guests would mostly be country club casual, but that two would really stand out: Adrian, worrying about competition, and Lavida, who didn't understand modern casual wear. Briana had decided to wear a casual polo dress in a raspberry knit; the contrasting navy blue collar made her eyes stand out. She felt comfortable that she would blend in with the other guests whether they were casual or slightly dressy for the picnic. Seeing Melissa in a flowered skirt and trim T-shirt made her feel even more at ease with her choice. "Where did you ever find earrings to match that exact color of lavender?" she asked.

The women discussed fashion and shopping, while in the background Briana could hear the men talking about the cattle problems from the night before. Briana decided she liked Melissa and wondered why Adrian behaved so badly. She also wondered what Lavida thought of Adrian's provocative apparel.

The food was outstanding and Tyler was attentive to his guests. Briana sat next to him at a picnic table, but could hardly concentrate on her food. Sitting beside Tyler made it easier, in a way. She couldn't look at him unless she turned sideways and at that close proximity, she wasn't about to do that.

Tom and Shelly kept a steady flow of conversation going and others joined in cheerfully. Adrian's parents were seated opposite them and Briana found them to be interesting people. Adrian sat at another table close by, with an older boy and Mark. She was facing Ty and Briana about ten feet away, and Briana could feel the animosity seething from her at that distance. The older boy also faced Briana and once she met his eyes she began to chill. He looked so brazenly at her that she quietly asked Tyler who he was.

"That's Chad Roswald. He'll start college this fall and after that Dolan hopes he'll come back home to farm. He's pretty rowdy and spoiled, in my opinion."

Briana purposely avoided looking back toward the young man, but felt his eyes on her anyway. She wondered if he had been one of the men inside her motel room that night in Marysville. Perhaps he'd been too busy slashing tires.

She raised her eyes to study his face for a brief second and thanked God that at least it wasn't Tiny. As she looked at him, she became aware that his eyes were slowly taking in every inch of her body, from the waist up, in a blatantly lascivious manner. When his hazel eyes met Briana's startled expression, he smiled, shifting slightly, then ran his tongue provocatively across his lips. Revulsion swept over Briana, so she turned and spoke softly to Tyler, who studied her pale face in concern.

"Are you experiencing a 'happening'?" he asked quietly. "What were you looking at?"

"It's not that. I'm just being silly, I guess. By the way, how did I end up with your shirt last night?"

He shook his head in dismay. "You mean you can't remember? I must be losing my touch!" He watched as disbelief clouded her face, then added softly, "Or did I just dream I held you in my arms all night?"

She felt her body responding to him, though there was no physical contact, and she couldn't speak. Seeing the raw confusion on her face, he turned serious.

"Actually, I had seen you curl up on the couch on the patio, but chose to stay away. It wasn't easy, believe me. When I could no longer stand the temptation I decided to pull the drapes so I couldn't see you because I needed my rest!" His low, throaty chuckle made her smile in response.

"When I peeked out later, I found you had gone to sleep," he continued. "So to keep you from getting chilled I covered you with my shirt. I wanted to carry you to my room."

"Tyler! Don't talk like that. Someone will hear." She glanced at the Lancasters, who were involved in a discussion with Tom and Shelly about the stock market.

"No one is listening to us. Would you have been upset to wake up in my bed?"

"I don't....I wouldn't...." Words failed her as she stared at him.

"Oh, really?" he murmured softly as his gray eyes searched hers, then lowered slightly to take in her flushed cheeks. "I'm proud of you. Sometime we'll have to discuss this at length to make sure I understand."

Before he could add to this, Brenda arrived. She said hello to the whole table before squeezing in between Tyler and Briana.

"Are you going to dance with me?" Brenda asked Tyler. "They're getting the music ready. Remember last year when you taught me to waltz?"

"I remember you stepping all over my feet!" Tyler countered.

"Silly! I didn't either. I learned quick!"

Melissa looked up. "Brenda, leave the poor man alone. Can't you see he has guests?"

"But Grandma, Tyler still likes me best. Don't you?"

Tyler poked her playfully and assured her she was his favorite little girl in the whole world. "Any waltz you want will be yours, but you have to ask politely, and you can't step on my new boots."

Brenda raced off to meet Penny by the table of fireworks, where some of the men had gathered to get things organized before it got dark. Briana remembered the fireworks from her childhood. The fun stuff was outlawed, but the boys had sparklers and snap and pops. They delighted in scaring her with the latter. At least, she pretended to be scared.

The music began and couples drifted onto the cement drive next to the garage and began to dance. Some of them were doing a Western line dance that had always interested Briana. She was sitting alone for the moment, since Tyler had been put to work carrying boxes of rockets out to the launch site.

Irene sat down to chat for until a very elderly woman interrupted them.

"So you got sick in the manor?" she cackled as she peered closely to focus on Briana's face.

"Grandma, don't embarrass the child," Irene chided. "She wasn't sick, just too much sun. Are you enjoying the country life? Our men had one devil of a time rounding up the cattle this morning. I hope the fireworks don't spook them again. We should be far enough from them, but when they are nervous you never can tell."

"I never cared for fireworks. Too much noise," Lavida Roswald snorted. "Seems a big waste of money." She was obviously opinionated and a person who didn't mind voicing those opinions. "The only display we should be looking for is the return of Christ." She looked closely at Briana and asked bluntly, "Do you know Him, young lady?"

"Yes, I do, Mrs. Roswald. I grew up with Him in California and was thankful to have His company on the journey to Kansas. My parents made sure all of us kids were in Sunday School every week and youth group Sunday evenings. Jesus is my best friend!"

The old lady smiled a worn, crooked smile and said to Irene, "Your children should feel that way!" Then she walked stiffly away.

"Oh dear, please don't be offended by her directness," Irene said. "At eighty-five, I guess she has the right to say what she wants, but she still embarrasses people who don't know her. You will be one of her flock now that you have confessed a relationship with the Lord. She will probably ask you questions to see how much you know. That drives most people away and we've told her that, but of course, it doesn't stop her. Oh, here comes Chad. Chad, have you met Briana Sheldon?"

He was a tall boy, towering above his mother, and Briana wondered for a second if his father had looked like this as a teen. At close range and in front of his mother, he behaved well, not even really looking in Briana's direction until his mother's question.

"I thought everyone knew Miss Sheldon," he answered with a hint of sneer that Irene missed.

"Why don't you take her out for a dance?"

Briana was sure he would refuse with the first excuse he could find, but that didn't happen.

"Sure," he agreed.

As he reached for Briana's hand, she mumbled, "I really don't dance very much...."

But Irene was waiting and, to avoid a scene, Briana went with him. He placed both arms around her waist, pulling her roughly against his body with his face against her cheek.

"Never dreamed I'd have you in my arms," he began and she stiffened, trying to push him away. "I'll never forget the sight of you sitting cross-legged on that bed. You might as well have been buck naked for all you had on."

Briana increased her struggles and demanded, "Let me go!"

"I don't think so. I've held you like this. I've touched you...."

"In your dreams!"

The next second he was on the cement drive, looking startled and embarrassed as others laughed and teased him about his big feet. Briana walked away, leaving him to deal with the ridicule. Then Tom caught her hand and pulled her gently back to the dance area. He held her properly, and after a moment, she looked up to meet his concerned eyes.

"Is that mad passion in your eyes, or just mad?" he teased.

"I'm so angry I could spit!" she seethed.

"Now, now, spitting isn't ladylike but if you feel you must, warn me ahead of time and I'll duck." Tom chuckled lightly and Briana smiled, too.

"That little boy is cruisin' for a Sheldon bruisin'," she promised.

"Got fresh?"

"Got flat on his butt!" she quipped, then laughed outright.

This was how Tyler found them.

"I guess I'd better find Shelly," Tom decided after one glance in Ty's direction.

"The fireworks are positioned and ready to be set off about 10 p.m. The Roswalds sure went all out this year." He held out his hand to draw her to him but she didn't comply.

"What's going on?" he asked, dropping his hand and looking closely at her.

"I guess nothing right now. I could use something to drink." This was a diversionary tactic until she could decide whether or not to tell him about her dance floor antics.

Like a good host, he turned and headed for the beverage table. Briana watched him go, wondering if he would take Chad aside and give him a talking-to if she told him, or if he would go straight to Dolan about his son's misdeeds.

"Hi," someone greeted her, rousing her from her thoughts. Brenda's friend Penny was standing quietly, smiling up at her.

"My name is Penny Roswald, Brenda's cousin," she began. "You're a friend of Tyler's?" The young girl seemed hesitant, as if she wasn't sure if she really wanted to talk now that the conversation had begun. Briana wondered what was in store for her with this Roswald child. Tyler was in a conversation at the refreshment table. Maybe she would have time to assure Penny their conversation wouldn't be interrupted.

"Why don't we move out of the crowd so we can hear each other?" Briana suggested as they distanced themselves from the dance area.

"That's better," she said, pleased that the child had followed.

Without preamble, Penny blurted, "I saw what you did to Chad!"

Briana felt her heart sinking, realizing the girl had probably come to tell her off, but before Briana could venture an explanation Penny asked, "How did you do that? That was great!"

Briana opened her mouth to speak, but Penny was still talking.

"It was so quick! One minute he had you in a bear hug while you were trying to push him away and then, wham! He was on the ground! You were great. Is that karate?"

The open admiration brought a smile to Briana's lips. "No, not karate. It's a self-defense technique I learned when I was a railroad cop."

"You were a cop?"

"We were called railroad agents. I'm a lawyer now but I still retain my status as agent for one year."

"So can you show me what you did, or is it a big secret?"

Briana smiled again. "The self-defense move is called Pain Compliance. You probably didn't see me reach behind my waist to grasp his fingers. I gave no warning that I was going to do anything, but I grabbed his thumb and bent it backwards. The pain concentrated his thoughts on that while I ground the heel of my sandal on the instep of his foot, causing massive pain. His body weight and gravity did the rest."

"Wow!"

"I'll show you some holds sometime when we have a chance, but right now Tyler is getting me a drink. What grade are you in?"

"I'll be in the sixth grade when school starts next month. I heard about those men breaking into your motel room. Dad said you had a gun. Is that legal?"

"Yes," Briana answered. "It's my service revolver and I was glad I had it. It was a bad scene."

"But you weren't hurt, were you? You scared them off!"

Bri could see that Tyler had shaken loose from the men and was looking for her, so she raised her hand and he started in her direction.

Penny turned to see who she waved to and said, "He's a sweetie, you know. I miss Deb so much." Then she looked up at Briana and added, "I wish you were marrying him instead of Adrian!" Then she darted off, leaving a stunned Briana to face the happy-go-lucky guy delivering her drink.

"Here you are. Hope Coke is okay?" He wiped the moisture from the can and handed it to her. She avoided looking at him and was glad she had the pop to hide her quivering lips. She willed herself not to show any emotion and turned toward the dancers with intense interest while Tyler, unaware of her pain, filled her in on the fireworks plan.

Tom and Shelly found them and helped breach the strain. Shelly was bubbly and carried the conversation, with Tom adding tidbits. *Thank you, God,* Briana thought. No one noticed her heart breaking and no one saw her pain.

Briana wanted to leave, but she could see no way to achieve that without having someone drive her back to Ty's house. Tyler would volunteer and they would be alone again. She must never be alone with Tyler again. Not now.

She should have suspected his relationship with Adrian was serious—no wonder the poor girl was so rude! Tyler was not without blame. Her face burned with shame as she remembered their passionate kiss and their stilted discussion about her virginity. How could she have been so naïve? *Oh, God, please help me get through this night,* she prayed.

The word went out that the fireworks display was about to start, so everyone converged on the side of the hill. There were benches and lawn chairs to sit on, and at the earliest opportunity, Briana chose a lawn chair. There was no way she would chance sitting beside Tyler in the dark.

As soon as the colors stopped exploding in the Kansas sky and they rose from their chairs, Briana told Shelly she had a headache. This was true, but she hoped it would be an excuse to go home and right to bed.

"Do you have any aspirin?" Shelly asked. "I have some in my purse if you don't."

"We'll be leaving before long, I expect. I'll wait until I get home."

Home. Briana groaned inwardly. She wished she were in her borrowed bedroom at Shelly's place where she could cry and no one would know. Her heart felt bruised and her body was trembling. She had begun to love that tall man with the quick smile and sexy gray eyes. How could she have allowed this to happen? She should have kept their relationship on a business level.

Tyler strolled over to where the girls were standing.

"If it's okay with all of you, we'll leave in a few minutes. Cecil and I had a short night last night."

They said their goodbyes, getting into the van for the return ride. Shelly and Tom rode in the rear seat of the van; Briana heard them murmuring quietly and then suspected they were kissing. It was pretty quiet back there.

As Tyler sat beside Briana on the middle seat, he put his arm along the back of the bench seat. She shivered as his hand briefly touched her shoulder. He asked what she thought of the Roswalds and she said they seemed pleasant. It sounded pat, but she didn't want to enter into a discussion about them.

He probably wasn't aware that his fingers were stroking her upper arm. If she moved slightly perhaps it would break the contact, but they had only a short distance to go and she could endure it for that long.

He's marrying Adrian, her conscience reminded her, but her heart replied, *Who cares?* She felt the tears well up in her eyes and she knew they'd be seen when they entered the house.

After they all disembarked by the three-car garage, Tom and Shelly announced they were going for a late-night swim and headed for the house to change. Cecil and Bea faded into the shadows leading off to their mobile home, leaving Tyler and Briana to enter the house alone.

"Want to see the pups before you turn in?" he asked as he opened the utility door from the garage. Spunky was feeding her puppies and was delighted to have guests. She struggled free of her brood and came out to greet Tyler. He scooped up the little dog in his arms, holding her toward Briana to be petted. The little gray poodle licked her hand, then glanced up at her master again.

"She is so precious," she said, keeping her eyes on the dog.

Ty's lips seemed to brush her forehead of their own will, but Briana knew she must step away. This was the time to put a stop to this, but somehow she had become rooted to the floor and even felt herself sway in his direction. He wasn't touching her now, just watching the confusion and indecision play across her face. He lowered Spunky to the floor, then searched Briana's face. A strange helplessness filled her, then she was in his arms and his lips were claiming hers.

One last kiss, her conscience promised. Or was it Satan at work again?

She finally stepped back and looked up at his handsome face. Tears were flowing down her cheeks, and he wiped them away with his fingers.

"What's this?" he asked, searching her eyes with his brow knitted.

"Tyler, that was not supposed to happen again," she began, avoiding the hand that reached out to draw her near. "I can't even consider getting involved with you or anyone right now with my life in such a turmoil. There is something happening to me that I can't seem to deal with and, until I can, everything else has to wait. It frightens me to think that any minute I could be reduced to terror and tears by something that's not even familiar. This is so scary for me, because I'm basically pretty tough and self-assured, yet here I am letting an old building and a staircase devastate me. I'm sure I seem like an immature child to you but...but...." She couldn't finish.

He caught her shoulders and declared, "You don't kiss like a child!"

She refused to meet his eyes, but felt color flush her face.

"I don't care if you're experiencing some problems. We can solve those and I can help you sort it out. All that matters is right now. Today!"

Then his voice lowered to a caress and he added seductively, "Tonight!"

Briana pulled free and ran swiftly through the house to her room. Briana was glad Shelly was elsewhere because she flung herself across the bed and sobbed into her pillow. How could he make advances to her, then turn around and marry Adrian? Did he really expect that she would waste herself on a cheap one-night stand—even if it was with him?

Maybe he'd misunderstood their odd conversation at the picnic table. Maybe he really believed what he thought earlier about her and the truckers. Anger overcame her misery and dried up her tears. How dare he?

As she calmed down, Briana realized that she was totally at fault. This whole friendship should never have started. She should have kept it all on a business level, and now she must strive to go back to that. She only had breakfast and the flight back to endure, and then this nightmare would be over.

Her thoughts then turned to Adrian and she wondered if Tyler loved Adrian enough to marry her. Why weren't they together? Why was Tyler putting the moves on Briana while Adrian planned their wedding? Briana couldn't see herself standing by quietly while her fiancé entertained an unattached female for a weekend, even if there were other people along. Was that being possessive on her part? Perhaps, but she didn't think it was unreasonable.

She should have come right out and asked Tyler about his engagement, but the moment was gone. She couldn't decide if it was even her business to ask. What did she really know about Tyler?

CHAPTER 15

Briana was glad to be back in Topeka. The weekend was a bittersweet experience she never wanted to encounter again.

The first few days after they got home, Shelly was quiet and distant. Either she sensed Briana's withdrawn attitude or she had problems to solve and decisions of her own to make.

Briana was happy when her shipment from California finally arrived, bringing the small amount of furniture that she owned. She planned a shopping spree to buy other necessities after she moved in over the weekend.

On Friday, Kyle came into the office after his doctor's appointment and said he was released to work a few hours each day until he recovered enough to resume normal duties. He complimented Briana on her handling of the Blue Valley spur case and offered to take that over, which would free her up to do research on another pressing case. That would mean no more trips to Marysville and no more contact with the Roswalds. No more dealings of any kind with Tyler. Briana gladly handed it over to him.

She spent Thursday night in her new house. She had only odds and ends to move Saturday, but it was fun to sleep in her own bed from California, and she had just dozed off when the phone on her nightstand rang. It was Shelly.

"Were you asleep?"

"Not really. What's up?"

"I miss you. You've never slept away from home before," Shelly joked lightheartedly.

"I wish you were here, too, so we could have a slumber party. What have you decided to do about Tom?"

Shelly didn't answer for a second, then sighed audibly. "He's pressing me for an answer. I just don't have one yet. I'm so scared!"

"Don't be forced into something you'll live to regret," Briana advised. She would start praying about this for Shelly. There was bound to be a solution.

"Tyler sure seemed to enjoy having you with him last weekend. Is this getting serious?"

Briana visualized his face when he bent over to kiss her parted lips. She remembered the laugh lines by his mouth, the twinkle in his gray eyes, and her heart fluttered with the desire stirred up by just the memory of his kiss.

"Bri, are you falling asleep?" Shelly's voice roused her from her reverie. "If you don't want to tell me, it's okay. I don't mean to be nosy. Much!"

"I...er ...we...." Briana wasn't sure how to begin. "I can't get involved with Tyler. We are just going to be friends. Acquaintances, perhaps. We're on opposite sides of the table on the spur line problem, so it would be unethical. It's okay. Really!"

"Poppycock! You should see the way that man looks at you and there is so much static in the air you couldn't possibly be unaware. Just friends? Not!" Shelly rambled along on the same theme until Briana began to laugh.

"He was just being a good host and thought I needed some romance on the holiday weekend. Trust me, nothing happened!" She thought about telling Shelly about Ty's engagement, but just couldn't bring herself to do it for fear of crying.

"So did you ever find out how you came to be sleeping in his shirt?"

"Shelly, I wasn't sleeping in his shirt! It was over me, remember? He found me asleep and was afraid I would get chilled."

"Yeah, right, and I believe in the Easter Bunny, too!"

The girls began laughing and joking back and forth.

"Tom told me today that you had a tiny little problem with Chad Roswald on the dance floor," Shelly said, changing the subject away from Tyler. "He said you were a little upset."

"Actually, I was the one who upset him—literally! The rude jerk."

"But why did you dance with him in the first place?"

"Believe me, it wasn't by choice. I had made such a fool of myself at the manor, I felt I should try to behave when Irene suggested we dance. We were in a crowd of people, for Heaven's sakes, so what could possibly happen?"

"I have never in my life met anyone as interesting as you, Bri. No wonder I miss you!"

"I could stand for less excitement and more answers. I live in fear each day that the feeling will come back that I had at the manor house and at Marysville. I'm going to talk to Pastor Woods Sunday and see if he can help me. I can't go through life wondering what will trigger this déjà vu stuff."

"That's a good idea," Shelly agreed. "Do you need some moral support? I'll come with you if you need me."

Briana smiled. Yes, Shelly would be there if she were needed. A true friend.

When they finally hung up, Briana turned over and settled down for the night. Again the phone disturbed her. She suspected Shelly had forgotten something.

"Okay," Briana answered without greeting, "If you aren't going to let me sleep, you might as well come spend the night!" She was laughing when she blurted this out, but the mirth died when Tyler's low-pitched chuckle began.

"That's the best offer I've had lately."

"I thought it was Shelly calling again," she quickly explained, then asked, "How did you get my phone number?"

"I called Shelly. She said she had been talking to you and you were still awake. I know better than to wake you!" He was teasing her about their previous major disagreement, which wasn't fair.

"I was calling to see if we could get together this weekend and talk about your strange happenings. Dinner, perhaps?"

Briana's heart lurched and she opened her lips to refuse, but instead asked, "Can't you tell me what you've found out over the phone?"

There was no way she was going to go out with him, even if it was just dinner. Furthermore, she resented the fact that he thought she would. Had he forgotten about Adrian?

"No, I can't tell you over the phone. I have some papers for you to see. This is very important, because I've been doing some checking on you and have some statistics I would like you to see. How about it?"

She felt the trap closing. There was no way she could avoid seeing him, but she could pick the time and the place. "Why don't I meet you at Burger King at 11th and Kansas Avenue tomorrow? I need to run an errand on my lunch hour so I could meet you at 12:30."

"Okay, I'll bring the documents and see you tomorrow. If you're sure about only lunch, I'll see you then. Sleep well."

Briana held the receiver a second longer than necessary. He had hung up rather abruptly, she thought. Or was it just her imagination?

Tyler was seated in a corner booth when Briana entered the restaurant exactly on time the next day. His smile started to melt her and she hesitated, experiencing a sudden longing as she realized how much she had missed seeing him. How had she ever allowed herself to care this much?

He rose to his feet and extended his hand, but she slipped into the seat across from him without touching him, knowing what a disastrous mistake that would have been. She would have made a real fool of herself, by either throwing herself in his arms or crying. Possibly both! The vision caused her to smile, and Tyler responded in turn.

"Tell me what you want, and I'll order for us," he said.

I'll have you, her brain was saying, but her voice said, "Just a Coke, I skip lunch sometimes."

"You need a noon meal," he preached. "Research shows that food keeps the brain sharp so you don't get dull at three in the afternoon."

"Are you saying I'm dull?" she asked defiantly.

"It's not three yet!"

Briana watched him place their order and noticed the glances and giggles as the girls working at the counter eyed him. When he returned he brought her not only the drink but a small cheeseburger as well.

"It will help you face three o'clock," he teased. "I knew you liked them from the way you scarfed the one on the turnpike." He laughed out loud at her expression. She had to laugh with him.

"Men!" she muttered.

"Speaking of the superior gender," he began, grinning at her flash of disgust, "what did you think of Dolan?"

"He seemed very civilized. I can't believe he and Chad are related."

"I heard about the trouble you had."

"Hey, I wasn't in trouble. I didn't end up sitting on the concrete!" She bristled at the pity in his voice. His hand went up and he smiled, calling a truce.

"Wish I could have seen it. Tom says you're pretty quick!"

"Keep picking on me and I'll give you a demonstration!" she promised and turned her attention to her burger. After that, their meal was comfortable and conversation flowed freely as it does with friends. When they were through eating, Tyler pulled out a business-sized envelope from his suit jacket and laid it on the table.

"I've been doing some research on the name 'Briana Sheldon' and have turned up quite a few." He opened the envelope and extracted four sheets of white folded paper.

"There happen to be twenty-eight Briana Sheldons in your age group in California, and eight of them have Lee as a middle name. Here's the breakdown."

He handed her one of the sheets and she perused the list, noticing that beside each one was an address, age, and marital status. Four of the Sheldons were married names, leaving four that could be hers, but none of them were.

"So why didn't my name show up?"

"Briana, you are not Briana Lee Sheldon of California." He took hold of her hand as he spoke and waited for the message to sink in. Her confused and fearful blue eyes met his.

"Then who am I? This can't be true. I have a family. My mother...my father...and I have two brothers!" She felt like a vise was squeezing her heart, as if she'd been suddenly abandoned. "There has to be an error somewhere. I don't understand!" She looked pleadingly at him.

"I don't either," Tyler said softly, "but we are going to get to the bottom of this. I'm sorry I had to break this to you in a public place, but these accounts are accurate and conclusive. Now don't panic, because it's possible you weren't born in California. Paula Irving, a woman at the Bureau of Vital Statistics who does freelance searches for people, has worked for our firm many times. She's extremely efficient, and when she did the first search for you on Tuesday and couldn't locate you where you should have been, she broadened it to encompass the whole state. As you can see, you aren't there either. Starting Monday, she'll expand her search and will find your records, I'm sure."

"But Tyler, I was born in California. It has to be a clerical error."

"We'll see. Meanwhile, call your parents and make sure all your facts are correct."

"I surely couldn't have gotten through life for twenty-five years without knowing my birthplace and birth date, could I? Ty, I'm scared. I can't believe this is happening. I feel like my whole world is collapsing." She closed her eyes momentarily while the magnitude of the bizarre tale sunk in.

"So if that isn't my name, how could I have a birth certificate, Social Security card, and driver's license?"

"Anything can be forged, duplicated, or stolen," he began, but she broke in.

"Forged? But why? I got my driver's license myself. I remember that and no one questioned who I was. Tyler, tell me this is a dream!"

"I wish I could. I've got to be in court in a half hour, so let me take you back to work, unless you want to go home."

"I need to finish some briefs at work this afternoon, and anyway it probably would be better to keep busy. I feel numb."

He squeezed her hands and rose, waiting for her as she collected her purse and slid out of the booth. She brushed away the tears that were trickling down her cheeks and, trembling, stood to follow.

When she got home from work that night she pulled out the papers Tyler had given her at noon and went over them carefully. Perhaps her records had been destroyed in a computer mishap, or even a fire. She needed to call home, be more persistent about her records, and make sure the dates were correct.

Her mother answered the phone and, as always, was delighted to hear her daughter's voice. After minutes of catching up on family news and a discussion about Briana's house, the actual reason for the call came forth. "Remember when I asked you about déjà vu or psychic experiences?"

Her mother recalled their previous conversation and asked why Briana was interested.

"This keeps happening to me," Briana said, then filled her mother in on the happenings at Marysville as well as the one at the Queen Anne manor.

"Tyler said I could have a twin somewhere. You didn't leave one of us in the hospital, did you?" Briana intended the question to lighten the conversation.

"No," her mother answered quickly, responding seriously to her daughter's jest.

"It's a strange feeling to freak out over a building and a staircase and not know why." Briana didn't go into detail about the sheer terror that went with those occurrences, for there was no reason to worry her mom unnecessarily.

"Really, I don't know what to tell you, Bri," her mom began hesitantly. "I can't think of anything that has happened to you at places like that, but I suspect you saw a movie or TV show when you were little and are recalling that as a child would, in parts."

"But Mom, how do you explain that fact that I have no records? For all general purposes, I don't exist!"

Her mother was silent for a second longer than necessary. "Can you remember the name of the hospital where I was born?" Briana asked. "It was in Fresno, right?"

"I can't remember the name. It was a long time ago and we moved shortly after that, but I don't suppose it really matters. Why are you pursuing this?"

Briana decided to soft-pedal now and said only that she had been doing some of her family history research again, like she had in California with her friend Lisa, and still found no record of herself. "I intend to get it sorted out before long. I'm sure it's some clerical error, like Dad has said all along."

When they rang off, Briana gave serious thought to telling Tyler to stop the search. The research lady must have missed something and it wasn't really that important. She recalled the time she and Lisa were doing family history research. It was for one of their college classes and Lisa found all kinds of people on both sides of her family. In fact, she had even located where the first generation of her people had entered the United States. Lisa had interviewed her grandparents, so was prepared with the basic knowledge, where Briana had none.

Why didn't I ask more questions? Briana wondered. Surely she must have had some statistics to start with. Her father had always been quiet about his childhood in orphanages, and her mother seldom made reference to her parents either. There were shirttail relatives in the

East somewhere, but living on the West Coast meant they had never met these distant relations, and eventually even holiday correspondence had faded away unnoticed. No wonder she lost interest. She had gotten too busy and then Jim had come into her life.

The weekend seemed to last forever. Shelly was busy and Briana was lonely. She had a good book she kept trying to lose herself in, but it just didn't work. She turned on the TV but there wasn't anything that could keep her mind off the fact that she didn't exist. This had to be solved!

Sunday morning she met Tom and Shelly at church and intended to set up a meeting with the pastor, but there was a replacement pastor that weekend so even that possible distraction was now out.

That night, a documentary about adoptions came on the TV set. Briana had gone to the kitchen for a drink and when she returned she heard: "Many adoptive families know nothing of their child's origin and in most cases, a fabricated story is concocted to hide the real truth. Regularly children are stolen and sold to loving, caring people who never know the truth."

Briana's heart seemed to stop. Surely her parents would have told her if she were adopted. That couldn't possibly be anything for her to consider. Or was it? Her mother had been a little cool when she had asked why Briana was pursuing this. Was there something to hide? She remembered her childhood and recalled incidents even at a young age. Or did she just remember being told about these things? There weren't any baby pictures of her, but supposedly they had been destroyed in a fire at her parents' house when she was very young. Had they ever existed?

How could she doubt any of this when it would infer her folks had been lying all these years? She felt instantly guilty, yet she still concentrated on the program and began taking notes. She'd call Tyler later to tell him about the phone call to her mom and maybe share a little about this program.

There was good money in selling children, the commentary announced, and it was not as uncommon as one would imagine.

"Babies born in prison have also been adopted out to unsuspecting parents who not only received a new baby, for an exorbitant price, but sometimes a drug addict as well. Some HIV-positive babies have been sold, too, and their problems were not detected until the child was older. But the most popular children for adoptions are from single mothers who are willing to give their children away to a couple in good standing instead of having an abortion. The young, unwed mother signs a paper relinquishing all rights to the child forever."

How could anyone give up flesh and blood forever? Could someone give up a twin and keep the other? Was Tyler right to question if she had a twin somewhere? Her parents would never separate twins or sell a child, since they had waited so long to have her. When the program concluded, Briana reached for the phone and dialed Tyler. She thought at first no one was there, but on the fourth ring a woman answered.

"Tyler Rainger's residence, Adrian speaking."

Bri wanted to hang up, but decided not to.

"This is Briana Sheldon. Could I speak to Tyler?"

"He's in the shower right now. Can you call back in about an hour?"

Briana was crushed. There was no way she'd call back—ever!

CHAPTER 16

Work was stressful on Monday. Nothing seemed to go right, and everyone was quiet and remote as if they were reliving the weekend. Briana couldn't even stand to think about her weekend.

In the shower! She burned with anger and humiliation just thinking about the pleasure in Adrian's voice as she relayed that message.

She needed to tell Tyler to cancel the search, but that would require another call. Perhaps she could go through Shelly?

"Shelly, can you come in for a second?"

The intercom voice answered, "Sure, give me a minute to finish a call."

When Shelly approached Briana's desk she looked at her friend closely. "Do you have the flu or something? You look run down. Are you having trouble sleeping?"

"I'm okay," Briana answered quickly. "Would you call Tyler for me and have him cancel the search for my records? I haven't had a chance to tell you that he verified that I have no birth records. Briana Sheldon does not exist and has never been where she should have been, so I'm not who I am but someone else!"

Shelly broke out laughing. "Is this some kind of lawyer lingo?" Briana lightened up a little and chuckled.

"Surely there's a mistake somewhere?" Shelly insisted.

"I think it's mine. I should never have involved Tyler in any of this, and really it was better not knowing my records are lost. I don't want him to bother with my personal business anymore."

Briana knew she was frowning so wasn't surprised when Shelly asked, "What brought this on?" Briana couldn't bring herself to explain so she just shot a curt "Nothing!" at her friend.

Not to be put off, Shelly said, "We'll talk about it tonight. I'm coming over for some in-depth girl talk, so please don't say no! I want to hear all about what Tyler found out, then you and I will do some digging of our own. You can't have been hatched or landed here from Mars, for heaven's sake. You aren't an alien, are you?"

Briana had to laugh. Shelly was a real morale booster. "I hope not, but maybe that would explain the weird feelings I experience sometimes. What time are you coming? I'll fix us a stir-fry dinner."

Knowing Shelly was coming over helped Briana feel better and, after a quick stop at the supermarket, she rushed home to start the meal. She flipped through her mail before putting the groceries away and found a letter from her folks, but instead of the usual small pastel envelope her mother normally sent, this one looked like a business letter. Perhaps her folks had found some records to send her. She would need to get dinner started first before she could curl up in the big overstuffed chair in the front room and relax.

Once the meal was simmering, she kicked off her shoes and slit open the white envelope. She pulled out just two sheets of paper: a typewritten letter. When she saw they were from her mom and dad, her heart took a constricted tumble in her chest.

"To our Darling Daughter," she read. The opening alone alerted Briana that this was not a normal letter. Her mom's usual "Hi, Sweetie" or just a "Hi" was the norm, and the fact that it was typed also surprised her. Bri hurried to the body of the letter.

> *Your father and I have a confession to make that I'm sure will change your whole life. We chose not to tell you this when you were growing up because of circumstances I'll explain later in this letter.*
>
> *First and forever the most important part is that we love you very much and are so proud of you. You are our only daughter and our first child.*

Because we love you, you will realize why this is the most difficult letter we have ever written or will ever write. We ask for your forgiveness because what we did was done only to protect you and make your life normal.

Briana felt fear racing through her bloodstream, but she still couldn't dream what all this was about. Glancing at the date in the top corner of the page, she saw it was written the same day that she called home. She picked up the discarded envelope and noticed the letter had been mailed the next day. With trembling hands, she went back to reading.

When your father and I married we intended to start our family right away. I was twenty-three and your dad was twenty-six, so we didn't consider ourselves old, but just eager to have a baby. That didn't happen, however.

When I turned thirty-two we panicked and adopted a beautiful little girl with big blue eyes and dark hair. She was four years old and had lost her family. They died in a plane crash, leaving this sweetheart for the courts to send from one home to another. An orphan wanting a mommy and daddy and she could have been caught up in red tape for months or years while they searched for just the right family.

We had an opportunity to adopt her, but not through the normal channels, and even though we knew it was illegal, we did it anyway. They refused to tell us where you came from, and the people who delivered you you didn't know or wouldn't tell.

They had papers for you: a birth certificate, Social Security card, and some health records. No one has ever questioned them. We never doubted their authenticity.

Two years after you came to us, I found myself pregnant with Richard, and two years later I gave birth to Mark.

Then the decision was whether to tell you or not. As you know, your father was an orphan and the children at school were cruel to him. He was shifted from foster home to orphanage and back again, disrupting his life and making him feel like a misfit. Each day he searched the faces of anyone he came in contact with, hoping they would see some kind of likeness and claim him as their own.

This never happened. He has no idea where his roots are or if he has siblings. See how cruel life can be? We didn't want that for you, so we created a life for you with us. From birth—forever.

We were shaken to the core when you discovered there was no record of you on the California books, and we spent many a sleepless night trying to decide whether to tell you or not. But because you trusted us, had such a family unity and love for us, we shrugged it off as a possible clerk's error in your birth records.

Briana rested her forehead on her shaky hands holding the now-crumpled letter. *God, how could you let this happen?* Tears coursed down her cheeks and threatened to dampen the letter from home. Home—yes, it would always be home. Mom would be Mom; Dad, Dad.

But now she would wonder, as her father had over the years, who her real family were. Why had she had been abandoned? Did her family really die in a plane crash? She could check on that. There were computers now with all kinds of available statistics. She could take over looking for her own birth records. Maybe Tyler's investigator could turn up something if she got the woman's phone number from him to deal directly with her. This wasn't his problem, anyway.

She opened up the crumpled letter and scanned it to the place where she had stopped reading.

We will help you in any way we can. If you choose to trace your people, we have a nest egg put aside for retirement that is yours for the asking.

All we can say is that we are sorry if we made such a wrong decision by not telling you. Perhaps when you marry and have a child of your own you will understand the feelings we had then and the love we still share with you, our darling daughter.

Please don't have hard feelings or any kind of hate for what we did.

Love, Dad and Mom (forever)

Shelly arrived just a couple of minutes later and found Briana sitting in that same chair, clutching the typed papers to her chest, but Briana didn't even acknowledge her friend's arrival.

"Bri, what's happened? Is your dad okay? You said he had tests run."

Briana didn't answer. Her mind was in turmoil and then it seemed to shut down, leaving her in a state of shock. Shelly took the crumpled papers and began to read them. Briana had begun to cry by the time Shelly folded the letter and returned it to the envelope.

"Bri, you are a chosen one!" she said positively. "Most parents have to take what they get in the maternity ward, but you were selected, chosen carefully by two people who wanted a child very much."

Shelly put her arms around her friend and Briana began to sob. Her whole world was being turned upside down. She could not believe anything anymore. Her parents were not her parents! Her brothers were not her brothers!

Shelly went to get Briana a tissue, then checked on dinner before she returned.

"You had the stove on low so at least you didn't burn my dinner!"

The hint of normalcy roused Briana. "I don't know which way to turn anymore. How could they have kept this secret so long?" She blew her nose and the tears began all over again.

"They explained that in the letter, and they love you. You surely don't doubt that, do you? You need to call them and let them know you love them too!"

"I can't. I'm angry, hurt. And don't you see? I really don't exist. I don't know who I am. It wasn't a clerical error and they knew that years ago when I discovered that my records were missing, but they lied and glossed it over. I would rather have never known the truth than feel this pain!"

Tears streamed down her cheeks so Shelly gathered her into her arms and let her cry.

The evening was a blur and when Briana finally woke up, she was in her bed with Shelly beside her.

"Are you okay?" Shelly mumbled in the dark.

"I think so."

"Then let's pray right now that God will take this episode in your life and turn it into something for His glory. He knows your heart and He will ease this suffering. Jesus knows all about suffering. He did that for us on the cross and he didn't even know us! You know when all else fails, He is always there and He sent a comforter to help us and to be with us at all times. He's here and so am I, Bri. If we keep our eyes on Jesus, we'll solve this mystery. I know we can find where you came from."

"But Shelly, I'm frightened. Where do I begin to search? Was I stolen from my birth parents? Was I a crack baby from some prison? Oh God!"

She began to cry again, so Shelly flipped on the lamp and got up. "The first thing we do is pray!" Shelly put her arms around Briana and together they lifted their concerns up to the Father.

"Now the second thing you must do is call your parents—right now! It's midnight here so that would mean it's ten there. Will they still be up?"

"Probably. Dad watches the eleven o'clock news before going to bed, but what should I say?"

"Explain that you love them and forgive them. Thank them for the wonderful life you've had and for the good parents you were blessed with. After all, you could have been adopted by unsuitable people. You are where you are today because of them."

Shelly looked down at Briana from her position on the side of the bed. "Come on, get out of bed and make that call! They are worried about this and only you can put them at ease."

Briana slowly dialed the phone, not sure what she should say. "Mom, it's Bri," she said softly before she began to cry, But that was all right, because her mother cried right along with her.

The next voice she heard was her father's. "Princess, we are so sorry about this. We thought about telling you so many times, especially when you got ready to leave for Kansas, but we just couldn't. I thought perhaps you could go through your whole life without ever knowing, but that didn't happen."

"It's okay," Briana heard herself say. "I've had wonderful parents and a good life."

"You sound like you're dying!" her father moaned. "Please don't dwell on this in a negative way. You will probably never know your real folks, but that isn't important. You'll marry and have a family of your own someday, and that will help. It did for me. I never did any searching for my folks. At first, I decided if they didn't want me, I didn't want them. Then I wondered if something tragic had happened. After a long time had passed, I just didn't care."

"I know you thought you were doing the right thing by not telling me, but it was such a blow," Briana said.

"I know, honey, I'm sorry. Here, your mother wants to speak to you again, so I'll say good-bye for now. I love you."

Bri felt the tears coursing down her cheeks again when she heard her dad's voice crack and knew that he, too, was crying. Her mother took some time coming to the phone and Briana knew she was comforting her husband.

"Hi, sweetheart," she began. "You'll never know how much this call means to us. We didn't know how you would feel after you read our letter, but we just didn't think it was fair to tell you all this on the phone. With a letter, we could be precise so you were sure to understand our side of it. Can you ever forgive us?"

"I do, Mom. It's just that I'm in a state of shock. All I know is that you and dad are my parents and Rich and Mark are my brothers, but I think I need to search for my birth parents in case there was a twin, as Tyler suspects. What if she or he is having these 'happenings' also? What if I was stolen and my biological parents search each face of girls my age like Dad did, looking for their lost daughter? How sad!"

Briana felt determined to search for her roots. She had to! Her parents promised to help in her search and in the next letter, they would write anything they could remember that might mean something from her past.

"I still have the clothing you wore when you arrived," her mother said. "You had a few items in a paper bag and I can describe the couple who brought you to us in the taxi. It was a long time ago, but Dad and I will work on this together."

When Briana finally hung up, she turned to look at Shelly.

"Now that's what I wanted to see!" Shelly cheered.

"What?"

"We're on a quest, aren't we? You're a fighter and we're going to win!"

The rest of the week went fast. Shelly called a local genealogy library about how to begin tracing ancestors. They expected her to be searching for old dates and were surprised when she explained it was the mid-sixties she was interested in. They explained that birth and death statistics were all listed in the records at the Bureau of Vital Statistics. She would need names, dates, and state. They, of course, only had Kansas records, but forms were available for out-of-state queries.

Shelly hadn't explained that there were a few problems with that part, since she had no name or state and was unsure of the dates.

Briana shared her discouragement with Shelly when they met for a quick evening meal at a local restaurant.

"We need to get help on this," Shelly admitted. "Has Tyler ever called to tell you anything more about his search?"

"But Shelly, didn't you call and tell him to cancel it like I asked you to?" Briana was incredulous. "You didn't!"

"After you got the letter I just made an executive decision and decided we needed all the help we could get. It wouldn't hurt to see what his contact has dug up! He really does want to help, you know."

"Have you talked to him?" Briana asked pointedly.

Shelly smiled at her friend's curiosity. "Actually, I just talked to Tom. Tyler has been very busy with a case that has just gone to court. Does he call you?"

"No. I told him I was not interested."

"You *what?*"

"Well, not in those exact words."

Shelly shook her head and gave Briana a look that said, "I don't believe what I'm hearing!"

"And you give me advice about Tom! Bri, you are in love with Ty! You have to be honest with yourself and him. What has happened?"

Briana wanted to say, "His engagement to Adrian," and then add the fact that they spent last weekend together in their love nest here in town. The words that she actually said were the same lame excuses she gave Ty.

"I have to get my life in order. I not only have to discover who I am, but why I keep experiencing déjà vu. Where did I come from? Where are my people? Shelly, what if I never find them? What if my mother sold me just for money? I have been giving this some very deep thought. I might not like what I find. Something else, too—I don't want anyone else knowing about this. Adrian would have a real blast looking down on me from her lofty 'best family.' That's another reason I don't want Ty involved."

Shelly could not see any connection there, but Briana was adamant.

The weeks began to slip by and before long it was the end of July. They had seen Tyler twice at church; each time he was with Adrian. The last time she had seen him they had chatted a minute in the church parking lot and he told them his mare had finally had her foal. Then Adrian dragged him away.

The pain in Briana's heart told her it was too late. She was past fighting to stop the attraction; she longed for his company almost as much as she yearned for his touch. She could not keep him out of her thoughts, yet she still would not return his calls.

Briana was pleased to get a long letter from her parents but was sad to hear their vacation to Kansas would be delayed one month. They hoped they wouldn't arrive in Topeka in time for an October snow! The letter also contained some of the information they had told Briana about on the phone earlier regarding her arrival over twenty years ago.

These are a few of the things your Dad and I remember about you as a child.

You said you came on a long trip in a car with a bed in the back. At your age that could have meant a car where you slept on the back seat or possibly a station wagon with a bed in the rear.

You didn't like the people who brought you, but they were probably only hired to transfer you from your home state to us, so they didn't have to form a bond with you.

We thought you might have come from the Midwest, because shortly after you came to us we took you to see The Wizard of Oz. *When the tornado struck Kansas and Dorothy got whisked away, you said you had seen a tornado. You said it was big and you had to hide. They can be most anyplace, but they are more prevalent on the Central Plains.*

The couple that brought you to us hinted that your parents had been killed in a plane crash, but we felt then and still do that it was a false statement. It could be something for you to check on. I would think the news media would cover a tearjerker about a child left alone in the world after such a disaster.

I will send you the clothing you wore and the few nightclothes and garments from the sack.

You cried for your baby, so we knew your doll had been left or lost, but when we took you to the store for a new one you were sad not to find your own. We can't remember the name you called her.

You knew your name and could write 'Bri.' You were so unhappy but we loved you right from the start.

We paid close attention to the nightmares you had, but could never figure out what caused them. You would scream and thrash about in your bed until they subsided, and only then could we hold you.

So, my dear. you have quite a job ahead of you and I hope for you that it will be successful. Sometimes, however, the past is best left undisturbed.

Briana's eyes brimmed with tears as her mother told her again how much they both loved her. They had told the boys about Briana's adoption, and her brothers felt sad that their sister had to learn the truth so bluntly in a letter. They sent their love as well.

One night in the second week of August, during a violent storm, Briana heard the doorbell rang. She peered through the curtain to see Tyler standing on her porch, drenched with rain. When she opened the door, one look at his penetrating gaze made her step back to let him enter.

"I have something for you in the car, but first I want to know what I could possibly have done to you that has caused this breach in our friendship. If I could send you a white truce rose and say 'I'm sorry I woke you up,' I would. But I didn't wake you! Whatever I did, I'm sorry. I fear a rose would never make it in this deep freeze anyway."

He was glaring at her and she could see his anger, but Briana was past being angry, hurt, and embarrassed. She had coped with his omission about Adrian and had lived through it. She would never allow that wound to be opened again.

"I wasn't mad because you woke me up that day. You don't know how angry I was about the whole episode, and then you had the nerve to apologize for them! The good tires—no, 'the best,' I believe you called them." He softened and seemed to be doing a mental rerun.

"Tyler, I am sorry, but my life is just not in very good order right now, but I still consider you a friend and I had a wonderful holiday weekend on the Fourth.

That does not mean we will see each other on a regular basis because we have other interests and other commitments." She thought that sounded good. Her lips had not quivered and her voice had been strong.

But Tyler saw through the bravado and caught her chin in his hand, forcing her to meet his eyes.

"You know that's a lie!" he challenged as he encircled her with his strong arms. "We are more than just friends, and don't try to deny it!" he growled against her cheek.

Briana knew it was true. She wanted nothing more than to be assured of that and to forever feel his arms around her as they were now, but she mustn't be tempted.

"Ty, my whole world has crashed down around me and I'm frightened," she admitted as she relaxed against him, feeling her reserve begin to crumble.

His hand came up to stroke her golden hair and she felt his lips on her temple. "Shh," he whispered as he trailed kisses across her cheek to her lips, which he then covered with a long, passionate kiss.

Briana didn't respond at first, so he lifted his head and raised his eyebrows in question. She had made her decision, however, and her arms went up around his neck to pull his head back down to her waiting lips.

"I'm getting you soaked," he finally said and stepped back. "Plus I have something for you in the car, which means I have to get wet again." Then with a quick kiss he added, "But you're worth it!"

She watched him from the door as he ran to the car, waiting expectantly to see what he was bringing her. She would never have guessed. It was a puppy!

"Spunky sends her love and one of her babies. I hope you want it. I should have asked but…"

"It's adorable!" She took the small, furry creature in her hands and looked closely at its face. "How perfect. Of course I want it, silly."

"It's a female but I'll have it spayed for you in a short while. She's had all of her shots so now all she needs is some TLC."

"I'm good at tender loving care," she bragged, laughing as the puppy tried to lick her face.

"I know," Ty said softly as he met her bright blue eyes over the puppy's head.

"What's her name?" Briana asked breathlessly.

"She's your pet, so name her whatever you like. Of course, she has papers and a long legal title, but she doesn't know that."

Briana couldn't think of a better present. She had loved dogs all her life, but since she had been away from home she had been unable to have one. Apartments are not the best place for pets, especially when you're working crazy hours. They fixed a box for the pup's bed, but she only stayed there a second before coming out to find them.

"I would have stopped to get some puppy food if it hadn't been storming," Ty said apologetically. "Give her some milk and we'll see about food later."

They went back to the front room and Tyler sat down on the sofa. Briana went to the desk and extracted some papers, then pulled the hassock up in front of the sofa and handed them to him.

"Shelly is the only one who knows about this," she began hesitantly. "It has just devastated me. Read this first." She pointed to the first letter from her parents. When he finished she could see emotions playing across his face.

"I'm sorry," he said huskily. "They only meant to make life easier for you and to shield you. The choices we make are not always the best, but we survive."

"That's what Shelly called me the other day: a survivor. Now read this."

She handed him the second letter her parents had sent explaining her arrival.

"This could explain why Paula couldn't find you anywhere. Do you still want to find your birth parents? Sometimes it's better to let sleeping dogs lie."

Briana looked at him so sadly that Tyler reached out and grasped her clenched hands.

"I have to," she said. "I don't want to be like my dad, searching faces all my life or seeing people who look like me and wondering. Will you help me?"

"Of course I will. Tom and Shelly will too. We'll make this our quest and if we don't find anything right away, we'll keep trying until we do."

She leaned forward and kissed his cheek. "Thank you!" The kiss on his cheek led to one on the lips. Briana was glad she was already sitting down because his kisses left her weak in the knees. She pulled away from his touch and, trembling softly, stood up. The rain had let up and she knew she'd better wrap up the evening before the temptations of his arms and lips grew even stronger.

After she went to bed, Briana decided she would live to regret this evening. She knew this relationship was wrong and that Adrian would not be pleased with Tyler's interest in her. She thought again of Jim and wondered if this was how he felt about her bridesmaid. Briana was now in the role of the other woman, and it made her feel cheap. She would have to ask him about Adrian, then find out where he expected this new relationship to go. Tyler might even have other women in his life besides Adrian and herself. Her heart ached at this thought.

Sleep was slow in coming. While she lay awake waiting she thought of her new little puppy. Such a thoughtful gift! There would be no more nights of coming home to an empty house. Then she gave some thought to a name for her. Something high-class to go with her pedigree, but it had to be ladylike as well.

Tiffany, she thought. Yes, Tiffany Dawn would be a fine name for her new pet. And she could call her Tiff for short.

CHAPTER 17

Tyler contacted Paula Irving to give her the new information, but even after widening her search to the whole mainland United States, she still drew a blank. Knowing that the last name wasn't correct, she began checking given names with the same birth dates.

On the nights when Tom, Shelly, and Tyler came over, Briana fixed a meal. After clearing the table, they would spread their papers out and brainstorm.

The clothing her mother sent was found to be a K-Mart brand sold all over the country in the mid- to late-seventies.

The plane crash theory went nowhere. They all agreed with her mother on the tragedy angle, but no major news reports had been documented. The child could have been in other homes after the accident, which would make the dates impossible to check.

With tornadoes prevalent in so many areas, it was impossible to pinpoint any one state to search. One storm system could spawn a number of twisters in numerous states at one time.

"We need to make an outline of things that could give us clues," Shelly said.

"So let's pretend we have a child to market," Tom suggested.

Briana gasped and cried, "You make it sound so commercial! Like I was a TV set to fence or a sack of flour to deliver."

"Tom does have a point, though, however crude it may sound," Shelly said.

"What would you most likely leave the same if you were sending a child away to a new family?" Tyler asked, pulling out a fresh sheet of paper to start the list.

"My niece is four years old," Tom offered. "She knows her name so it seems logical they would keep that the same. If you came across a child who kept correcting you when you used her name, wouldn't you be suspicious?"

"And maybe the child could even write her name at that age," Briana said. "Some do. Some even know their address, town, and state. Mom said I could write 'Bri' when I came to them."

"So if Briana was her real name, Paula should have found a link-up," Shelly decided.

"But only if they kept my birth date and year the same," Briana added.

"You could be older than you think you are!" Shelly giggled.

"I could be younger, too," Briana quipped, poking at her friend.

"Okay, let's assume they kept her dates the same. Who would ever question that, and how would they know, unless her family gave them to the adoption people?" Tyler's pen was poised in mid-air.

"There is a birth certificate," Briana announced. "I must have had a real one originally, but if I were stolen, this one would be false. Yet if they just gave me away, my birth parent would probably have sent that information along. What do you think?"

"Bri, you've hit on something there. So if we find that your dates check out, we can be pretty sure you were not stolen, but given up willingly." Tom looked at her, his expression sympathetic at the tears in her eyes.

"You can't give up," Shelly said, seeing her friend's dilemma. "We'll find you!"

Tyler picked up his pen again and said, "We have to begin somewhere, so let's assume her dates are the same, because we'll know soon enough if they aren't. That tornado thing has me curious. We are called the Tornado Alley here in the Midwest, so let's centralize our search to Texas, Oklahoma, Kansas, and Nebraska. We can add Missouri, Iowa, and others later."

"Her name has me stumped," Tyler added. "What other names would Bri be derived from besides Briana?"

"Hey, Tyler, that's good. My niece Amanda writes her name as Mandy," Tom said.

Shelly suggested Gabrielle. Briana thought of Aubrey and Brietta. After some more brainstorming they added Ambria, Mabry, Sabrina, and Cambria to their list.

"Maybe it could be a nickname for her middle name?" They groaned in unison when Tom mentioned that. This was not going to be easy!

Bri was very grateful for the support of her friends, and she was also pleased to see Tyler on a regular basis. He was not pursuing her actively or pressing her for a commitment in any way, though she would have felt better if he had. She knew he realized that, until she got to the end of her search, she couldn't consider a relationship. Eventually they would have to discuss Adrian. She had a hard time believing Tyler would make advances toward her while engaged to Adrian, but then their attraction had been rather spontaneous and overwhelming.

The group decided to research Kansas first, since they had easy access to the state records at the Historical Society as well as the Bureau of Vital Statistics. It was discouraging to see so many births on that date.

Tyler called one day while she was at work and asked her to write down every feeling, thought, or word that had come to her during her "happenings." She and Tiffany worked on those that evening. It was so pleasant having the puppy's company. Though Tiff was a poor substitute for Tyler, she was a constant reminder of the night when he arrived with the puppy. Tyler had been hurt and bewildered by her coolness, but that hadn't lasted long! In the back of her mind was a subtle plan to oust Adrian from his life. She did not have her plan formulated, but she'd work on that when the rest of this search fell into place.

She looked up to find Tiffany looking at her with her head cocked to one side as if she was saying, "Are we working or dreaming?"

"Okay, you slave driver!" Briana laughed.

Many different emotions flitted to mind as she relived her first experience in Marysville. It had caught her unaware and she hadn't been prepared for the terror or the panic, the tears or the desolation.

Now that she thought about the experience at the manor, she realized that it was anger she had felt there. Had she been angry at the courthouse building? She didn't think so. Hmm! So what did those two places have in common? Neither of them was anything to fear.

Since coming to Topeka, she had been through many tornado watches and two warnings. If anything were to scare her, that should have done it, but she had watched the clouds boil and felt the heavy, erratic air. She had watched the green cast to the sky, suggesting hail or worse, and had seen the dark layers of clouds as they went in different directions: top layer east, bottom layer west. Yet, she felt no overwhelming fear as she did during the déjà vu episodes—just apprehension and amazement.

If she had been in a tornado as a child, why didn't she fear them?

The next night, the group gathered to consult over the findings collected by each person. Shelly had not been able to locate any names and dates that matched up the list of sound-alike names. She had completed her search through the R's, ending with Rabrina, but the dates always let her down.

"I got discouraged mighty fast," she admitted. "And this is only Kansas we are working on!"

Briana felt guilty about the time and effort her friends were spending for her benefit. "Why don't we just abort the whole mission, guys?" Briana suggested. "It doesn't really matter anyway, I guess."

"Yes, it does," Tyler growled. "We can do this!" He looked at the others and smiled. "How hard can it be to find someone who is sitting here in this very room?"

"Sure, that's the easy part," Tom said. "But we need to know the information about the circumstances of her adoption. Why she was given up, by whom, then find out her correct name. Who knows what Briana could stand for?" He flipped through the pages in his tablet. "We must be missing something. Shelly, do you have the list of the rest of the names? Surely there can't be many more!"

"Only six or seven," she answered, scanning the page.

"Read them!" Tyler took a pen to jot them down for future use.

"There is a Sabrina Barton, in Marysville," she began and followed with two more names with the same dates.

"Wait a minute here!" Tyler sat up straight and circled the Marysville name. "Is this just a coincidence or a full-blown lead? What if Briana is Sabrina?"

Everyone looked at Briana.

"So now what do we do?" she asked. "How can we find out about Sabrina?"

"I'd like to go up to Marysville," Tyler said. "We could use the Historical Society here in Topeka, but I have a friend in Marysville who can help us, too. This is the best lead we've had. Especially when you had those 'happenings' when you were there. How about this weekend?"

Tom had a meeting in St. Louis Saturday morning so he couldn't go, but the women were free. Friday evening they lifted off in Tyler's Piper Arrow once again, but this time Tiffany went along, sleeping during the flight. When they entered Tyler's house they could smell the cozy aroma of dinner being cooked, and Briana felt she had come home.

After the delicious meal, Bea served their coffee out on the patio by the pool. It was very calm and humid; Tyler observed that they would have storms by midnight. The weather reports had announced storm warnings earlier in southern Nebraska, heading south for northeast Kansas. Ty had monitored the storm earlier from the air to be sure they could reach their destination before the thunderheads arrived.

Tyler excused himself after coffee to make some phone calls, so the girls chose this time to go swimming. The air was so heavy Briana felt she could hardly breathe! They were toweling down when Tyler returned to the poolside with a paper in hand.

"I think tomorrow morning we'll drive into town and see what we can find on this Sabrina chick," he teased, winking at Briana. "Dorothy Baldwin at the courthouse has the birth records and will meet us there at nine. Sabrina's father was killed in 1968 in some sort of a farm accident, so we'll need to check that in the old newspapers at the library."

"Oh Tyler, do you think I'm really Sabrina? I think I'm getting scared. If my father is dead, then where is my mother?" Briana was shivering, so Tyler took the beach towel from her and wrapped it around her body.

"There is nothing to be afraid of," he said, laughing briefly as Tiffany took interest in the towel and began tugging. "Looks like your guard dog isn't happy about my attentions. You, little Tiff, were given to this woman as a truce, not to scare me away!" Tyler dropped a kiss on Briana's forehead and she swayed toward him.

She had to stop this, she reprimanded herself. He had never said he loved her, which was a good indication that he had other commitments.

The next morning they traveled to Marysville in the farm van, and Tyler told them he wanted to enter town the same way Briana had when she first came to Kansas.

"Shelly, I want you to write down anything Briana says about the old courthouse."

"But Tyler, I'm on guard now, so it won't scare me," Briana explained. But it did. She couldn't see it until they were almost upon it, as had been the case before, but when the tall red towers became visible, Briana began to shake. Tyler parked the van at the curb and turned in the seat to watch her. Tears began, but it wasn't as intense as it had been before.

"Talk to me, Sabrina," Tyler said, using the new name.

"I'm scared," she wept. "I don't know what to do! Please help me," she pleaded, then covered her face with her hands and sobbed.

Tyler started the van and drove around the block, parking on the west side in front of the new modern courthouse where the meeting had been held about the spur line.

"Are you all right?" he asked as he turned to look at her again.

"I guess so. It's getting easier, but something came to me that I forgot about until now. I called it a castle when I was here for that meeting. Why would I call it a castle?"

Shelly was scribbling all this down in her notebook. "A child would think of it that way," she said. "What do you think, Ty?"

"It's possible. I just feel we're on the right track, and I think this building means something to you. Maybe just one that looks like it, but there is a definite connection. Have you seen that red brick cathedral in downtown Topeka? It's on Fourth Street, I think, and has twin steeples."

"I did see that one day, but felt nothing. In fact, I have gone back a few times since then on my noon walk and even walked around the property. The priest raises lilies on every inch of land that surrounds the church, and they are so beautiful! But the building doesn't affect me in any way." She looked up at Ty and asked, "What if my mother gave me up after my father was killed because she didn't want me?"

"We'll find out. Let's go see what Dorothy has dug up in the files."

The birth records of Sabrina May Barton were on film and Shelly copied the full name and dates, which matched Briana's exactly. Her mother was listed as Mary Jeanette Barton. Father, Jack Barton. Both from Marysville. Briana's heart began to pound. Were these her parents? Was her mother still alive?

"I did some inquiring about the parents, but couldn't come up with anything concrete," Dorothy explained. "They didn't live in town, we are sure. You might scan the newspapers on film at the Topeka Historical Society. We have an abundance of social things, as well as other newsworthy pictures in our local paper, which would include the rural folks as well. I need to make a few more phone calls and see if anyone remembers the Bartons. Are you staying the weekend at the farm?" she asked.

"Yes, we'll be here till Sunday afternoon," Ty answered as he extracted his business card from his wallet. "Here are my office and home phone numbers in Topeka. Feel free to call at any time."

"Thank you for helping us," Briana said, reaching out to shake Dorothy's hand. "This is the best lead we've had yet!"

Dorothy walked with them to the front door, chatting about local news with Tyler.

"Has she set the date yet?" she asked.

"Not yet, but it shouldn't be long. October perhaps. Some things can't be rushed," and he winked at Dorothy, not realizing Briana's heart was breaking into a thousand pieces.

The person the woman had mentioned was Adrian, of course. October wasn't far off. Briana assumed that it was the tentative date for Tyler's wedding.

Everyone assumed that Briana was upset about the Marysville search, so no one questioned her. She tried not to be moody but she felt shattered once again.

Her life had seemed to be going quite well. She had felt confident about the Kansas bar exam she had taken. When she got her results in September, she could carve out a law career either with the Santa Fe or perhaps another firm. She could see a future for herself, but now the whole thing seemed hazy. Her dreams were put on hold while she searched for her lost family. Her visions of tomorrow were obscured as if she was looking through a foggy window. She must force herself not to look for Tyler through this glass. He could never be hers.

Back at the farm, Tyler took her to see his mare and her new colt. Briana was so wrapped up in memories of what had transpired the last time she was there that she could hardly appreciate the new addition.

"We named him Thunder," Ty informed her, patting the little foal. "He's going to be worth some big money in a few years."

"You won't sell him, will you?"

"Probably. That's my business up here. I raise Arabians to sell."

Briana reached out and rubbed the colt's head. "I would get too attached," she sighed. "I would make pets out of each one of them."

Ty's arms came around her and he buried his face in her hair. "You sound like a city gal to me," he accused, jokingly nibbling at her neck.

She was lost and suddenly had no resistance against this man. His kiss was a tender caress, surprisingly soft and gentle. Briana could sense Tyler controlling his passion and had mixed feelings about that. She tried to remember the wedding date in October and Adrian. She knew this was wrong, but she couldn't resist. Her hands spread across his broad chest and wound their way around his neck as she lifted her lips to begin the kiss anew.

Later, she decided she had been out of her league, but the passion that erupted from that kiss could keep her warm through many a cold Kansas blizzard. She had finally pulled away because the thought of Adrian intruded. Eventually, she would have to ask the questions that made her heart ache. She thought Tyler was battling with his conscience, also, since he had been quick to guide her out to the truck and even quicker to bid her good night at the house.

Shelly emerged from the shower just as Briana entered the bedroom. "There are tornado watches out all around us, so you might get to see a real tornado this time," she said, toweling her hair.

Just then Tyler knocked on their open door and said, "The watch has been upgraded to a warning, so we'd better take cover. Cecil and Bea are in my office.

It's our best shelter during a storm since it's underground and has no windows."

Bea had fixed a big pitcher of ice water and grabbed some chips and cookies. "This storm probably won't last long, but we might as well play some cards," she said. "We have a generator that will kick in if the power goes."

They enjoyed a game of Uno, and since Briana won, she had to endure the wrath of the losers. It was like having her family here. Family! She wondered if her birth parents had played parlor games during storms years ago. Were they fun-loving people like her family in California?

Thankfully, the tornado didn't materialize. As the rain died down, everyone drifted off to bed. But when the girls got up the next morning, Tyler apologized that he had to cut the weekend short. He had just received a phone call and had to get back to Topeka as soon as possible. Briana was relieved. Instead of clearing things up, as she had hoped, the trip had left her more confused than ever.

CHAPTER 18

Tuesday afternoon, Tyler called Briana at work to inform her that Dorothy Baldwin had called him with a possible clue. At a church women's circle the night before, Dorothy has mentioned that Tyler and the girls were doing a search involving Jack and Mary Barton and had asked if anyone knew them. One of the older ladies had asked Lavida if Jack wasn't the young farmhand who was killed on the Roswald farm. Lavida wasn't sure and seemed to become flustered, so they dropped the subject.

"We'll be able to check on that, easily enough. We can look up the Marysville papers for that year at the Kansas Historical Society and see what we can find out about the accident," Tyler suggested.

"Shelly and I can do that tonight after work. It will be a big job not knowing what date to look up, but it's a good lead. At least we have the year."

"Maybe Melissa will know something, Ty said. "Let me see if I can catch her at home. Perhaps she can narrow the time down for you. She's older than Dolan and she would have been in college then, I believe. I'll call you right back if she's there."

Briana was afraid to get too excited and felt sad knowing that, if she were Sabrina, her father was dead. The waiting began again. It was after five when Tyler called back.

"I've narrowed your search somewhat. Melissa was home from college when the accident occurred and she verified about when it happened. Possibly late June or July, she thought, since they were harvesting winter wheat when it happened. She said they had a little girl about three or four years old."

Bri felt hope leap in her heart. Could it be this easy?

Shelly and Briana sat in the darkened viewing room at the Kansas Historical Society and scanned the file of Marysville's newspaper, *The Advocate*. Small-town papers were always newsy with something about everyone— who did what, when, and why. It was Shelly who yelled "Bingo!" then quickly covered her mouth as people at the other viewers gave her dirty looks.

"Come see what I've found," she whispered unnecessarily—Briana was already on her way. It was a picture taken at the cemetery where Jack Barton was buried. Probably the main reason for the picture was because the Roswalds were involved, but it showed

Bevin and Gladys Roswald comforting a young woman, Mary Barton, and her small daughter, Sabrina. Shivers ran down Briana's spine as she looked closely at the child.

"Could that be me?" she whispered. "Oh, Shelly, I don't hope too much, just in case we can't confirm it. We need to go talk to Melissa and see what else she knows."

"Let's get a couple prints of this so we can show her. Will you tell your folks about any of this?" Shelly asked.

"Not yet. I don't want them on the same roller coaster I'm on. I'm afraid I won't find my birth parents, but almost as fearful that I will—and won't like it!"

Shelly called Melissa that evening and asked if they could come talk to her.

"I'm free tomorrow evening," she replied. "How about seven o'clock?"

The Lancaster home was in the Lake Sherwood area. Shelly told Briana it was one of the most prestigious locations for local rich folks; after one look at their home, Briana agreed. The neighborhood surrounded the small lake with boats and boat docks on the shoreline and their mansion was most likely one of the nicest and most expensive homes in the city.

Melissa answered the door and led them into the parlor, which was off the main entry hall. It was elegant, with cathedral ceilings and stained glass windows that allowed the fading summer sunlight to color the white ceiling between the rich oak beams. There were plants the size of trees dotting the large room, adding a healthy look to the all-white carpet and furniture. Even the brick fireplace was white, with a mantel of polished oak.

The huge painting that hung above the mantel showed a youthful Carter and Melissa with their young, dark-haired daughter and a boyish Mark. Briana looked at Adrian as a teenager and saw the same spoiled person she was today. Was she rude now because Tyler was paying attention to Briana? What had been her excuse as a child?

"Have a seat," Melissa said, waving them to an assortment of choices. "My housekeeper will serve some refreshments in a few minutes."

After they got situated, Melissa asked what questions she could help them with. "It's kind of weird to think you could be the Bartons' child. I remember her quite well, in fact. The accident was so tragic, and poor Jack was killed instantly."

"What happened?" Briana asked.

"There was a problem with the combine. Something had jammed the header, so Jack went back to unclog it. Somehow he got caught. There was nothing anyone could do."

Briana could see the accident in her mind and paled visibly. What a horrible death!

"His wife and child stayed at the farm only a short time after that. The folks had insurance that covered the accident, so Mary was set for life. I imagine the child would get Social Security payments until she was eighteen, also." Shelly was logging all this in her notebook.

"So the insurance company could have information about Mary even now," Shelly said. "I don't suppose you know what insurance company it was?"

"No, I don't, but I'm sure when the folks get home Dad will remember. They are touring right now in Europe. They just left France after a month. Their friends from France have their own yacht, so they'll be cruising off the shores of Greece next."

Briana thanked her for the update and murmured that perhaps she'd have the chance to visit with them upon their return. Then she pulled out the copy of the picture they had found and passed it to Melissa.

"Yes, that was taken at the gravesite. I didn't go to the funeral, as I recall, but Mom and Dad did. Mary was a nice girl. She was only a year older than me, but of course she was married and had a child. We saw each other at the farm once in a while."

"What did she look like?" Briana asked, wondering if this could be her mother they were discussing.

"She was of medium height. Maybe five-foot-six, blonde with blue eyes. Quite pretty and she had the most beautiful complexion!"

"What was her personality like?" Shelly asked, still writing the previous information.

"She had a sweet disposition. The folks were fairly friendly to her, but she was, after all, just the farmhand's wife so she stayed close to their cabin. I was in school when their baby was born. I only really got to be friends with Mary after the accident. She was afraid of being left all alone to raise the child, since they had no family in the area."

Melissa laughed. "I just remembered that Grandma Lavida didn't like her at all. They had some kind of disagreement years before all this happened and any chance Gram had to pick on Mary, she would. It was over something silly, Mom said. Something Mary did that could not be fixed."

The evening wasn't a complete waste, the girls decided on the way home. At least they had a profile on Mary Barton. "So if Mary had no family, yet left the farm, where could she have gone?" Briana asked as they pulled up in front of Shelly's apartment.

"If I had that old grandma mad at me, I wouldn't stay in the same area either! I wonder if she's in the phone book here in Topeka. The lady at the genealogy library said the first place to look is in your local phone directory. It's worth a try. Come on in and we'll look."

There were many Bartons listed. The one M. Barton that Shelly called was a Martin who didn't know a Mary. "Melissa said she was very pretty. Maybe she remarried?"

"Oh Shelly, we'll never find her!"

"Surely if she were here and remarried, she could be traced by her marriage license."

"But what year? That's a real long shot. She could have moved to Omaha or Kansas City. Where do we go from here?"

"Let's get Miss Irving to find her. Do you want to call Tyler when you get home?" Shelly asked, smiling smugly.

"I can," Briana affirmed softly.

"Bri, you are making your relationship with Tyler a very stressful one. Can't you just focus in on him and admit you love him?"

"It's not that easy. You don't know the whole story. He isn't free." Briana turned away, hiding the tears that glistened in her blue eyes.

"Not free? Oh, you mean Deb. It's been two years since she died, and he should get on with his life."

"We'll see," Briana murmured. After a long, sisterly hug, she left to go home.

Tiffany was glad to see her and it was wonderful having someone waiting for her when she arrived. Someone who loved her no matter who she was.

In the end Briana couldn't face calling Tyler at home, so she waited until the next day and called him at work. He took down the information and said he'd call Paula right away. It was eight o'clock that evening when he called back.

"Paula found a Mary Barton who applied for a license to marry James Duncan in Topeka in 1971. The age listed for her was twenty-five. How does that work out for our Mary?"

"She was twenty-two when Jack was killed in 1968, so she would have been twenty-five in 1971. Do we have a lead or what?" Briana was so excited that she could hardly control herself. This had to be her mother! It all pointed in the right direction.

"I have a phone book here," she said opening it to the D's. "Oh, Tyler, there must be fifty Duncans listed! There are a couple of Jameses and two J's. It's not too late to call, is it?" Tyler assured her that 8:15 was still a respectable time to call, especially to one's possible birth mother.

"Call me back when you're through," he requested, then added, "Not tomorrow. Tonight!"

"Yes, sir!" she laughed.

She copied the numbers down from the phone book and carefully made the first call. She asked if Mrs. Duncan was home, and the voice answered that she was Mrs. Duncan.

"Are you Mary Duncan?" Briana asked.

"No, my name is Joan. Sorry."

When she dialed the next number, a child answered. "Hello," Briana began, "Could I speak to your mother?"

"She's not here now." The voice sounded like a boy's.

"My name is Briana Sheldon. I'm looking for a Mary Duncan. Is that your mother's name?"

There was some confusion and a conversation began on the other end of the line that did not include Briana. Then a new voice came on the line. "I'm Janet Duncan. May I help you?:

Briana repeated the purpose of the call and the young girl asked, "Why are you looking for her?"

"It's a private matter. I'm looking up some family history, and I think she might be able to help me. Is her name Mary?" Briana prayed the girl would answer.

"Yes," she finally answered. "My mother's name is Mary. Just call back another time. Could I have your name once more and I'll tell her you called?"

Briana was disappointed, but gave her name and said she'd call back the next day. She called Tyler and told him of her news, or rather the lack of any.

"That sounds pretty good, though," Ty said. "At least the name is right. I'd like to take you back up to my farm. This time we'll go over to the manor and walk around the outbuildings and see the area where the old cabin was located. You might remember something. Children forget the things adults think are important and remember the ridiculous, like a big rock or a tree. Something that was only important to you as a child. How about in the morning? We'll come back before dark since we don't want people talking."

Briana laughed, yet wondered who would care. He couldn't be very worried, with Adrian at his apartment while he showered. Against her better judgment they flew up to the farm and while it was still cool, went up to the manor to walk the grounds. Behind the big Queen Anne house was a large barn and beside that, standing almost in its shadow, was a smaller barn that was a part of Stone Haven. It was constructed of native stone like the house, but the doors and windows had stone arches instead of the usual straight angles. It was an intricate bit of stonemasonry that gave the barn character; Ty said that a local Indian had done the rockwork for the pioneer family.

Briana thought it strange that the barn had the beautiful rockwork and not the house. Tyler explained that the barn had come later and the stonemason might not have been in the area when the house was constructed. It was interesting to see the original wood on the floor and stalls. The two-by-fours were thicker than usual and the beams were of primitive planed wood from a time gone by. There were lambs in one stall, giving Briana a glimpse of what it must have been like back then.

"Dolan's not too pleased about the sheep, but Lavida insists and what she says still carries some weight. Do you see anything that looks familiar?"

Briana looked all around. Surely if she were Sabrina she would remember the old house and barn. But she didn't. Nothing looked familiar or frightening, causing her to doubt she was Sabrina after all.

Dolan arrived in a well-used, older pickup and Tyler walked over to the road to converse with him. Briana turned and walked back around the area where the large trailer was set up on concrete blocks and tried, once more, to visualize a wooden structure in its place. Nothing came to her. She was so engrossed in her thoughts that she didn't see Chad emerge from the big barn behind the manor until he was almost to her.

"Well, if it isn't the tramp," he sneered.

"Leave me alone, Chad, and we'll avoid future problems!" Briana started walking toward Tyler, but Chad wasn't through.

"You made me look like a jerk!" he accused, sounding like a petulant little boy.

"You are," Briana told him. "And I take no responsibility for that."

She had taken a few steps when she felt his hand on her shoulder. She whirled around, knocking his hand away. "Don't you dare touch me, Chad Roswald!"

"You cause trouble everywhere you go, so why don't you just go back to California where you belong? My grandmother has your number. She says you're evil!"

Briana's skin began to crawl and she felt the presence of a power that seemed satanic. She could see hate in Chad's eyes and recalled Lavida as she quizzed Briana about the Lord. At the time she had been certain the old woman's impression of her was favorable, not one of evil. Why did this young brother of Adrian also hate her?

Briana opened her lips to reply, but the only words to come were, "Be gone, Satan. You have no power over me. In the name of Jesus, depart!" Her voice rang with knowledge and truth.

Chad's mouth gaped open for a brief moment, then Tyler called out "Hi, Chad!" and walked toward them. The spell was broken.

Chad had been so intent on Briana and her words that he hadn't seen Tyler coming.

"Er...oh. Hi there," was all the boy could mumble. He turned and walked away, slapping his old cowboy hat against his dirty jeans as he went.

"I asked Dolan about Jack Barton," Tyler began, unaware of the tension he'd walked into, "but Dolan was in college when he was killed. He was having some problems of his own that year since Irene was pregnant with Deb, and they had to get married. I guess Bevin, Dolan's dad, told him Irene could come here to the farm to have the baby, but only after their marriage, and the second condition was that Dolan would complete his schooling. I guess it all worked out. He and Irene are still married, he finished college, and he's a very successful farmer."

Tyler looked toward the disappearing boy and asked, "Was he getting fresh again?"

"I can handle him. I wonder if Dolan was like Chad when he was that age?"

"It's possible. Deb told me Dolan had quite a reputation with the ladies. I'm surprised Irene was able to keep him at home back then."

"I wouldn't put up with infidelity for one second," Briana stated bluntly.

"Sometimes love—true love—has no boundaries," Tyler said softly as he looked intently at her.

"For the women?" Briana asked. "Men can two-time, but we women have to stay home and wait. Well, that isn't for me! I couldn't handle that again." The last sentence just slipped out and Tyler studied her face.

"Just because one man let you down, that doesn't mean you should judge everyone by him." He reached out to pull a strand of hair back from her face.

The mere touch of his hand on her cheek made her heart race. She closed her eyes for a second and thought of their conversation. All her bravado about not sharing a man was just talk. Adrian was still in the picture and here Briana was swooning over Tyler's touch. Maybe he was right about true love.

"I have to drive over to Frankfort for a machine part Cecil ordered, so you can come along or lay around the pool and relax. We'll return to the city when I get back."

She chose to go with him in case Chad or Lavida might find her there alone. Some strange tension seemed to haunt this family, but she had problems of her own and they were going to have to be resolved.

They headed south on Highway 77 to 9 and turned east. The country was a beautiful contrast with wooded areas in one section, then fields, crops, and cattle in the next. In some places there were rocky hills, which seemed out of place in the Kansas landscape. Everyone had assured her that Kansas was a flat prairie land with no character. They were wrong!

Tyler pointed out earth silos where grain was stored underground and showed her an old round barn with a green roof. She wondered if she had seen that before. Maybe. Maybe not.

Frankfort was up ahead, and as they entered the town from the west on the left side of the road, she saw a playground. It was small, grassy, and had a swing set and a slide.

"Oh Tyler, please stop! I have to walk in that playground." She was already opening the door, even though the truck had not completely stopped. She ran across the pavement and up a small incline, then stopped and stared at the swings. There were three swings hanging from metal chains connected to an old, rusted metal framework.

"I've been here!" she cried. "I've been right here!"

Her fingers ran lightly up the links of the chains holding the wooden seats, and then she went over to the small slide and touched the partially rusted steps. The slide had stayed shiny with frequent use, but the years had weathered the rest. Nearby was an old-fashioned merry-go-round with a wooden platform that twirled and metal bars to hang onto. Briana sat down on the wooden floor and pushed it into action with her foot. Her mind was remembering another time, a happy time, but then her smiling face crumpled as the tears started flowing.

"Tyler, who am I?" His arms went around her as he pulled her up to him. She sobbed as he held her in his arms until she was exhausted.

On their return trip, Tyler asked her if she wanted to stop once more at the park, but she said no. She knew now that she had to be Sabrina, and that was enough.

CHAPTER 19

Briana called Mary Duncan again when they returned to Topeka. Tiffany had greeted them noisily when they arrived but soon calmed down and sat curiously watching as Briana dial the numbers on the phone. Tyler watched her also, sitting across from her in a big overstuffed chair that she had brought from California. He was leaning forward, forearms on his knees and his strong hands clasped together before him.

"Hello, I'm Briana Sheldon," Briana began nervously. "I called the other evening to talk to you about Jack Barton." When there was no reply from Mary Duncan, Briana went on. "You were married to him before your present husband?"

The woman on the other end of the line said coolly, "May I ask who you are and what your business is with me?"

She wasn't being rude, Briana realized, just wary. "I'm sorry, Mrs. Duncan, I should have explained before that I'm doing some family history and was hoping I could come and talk to you or meet you somewhere to discuss the Barton family."

There was a pregnant silence that caused Briana to glance at Tyler with concern.

"I don't know much about Jack's people, but I do have some of his old pictures in a box in the attic. They might help you. Can you come over tomorrow afternoon? We're having a fellowship dinner after church, so three o'clock would work out best for me."

Briana said that would be fine, and, after getting directions, thanked her and hung up.

"Tomorrow at three," she said, grasping Ty's hands in hers. "Oh please, Lord, let this be something concrete!" she prayed aloud.

It wasn't until she was at church the next morning that she began getting cold feet. Briana hadn't been fully honest with Mary Duncan, but she also hadn't exactly lied. She hoped to stay focused on Jack at first; she had no intention of claiming to be his daughter without more facts. Eventually, she also needed to find out if her mother had willingly given her up or if she had actually been abducted. The mystery had to be solved, but Briana planned to take it one step at a time—she knew it was up to her to discover the truth about her past. She would be going alone to this meeting, even though Tyler and Shelly had offered to go with her. This was something she had to do by herself, no matter how frightened she was.

The small wood frame house was in a pleasant, older area of Topeka. Huge trees shaded the homes, streets, and the small, well-trimmed yards in front of each house. The mailbox had the street address displayed quite visibly, so Briana pulled into the cement driveway and parked in front of the Duncans' attached garage. No other car was in sight, and she wondered if Mary would be alone.

The woman who opened the door was a few inches shorter than Briana and very pretty. Melissa had mentioned her complexion and it was still lovely. Briana felt her heart pounding as she cordially greeted this stranger who might be her mother.

"Come in. Briana, is it? I have the house to myself this afternoon, so we won't be disturbed. Baseball games are an ongoing thing when you have three children."

Briana glanced around the neat, welcoming home and was aware of the contrast between this and Melissa's elegant house. But Briana felt at home here. It was a lived-in house, with a toy car partially visible under the couch and a candy wrapper beside a half-empty candy dish on the end table.

"I found the box of pictures I mentioned," Mary said, motioning Briana to follow her into the dining room, where a small cigar box sat on the polished table. "Let me fix us some iced tea first. Do you use sugar?"

"Plain will be fine. My folks say I'm sweet enough," Briana laughed and wished she'd said something else.

"I like mine plain too, but Jim always heaps sugar in his. Yuck!" Mary sat the glasses on coasters, then reached for the box.

"Are you from Topeka, or have you just traveled here for your search?"

"I'm originally from California," Briana said, not ready to divulge any facts just yet. "I was transferred here recently by the Santa Fe to work in their law office."

"Are you an attorney, then?"

"Yes," Briana answered and told her about recently taking the Kansas bar exam and how she was enjoying the work thus far.

"This will be a big change for you weather-wise," Mary said. "Come January you'll wish you were back in sunny California, but you'll learn to enjoy having four seasons before long. Each one is so different."

Mary opened the box and Briana saw the first pictures of her father. He was a tall, good-looking young man in a rugged sort of way. "Jack loved farming," Mary said softly as she looked fondly at the image in the picture. "He was killed in an accident one summer, and I was left alone with a child to raise and nowhere to go."

Briana's heart began to chill, and she dreaded hearing the next words. Would her mother admit that she had gotten rid of her?

"I didn't want to live without Jack," she went on. "We had been high school sweethearts, and I was only a freshman when we met. He was a senior, a football jock, and so good-looking. My guardian seemed to consider me just a cross to bear until I was of age. We got married as soon as I was eighteen and I dropped out of school. And then we had the baby that first year. I have preached to my children about finishing their education, yet I didn't get my GED until after I came to Topeka. I had free time and a small amount of money, so decided to make something of myself." Briana wondered—was the money from insurance, or the sale of a child?

Mary laid out the rest of the pictures so Briana could see the faded ones, describing Jack's people. There was one photo of an older couple in front of a farmhouse, who Mary said were perhaps his grandparents. She thought they could have come from back East. but she wasn't sure.

"So what are you looking for in the Barton family?" Mary asked as she sipped her tea.

"Well, I don't have much to go on except that Jack Barton lived up by Marysville and died there. There was a picture in a paper showing you and a child at his gravesite. Where is that little girl now?"

Mary sat her tea glass down and got up to adjust the mini-blind on the large window to filter out the streaming sunlight.

"Our daughter died less than a year after Jack's accident. I don't know if I will ever forget the pain." When she resumed her seat, Briana saw tears glistening in Mary's eyes. Briana herself was close to tears, because she wasn't Sabrina after all. Sabrina was dead! *Oh, my God, now who am I?*

"What happened?" she felt compelled to ask, trying to fight the emotions that were coursing through her body.

"I moved to Topeka a few months after Jack died when I couldn't bear the memories in Marysville anymore. I had enough with the insurance settlement that I hoped to stay home with Sabrina till she began kindergarten. We played at the park, visited the library, and I began looking for work. Sabrina and I lived in a small apartment, and we were happy in spite of our loss. Sabrina was almost four years old and was such a sweetheart. Having her to live for helped me through many a lonely night. Then I got sick. We thought it was just pneumonia, but then I was hospitalized after taking a turn for the worse. What was I going to do with Sabrina? I had no family to turn to. An elderly neighbor had befriended me when we first moved in and Connie volunteered to look after my little girl. Then when the tests came back that it had turned to meningitis, I was told I was dying." Tears ran unnoticed down the woman's face. "Connie said she would take care of her. She was so kind to us." Mary finally brushed away the tears at that point and reached for a tissue to blow her nose. "You didn't come to hear all my sorrows. I'm sorry."

"That's all right," Briana assured her. "You quite obviously didn't die. How did you recover?"

"I was in the hospital on my deathbed, comforted by the fact that Bri would be taken care of so I could die in peace." Briana's heart lurched when Mary called the child by her nickname.

"They called in a specialist who tried an experiment, and I responded, living from hour to hour, then finally day to day. Somehow, I got stronger and eventually asked to have Sabrina brought to me. The young doctor who saved my life had to break the news to me that while I was fighting to stay alive, pneumonia had snuffed out my child's life!" Mary's face crumpled as the memories returned, and tears blurred the vision of both women.

"I'm so sorry," Briana murmured and took the woman's hand in hers. She felt the loss acutely—not only for the mother and child, but for herself. She was not this child. Sabrina Barton was dead. Some time went by before Mary Barton was able to speak again.

"The babysitter, Connie, was so upset that after I was released from the hospital, she moved to Minnesota to live with her married daughter. She died soon after. I told her I didn't hold her responsible for what happened. Children get sick so quickly!

"Janet got the flu when she was about four, and I could see the same thing happening all over again, but she was fine. In fact, I have a recent picture of all of us I'll show you. The church puts out a directory every few years and we get a free picture if we go in for a sitting."

Briana looked at the group picture slowly and could see they were a very handsome family, not unlike Briana's own family. But her family wasn't actually her own! Suddenly she felt adrift and wished she had never been told. Jim was an average-looking man, a few years older than his wife. According to the marriage license, Briana had Mary's age figured out to be forty-three.

"Greg is seventeen," Mary said, looking fondly at her oldest child's image in the picture. "This will be his senior year in high school. Janet is fifteen and hates boys!" Mary laughed. "Of course, it's only a matter of time until all that changes. Doug is ten and seems to grow a foot taller each week. But though I'm very proud of my family, I will never forget my firstborn."

"Do you have pictures of her?"

"Yes, just a minute." Mary left the table and came back shortly with a small album of pictures, many of them black and white. "We were pretty poor when we lived up north, but we didn't care. We could live on love, we used to say."

The pictures of the child were typical: a new baby, then her first steps and birthday parties. Sabrina had dark hair and though the pictures didn't show it, Mary said her eyes were blue. Briana commented on each image but soon excused herself. She could see how hard it was on Mary to relive this painful chapter, and she wasn't sure she could hide her own emotions much longer.

"It could have been me!" Briana sobbed, later that evening, in Tyler's arms. "I should never have let myself get this involved. Who cares who my parents are? I don't! I'm not going to search anymore!"

One evening later that week, after Shelly and Briana had been out to see a movie, Shelly asked, "Did Mary say where Sabrina was buried?"

"I didn't ask her—I caused her enough misery with all those questions. Imagine how much she loved that child to mourn her so deeply after twenty years!"

"But Bri, it was the only child she and Jack had and she lost them both so suddenly. How cruel life was to her." Shelly was quiet for a second then asked, "Briana, what if the child didn't die?"

Briana looked at her friend and said, "But she did. Mary said she did!"

"Then let's find out where she's buried. "

"It's just so utterly useless, Shelly." Briana leaned back in her chair and sighed. "I'm not her!"

"Then why the flashbacks? Why does that big red building you called a castle frighten you? You can't deny that you freaked out at the sight of that fancy staircase! And why did you say you had been to that playground in Frankfort? Call Mary and ask where the child is buried. Tell her you need it for your records on Jack's history chart. It can't hurt!"

Later, Briana called Mary and was told that Sabrina was buried with her father's grave in Marysville. Not expecting the ailing mother to recover, the people in charge had the child cremated, and her urn was buried with her father. Another dead end.

Briana's tears erupted again. "I knew it was too easy," she said.

So the search was called off. They all had to get on with their lives and Briana called her parents to let them know the results. It wasn't important, she lied, hoping to put them at rest. Tiffany was her constant companion during this time. How many friends do laundry with you or watch you fold clothes? How often do you have someone who loves you so much they want to be with you all the time?

One night the phone rang, and Tyler asked, "Are you sitting down?"

"Why?"

"Paula looked for the death records of Sabrina Barton and there are none. What do you make of that?"

"Tyler, I can't go through this again! Mary said the child was buried on Jack's grave. Well, her ashes anyway. I assume Marysville will have the record?"

"Trust me, if she died in Kansas, Paula would have found it. Why didn't she? I wonder if there is a marker on the grave? If Bevin and Gladys were home they would know."

"Tyler, are they very, very rich? I can't imagine them taking an extended European vacation when they're just farmers."

When Tyler quit laughing, he explained, "The friends they are visiting are very wealthy and have their own yacht and live very well. I'd say you could refer to Bevin and Gladys as comfortable. Wealth is in the eye of the beholder in most cases."

"Then where do we go from here?" she asked. "If there is no record of Sabrina's death, are you thinking she didn't die?"

"She might have died somewhere else—in Kansas City, Missouri, for instance."

Briana remembered what Mary Duncan had said. "No, she died here in Topeka while Mary was in the hospital. Wouldn't the hospitals have records?"

"Maybe she wasn't in a hospital. Did Mary say she died in a hospital? We need to know which one."

"No, she just said she died of pneumonia."

"Maybe she would know the doctor's name or even which mortuary handled the funeral."

"Oh, Ty, this is so pointless. I can't bear to resurrect this subject again and call her to interrogate her further. Mary saw the marker on Jack's grave that had Sabrina's name on it. She said it was one of the small metal stakes with a written card on the top. She and Jim drove up there one time, and they looked it up. Would someone put a marker on a grave when there is no body?"

There was a pause as the question hung on the line. Then she asked again, "Would they?"

CHAPTER 20

Tyler was scheduled to go out of town over Labor Day weekend, so Briana stayed around the house. Shelly and Tom came over on Labor Day and they had a cookout. Tom grilled the burgers while the girls set out baked beans and salads. As usual, they had too much food.

They had just started to eat in the backyard when the doorbell rang, sending Tiffany into an excited frenzy. It was Ty. When Briana opened the door, he wrapped her in his arms and began kissing her. She responded instantly, throwing caution to the wind.

"I missed you," he murmured in her ear.

"Yes," she agreed. She would miss him all the time very soon, and she hated herself for being weak. *October is a month away*, she groaned silently, *then I'll have cut all ties with him.* Though it now seemed impossible, perhaps down deep she thought she could still take him away from Adrian.

"Shelly and Tom are here for a picnic," she explained when he loosened his embrace. "There's plenty of food—please join us!" Tyler reached down to pet the anxious poodle, then followed Briana out to the shady backyard.

"Hi!" Tom greeted Ty from the picnic table. "I hope you've come to help me out on horseshoes. These girls are beating the socks off me! Of course, I'm not trying very hard." He cleared his throat as if he had choked, then laughed. "It isn't good to beat the homeowner lest she asks us to leave before the food is gone."

"Oh give me a break!" Briana wailed. "I'm beating you fair and square!" They all laughed, enjoying their easy camaraderie.

While they were all sitting around the picnic table later, snacking on the leftovers, Tyler looked serious all of a sudden. "I had Paula look all over the country for the death records of Sabrina Barton, and there are none. Bri—she didn't die." They all stared at Ty, then turned to Briana.

"Why would that old lady tell Mary she had?" Briana asked, incredulous. "How cruel! How could a person tell such a lie to a mother?"

"Did the sitter sell the child?" Tom wondered.

"I don't know, but nothing is adding up here," Tyler said.

Shelly reached for a chocolate chip cookie. "I can't understand why Mary didn't demand the death certificate or information about the hospital, the attending physician, or the funeral home. Wouldn't any mother do that?"

Briana knew why. Mary's baby was dead and the young mother's life was crumbling. She was in pain from her loss and still weak from her own illness.

"I wonder if she knows something important, yet hasn't recalled it?" Ty asked. "Bri, how would you feel about me going with you to see her once more—would you mind?" He frowned, then added, "I'm sure you're Sabrina Barton. I don't understand why you're buried in Marysville when you were brought up in California, but I feel there has been a crime committed somewhere, and you and Mary are the victims. What do you think? Bri, will you give her a call?"

Briana could see now why Tyler was such a good lawyer. With those few words, he had all of them believing it was true.

"But should I bother her on the holiday?"

"It won't hurt to ask," Shelly said. "If she's busy, just make it for another time."

When Mary answered she seemed pleased to hear from Briana and willing to see her again. "I've thought many times about our conversation and am very pleased you called. You had said you were doing Barton family history and I've been wondering why you were so intent on searching for Sabrina."

Briana hesitated briefly, then explained: "I just turned up that lead and decided to trace it to its roots in case she had family in this area. Would you mind if I bring a friend of mine with me this time? His name is Tyler Rainger. He's a lawyer here in Topeka."

Mary said that would be fine, and they agreed to meet two hours later.

"Now we need to write down some questions to ask and think of things to jog her memory. I feel sure she'll help us," Briana said on the drive over. She glanced toward Tyler and caught him looking at her with such love in his eyes that she could hardly contain herself. She would have to be careful and not let her heart rule her life.

Mary answered the door and smiled as Briana introduced Tyler to her.

"How do you do?" she greeted Tyler. "I've heard of you, Mr. Rainger, but never dreamed of meeting you, let alone having you come to our home. Please make yourselves comfortable in the front room, and I'll be right back."

When Mary returned her family came with her and she made the introductions, smiling proudly at her three children and husband. "Greg is seventeen," she told Tyler. "My Janet is fifteen and Doug," she said as she ruffled his hair, "is ten. This is Jim, my husband." It was plain to see the great love Mary had for her husband.

"You're lucky you caught us at home," Jim said cheerfully as he shook Tyler's hand. "We had ball games until four, and if I might use this opportunity to brag just a bit, Greg's team won the tournament!"

Tyler and Briana said the expected congratulations, and Tyler shook Greg's hand.

"Janet's team was in the playoffs," Mary added, "but lost out in the last inning. They'll take it next year."

Briana felt like she was seeing the positive result of a second marriage. These people were caring and loving, and the children were bright and well behaved. Mary had said before that Jim worked long, tedious hours as a construction supervisor, but always had time for his family.

"I'm really sorry to have to bother you again and on the holiday, but we promise not to stay long. You see— well, this is very important." Briana didn't know how much to tell them, and somehow she felt like she was lying by not explaining about her birth parents.

Seeing her confusion, Tyler broke in and said, "Maybe we could just sit down and see if we can find out some things to help Briana."

That was fine with Mary. As the family left the room the three of them sat down at the dining room table. Tyler got out his yellow legal tablet and scanned down the pages.

"Mary, we need to know if you've ever seen the death certificate for your daughter?"

Mary stared at Tyler for a second and then said, "No."

"Why not?" he asked.

"She was dead." Mary looked down at her hands on the table in front of her. "I thought my world had mended itself when I got better and would be able to come home, but then Connie told me about Sabrina's death and it all fell apart again. I felt guilty because I lived and she didn't. It wasn't fair!"

Tears began to build up in the woman's eyes. Briana reached over and took her hand.

"That time in your life must have been very painful. I'm so sorry for you, but there is a saying my mom used to repeat. 'When God shuts a door, He usually opens a window.' Your window seems to be a happy marriage and three fine children." Mary nodded in quiet acknowledgment.

"Can you remember the name of the doctor who cared for Sabrina before you went to the hospital?" Tyler asked. "Did you have need of one after you came to Topeka?"

"No."

"Did the babysitter have a physician that she might have contacted to care for your child?"

"I don't know." Mary's voice was a whisper as she realized how little she had known about what happened all those years ago. Finally she asked, "Why is all this important now over twenty years later? I don't know how I can help you after all this time."

Tyler reached over and touched Mary's shoulder as he gave her his warm, lovable smile.

"Mary, you are not to feel guilty about what happened twenty years ago, but we have something to tell you—yet we can't prove it. The one thing we do know is that your little girl did not die in the United States, and we don't believe she is dead at all."

Mary's mouth gaped open as she stared at Ty. "Not dead?" She sat up straighter in her chair and then leaned closer to Ty.

"Of course, she's dead! Her ashes are buried on Jack's grave. I saw the marker!"

Hearing the alarm in his wife's voice, Jim entered the room and asked, "Mary, is there a problem?"

"They said my baby isn't dead!"

Jim bristled slightly and asked, "Just what is it you are trying to do here?" Then he looked directly at Tyler and asked, "Are you representing a client who has some kind of claim?"

"Not really, we just keep running into facts that don't jive and we're searching for the offspring of Jack Barton. We found Jack's death records, but none for Sabrina, and hers should be there. We have the correct year and the location, but there are no records."

Tyler turned back to Mary and asked, "In the event of your death back then, who would have been notified? Who would have been responsible for Sabrina? Do you have relatives? Parents?"

"I lost my parents in a car crash when I was young, and my older aunt brought me up. I gave Connie the Roswalds' name and phone number, so she might have contacted them if she needed help. When Sabrina and I left the farm Gladys told me to stay in touch, but I wouldn't have called on them at all. But maybe Connie did when she found out how sick Sabrina was." She paused briefly, as if another thought had been jogged, then turned to Briana. "Do they all call you Bri?"

"Yes, my parents and brothers always called me Bri. It's a good name."

Briana wanted to confide their suspicions that she was Sabrina, but she had decided to avoid that until they solved the mystery. Mary had been through enough without raising hope again after all these years. Now it seemed as if Mary might have the same suspicions; however, she didn't comment any further.

The car was quiet on the return trip, but at Briana's door Tyler said, "I'll call the farm tomorrow and talk to Lavida if I can. She's the only one there right now who might remember Mary and her child. Gladys will know more, but we can't wait until they come home." He lifted her chin to brush his lips over hers.

"See you later in the week? How about a real date Saturday night? We could have dinner and go to a movie. What do you think?"

"You're a bad influence on me. I really want to, but...."

Her words were stopped by his lips as they covered hers. "Say yes, Bri," he breathed against her lips. The "yes" she whispered came quickly, before she could stop herself.

She wondered if Tyler felt as guilty about this infatuation of theirs as she did. Would he decide at the last minute not to marry Adrian? Maybe Adrian would find out about them and call off the wedding. This wasn't fair; she knew from experience how that felt. Briana wished her relationship with Tyler had never started, but when that thought surfaced, she knew it wasn't true. She would never love anyone the way she loved Tyler.

He called the next day while Briana was in a meeting, so Shelly took the message. Ty had called the Roswald's and talked to Lavida. She had given him some information that he would pass on to Briana that evening. She waited all evening, hoping he would come over, but he just called on the phone a bit after eight.

"Sorry I couldn't call you any earlier, but Adrian and Brenda are here."

Briana's heart tightened. *I won't be jealous*, her mind said, but she knew she was.

"Lavida wasn't very open about Sabrina. In fact, she was reluctant to talk about it at all, but she knew the child had died because she personally paid for the marker on the grave."

"Did she know at what hospital Sabrina had been treated, or which doctor treated the child? And Tyler, who took care of the bills?"

Tyler turned away from the phone to speak to someone who had just entered the room where he was. "Brenda says hi. She says you are special!" He lowered his voice and said, "I knew that!"

"Tell her hi for me," Briana replied with a catch in her voice.

"Anyway, Lavida didn't know about the hospital or the doctor and I didn't think to ask about bills. I told her there wasn't a death certificate, and she began going off about evil, stakes in the heart, and silver bullets. I couldn't get her back on the subject. I guess at eighty-five she can think what she wants."

"Ty, we still don't know anything more than we did. What was she saying about evil? Chad said something about me being evil that day at the farm. Sounds to me like that family has some major problems. I need to add Lavida to my prayers along with Chad. That 'stake in the heart' stuff seems like it would be for vampires or the living dead. Weird!"

"Brenda wants to talk to you, Bri. I'm going to have to go. I'll pick you up Saturday night at six, and we'll decide on a movie and place to eat. Here's Brenda."

"Hi," the child greeted her.

"Hello to you, too!"

"What have you been doing?" Brenda asked.

"Mostly working, I guess. Have you started school yet?" Briana was glad to get Brenda started on that because the child was quite vocal about beginning the second grade, talking incessantly till her mother made her hang up.

After that Briana couldn't seem to get interested in anything. Her thoughts kept going back to Adrian at Tyler's apartment and she wondered if he were taking her out this evening. Was she spending the night?

"Lord, are you trying to warn me that this is all wrong?" she implored that evening as she got ready for bed. She laughed and added, "I have no right to be jealous. I have no rights at all, do I? Please bless Tyler, and help him in all he does, Lord. You know how much I love him, but if he and Adrian are to marry, and You are in this union, then so be it." Tears welled in her eyes, and she blinked them away as she lifted up her parents and friends in her usual evening prayer.

"And Lord, I ask for one more thing this evening. You know about my search for my birth parents and how many dead ends I've come up against. If it's Your will that I accomplish this mission, then please give me patience. I get so eager! Thank you also for giving us Your Son, Jesus. Amen."

She had only just murmured "Amen" when she remembered to pray for Lavida and Chad, so added them quickly. Only the Lord could help with them, she decided. Evil was something God understood and dealt with every day. She felt at peace now, but somehow sleep was slow in coming. She read for a while and finally turned off the light around eleven.

Suddenly the phone woke her and as she reached for it, she saw that her digital clock radio said 12:08. Fear grabbed her as she tentatively said, "Hello?" No one liked a call at this time of night, because it usually meant accidents, illness, or something worse.

"Hello?" she said again, sleepily and fearfully. Her dad had been fighting a cold, she recalled and her mother's blood pressure had been up at the last doctor's visit.

"Who is sleeping with you?" the male voice asked.

"My poodle, what's it to you?" she blurted, and then hung up.

In a few seconds, the phone rang again, so she lifted the receiver and let it fall loudly in the cradle. For two hours the phone rang—sometimes two or three times in a row, sometimes with a fifteen-minute space between calls. Briana didn't answer it again. It was a short night. The calls ended around 2:30 a.m., but by then Briana wasn't able to relax or sleep. The calls continued the next night. The following day after work, Briana stopped and purchased an answering machine.

Tyler called one evening but Briana didn't pick up until after she heard his voice beginning to leave the message. Once she finally picked up the phone, he asked why she had gotten the recorder. She told him about the obscene calls and he was upset she hadn't called him about it.

"Tyler, I'm a big girl. I can handle this."

"Do you have any of the messages on tape?"

"Yes, I kept them just in case…." she admitted.

"I'm coming over," he barked and hung up.

Briana fixed the tape to begin at the place where the prankster had called the night before, so when Tyler arrived, Briana played the tape three times for him and he shook his head in disbelief. "I know the voice," he admitted. "It's Chad Roswald."

"What? Surely you're wrong. These calls would be long distance. Why would he want to harass me? Tyler, are you sure?"

"I'm positive and this is going to be stopped. I have to fly up to the farm this weekend and it will give me an ideal opportunity to have a man-to-man talk with Chad. He'll either choose to apologize or I'll go to Dolan about it. Chad has a great amount of respect for his dad, since Dolan holds the purse strings as well as the keys to the boy's future. Chad and Deb were close, and when we lost her he rebelled. Nothing major, just disrespectful and a bit wild."

"I know. He breaks down doors at motels and slashes tires!"

Tyler groaned and said, "When I think of you all alone in that room it makes my blood boil. You could have been hurt so easily."

"You forget, I was the one with the gun!"

"They could have overpowered you and…."

"Tyler, I'm trained not to let that happen, but let's forget it. I'm okay and if you can fix it so I can sleep again, I'd appreciate it greatly."

"Yes, ma'am," he answered. "By the way, Brenda sure thinks you're super. Well, *special* was her term."

Briana laughed and told him about their birthmarks and what her Mom had told Briana about being special.

"It's a secret, so don't let her know I told you."

"Where is your birthmark?" he asked in a more serious tone.

"It's on my side. I'll show you." She pulled up her shirt, exposing her waist, then turned to let him see the red mark.

"It's very similar to Brenda's," he said, touching it lightly, which made her squirm and pull away. "I'm ticklish!"

"So I noticed," he laughed, pulling her into his arms.

"We need to talk about us, Bri."

"What about us?"

"Well I was hoping…." His words were cut short by the phone. As the recorder began Briana could hear Shelly's voice saying "Bri, pick up the phone!" Her friend sounded very upset so she hurried to answer.

Shelly's father had had a stroke and she was needed in Texas. She didn't know how long she'd be gone, but probably a week. Briana assured her that they both would be in her prayers.

As it turned out, Tyler wasn't able to keep their date Saturday. Instead, he flew up to his farm to do some harsh talking to a rebellious teen.

He didn't mention that Adrian and Brenda went along, and Briana wouldn't have known about it except that it came out later in a passing conversation. Tyler didn't seem to hide it, and it was evidently nothing out of the ordinary. *Yet he was the one who had wanted to discuss us*, Briana mused. She hadn't been able to settle down all weekend—it seemed to go on forever. Shelly had called Friday morning to update Briana on her father's condition; after that, time stood still. Briana cleaned house, washed clothes, and called her folks. Still, the hours stretched ahead of her until finally she decided to do something she'd been planning for some time. She would tint her hair back to its original dark color, she decided. The change would boost her morale and she could end all the work it took to keep her hair blonde. It had served its purpose and had been fun, but now that she was a full-fledged lawyer she would need to concentrate on her work, not on whether she had dark roots showing!

It had been years since her hair had been dark and as she looked at her image in the mirror she wondered what Tyler would say. Shelly would laugh and accuse Briana of copying her kooky habit, and Frank and Kyle would make comments, but in an hour they would forget.

At church Sunday morning, a couple called out to her in the foyer, but used the name Adrian. When Briana turned to look for Adrian, they were looking at her and apologized for the mistake. Briana hoped she didn't look like Adrian.

Tyler got back Sunday evening and called to tell Briana about his confrontation with Chad. "He was upset that we were able to recognize his voice, but said you deserved what you got. At that point, I explained that he could go to jail for that and he was shocked. I told him we had the tape as evidence and wouldn't hesitate to use it. He won't be calling you again. I asked him why he dislikes you, but he wouldn't say. He also said he wasn't the only one who felt that way."

"But Tyler, why would these people dislike me when I don't even know them?"

"I don't know, but we'll find out eventually. By the way, I took a run out to the cemetery and saw Jack's grave. The marker with Sabrina's name on it is the kind you just stick in the ground like a stake. It has a small holder at the top in which a faded, typed card with her name was placed. Anyone could steal one from an old grave and put her name on it."

"This whole thing has me drained, Tyler. I'm on a roller coaster and can't get off!"

"I think we need to rattle some cages. Someone knows what went on twenty years ago and we're going to find out who!"

"When are Bevin and Gladys coming home?" she asked.

"A few days before the end of the month. In fact, they're having their annual Halloween masquerade party at the manor on October 31st. How about going with me?"

"I don't think so. It's too close to when my family arrives, and anyway, the less I have to do with the Roswalds, the better I like it."

"But your family might enjoy the party, too."

Bri could just see Chad calling her names and her dad and brothers beating him to a pulp. Nothing like being entertainment for the gala occasion!

"I think they'll be here after the first, and I hope they don't get into any blizzards. Dad has had to change his vacation three times now, but at least the boys will be able to come this time."

"I'm sorry we had to miss our date Saturday. Will I have another chance this week?"

"We'll see," Briana said hesitantly, "Maybe you could come over for dinner tomorrow night if you want. I have something to show you."

"That sounds interesting. Could it be another birthmark?"

"No, not that. I'll just keep you in suspense!" She laughed and added, "It's no big deal, Tyler. I'll see you about six. Bye."

CHAPTER 21

Briana was nervous the next day, wondering what Tyler would think of her dark hair. Kyle and Frank had both done double takes and commented on the change, as did some of her other co-workers.

When she got home from work, she stood in front of the mirror for ten minutes trying different hair styles, In the end, she left it loose, freshened her makeup, and dabbed on a hint of perfume.

The closer the time came for Tyler to arrive, the worse it got. She tried to concentrate on preparing dinner, but somehow that was impossible. The Lord must have helped her, because it was just completed when the doorbell rang. Tiffany began her usual greeting and impatiently danced in place until the door opened.

Briana would never forget Tyler's expression. He stared at her for a full ten seconds before struggling to say, "So you finally did it."

She opened her mouth to reply, but hesitated. His voice had been crisp, and he sounded disturbed, angry even. He reached out and touched her hair gently. She wanted to turn her head so his palms would touch her face, and she felt a rush of desire to be in his arms to feel his lips capture hers and send her into their magical world.

"Come on in," she said to cover her confusion. She could feel his eyes on her as she led the way to the dining room.

"I'll have to eat and run," he informed her quickly. "I have an appointment. Will that be a problem?"

Her first thought, of course, was that it was probably not an appointment but a date with Adrian. "No problem," she answered hesitantly, already sensing the evening was ruined.

"How's Shelly's father doing?" he asked while she brought in the food.

"She'll be back this weekend. Her dad is doing very well with only a trace of paralysis. He was lucky."

"No luck. Prayers," he mumbled as he followed her to the kitchen and picked up a bowl of vegetables to set on the table.

Their conversation was so strained throughout the meal that Briana was almost in tears. She tried to draw out of him what the problem was, but got nowhere. Finally she came right out and asked him if he liked her hair dark.

"If that's your natural color, it will be okay. It's hard to think of you any way but blonde."

Well, that was non-committal. After he left, Briana started on the dishes. Anger was her first emotion, followed next by hurt. Then while she was doing the pans, realization seeped in. Tyler was going to break off their relationship. He hadn't kissed her or even looked lovingly at her, which meant he was probably trying to build up the courage to explain about the upcoming wedding to Adrian. He told the lady in Marysville it would be in October and that was already here. Neither Tom nor Shelly had mentioned invitations, but Briana knew Adrian would not hesitate to send one to her.

Just before turning in, her phone rang and the answering machine clicked on. "This is Tyler. Call me when you get a chance. Night." She stared at the machine longingly.

"Oh, Tyler," she cried out to herself and the attentive little poodle by her side. She held back tears as she listened to the message once more, noticing the absence of caring or terms of endearment. He sounded like he was talking to a client.

No way would she call him, she decided. She was through. She had spent hours talking to God about this situation and though she knew it was wrong, she kept going back for more. Was she now getting what she deserved?

The next day he called her at work. "You didn't call me back," he accused her.

"It was late," she lied.

He sounded so curt. "I went out to see Melissa last night."

She's probably dealing with the wedding plans, Briana thought.

"There's been a new development," he began, and Briana's heart began to pound. *This is it. He's going to tell me about the marriage.*

"We need to go see Mary Duncan again."

She wasn't prepared for this and made him repeat it to be sure. "Why?" she asked, trying to follow the startling switch.

"Something has turned up," was all he said.

"What, Tyler? Is it about Sabrina?"

"I remembered something Deb told me a few years back. Something so bad that only a few people knew." She waited for him to go on, but he didn't. So she asked him a leading question.

"What does Mary have to do with that?"

He ignored her question and said, "You call her and see if we can visit with her this evening. I'll tell you both about it then. Bye." Then the phone was dead. This new habit of hanging up the phone before she got a chance to answer was really bugging her.

Mary wasn't home when she called, so Briana had to wait until after work to reach her. Mary said she would be glad to meet with them at seven that same evening. She sounded like she was eager to put this to rest.

Tyler picked up Briana in his big, comfortable Mercedes, and they headed across town to the Duncans' residence. Although Briana asked, Tyler wouldn't divulge any information about his find. He seemed quiet and strangely aloof.

Mary ushered them into the front room, glancing furtively at Briana and finally saying, "You've changed your hair color. I couldn't think at first what was different."

"This is my natural color, I think. I've been blonde for so long I've almost forgotten. Do you like it?"

"Yes," Mary replied, "but you remind me of someone. I can't think who, right now. Oh, well. Tell me how you're doing on your search for the Barton clan?"

Tyler answered for Briana by saying, "That's why we're here. I hope you won't be offended, but I have to ask you some personal questions. We're not here to cause you stress, but I'm sure you're just as eager as we are to find Sabrina."

"But she's dead, Mr. Rainger. There must have been a clerical mistake in the records."

Briana hid a smile as she recalled another family who had said the same things for years.

"Were you and Dolan Roswald lovers?" Tyler asked without preamble.

"I beg your pardon?" Mary was stiffly resentful and rose to her feet as if to flee.

"I have reason to doubt that Sabrina was blood kin to Jack Barton. I believe that Sabrina was Dolan's child, born out of an affair you had with him while working on the Roswald's farm."

Briana gasped and looked quickly from Mary to Tyler and back again.

"None of this is any of your business," Mary said angrily as she rose to her feet. "I am not going to talk about this at all. My child is dead, and I'm sorry you've wasted your time coming here tonight for nothing."

Briana felt the woman's anxiety and knew how disruptive all this was to her organized, comfortable life. But Briana was having difficulty following Tyler's intent.

"Tyler, what are you searching for? What does my problem have to do with the Roswalds? Surely Sabrina must be dead!"

"Mary, did your child have a birthmark?" Tyler was not put off by Mary's resistance.

"Why?"

"The Roswald family has a reoccurring mark that shows up every few generations."

Briana stared at Tyler and cried, "Tyler, no!"

"Did Sabrina have a birthmark?"

Mary squinted her eyes painfully and nodded.

"Was it on the side of her waist?" Tyler was not backing off.

"Yes. It was a red circle about the size of a dime. What does this mean? How do you know about it?"

Briana was shaking and Tyler reached out and caught her hand in his.

"This can't be happening...." she began, afraid to believe this woman could be her long-lost birth mother.

"I have a birthmark on my side," Briana whispered as tears began to fill her eyes.

"You *what?*" Mary gasped, unable to believe all that was unfolding.

"Mary," Tyler said softly, "I have reason to believe that Briana is Sabrina. Tell us if she was fathered by Dolan Roswald."

"But she's dead!" Mary repeated.

"No she isn't. She was made available for adoption to a couple in California. We'll find out who did this dreadful thing, but first we need answers. We only want to solve this so Briana can get on with her life."

Briana was in shock. Could this be happening?

"Would you recognize the birthmark if you saw it?" Briana asked. "Look at mine, and tell me if it is the same as your child's." Briana stood and lifted her sweater to expose the mark on her side.

Mary leaned closer then touched the area.

"Look out, she's ticklish," Tyler warned jokingly to ease the tension.

"Sabrina?" she murmured. "Oh my God, you've answered my prayers. My Sabrina! My baby!" Mary took Briana in her arms and they cried together. Finally she looked up at Tyler and asked, "Who could have hated me so much they would take my child? What a cruel, sadistic thing to do!" She looked deeply into Briana's eyes.

At that moment, Jim and the children returned home.

CHAPTER 22

Jim was instantly protective and visibly upset to see his wife in tears. The children took one look at the charged scene and went quickly to the back of the house.

"Jim, meet Sabrina! My daughter!" Mary wept unashamed against her husband's chest, but Jim's face had turned hard.

"I won't have you upsetting my wife. What kind of game do you people think you're playing here? We've seen Sabrina's gravesite, and we've accepted her death, so just leave it alone. There is no reason to stir all this up again and bring futile hope to Mary."

"It's not futile. Mr. Duncan. I was married to Briana's half-sister," Tyler answered looking at Briana directly. "She mentioned once that her dad fathered a child out of wedlock when he was sixteen years old, and there was a royal decree sent down from the Roswald hierarchy to hush up the matter. Very few family members knew, and the pressure was put on the young mother never to refer to Dolan as the father. Am I right so far, Mary?"

Mary was looking again at Briana. "My Sabrina, all grown up! Can I hold you again?" They hugged cautiously while Mary answered Tyler's question.

"It was such a terrible thing to have happen, but Dolan pursued me and turned my head with sweet talk. I was nineteen and lonely, and Jack was putting in such long hours on the farm. He was such a hard worker, but I wanted something to break the monotony. I did not intend to...I didn't mean to...." she found she couldn't complete the sentence.

"You were young and a sexy boy turned your head," Briana finished for her birth mother.

"He caught me unaware in the barn one day, but I could have stopped him. I'm not without blame in all of this. It only happened once, though he pressured me often. Dolan was so handsome and strong. He used to give me things, which I hid from Jack."

"What happened when you found out you were pregnant?" Briana wanted to know.

"I knew it was Dolan's. Jack had been tired and—well, I felt guilty also. He had always wanted children so it was a happy surprise for him when I got pregnant. At any rate, we were to have a baby and he was delighted. It would have never occurred to him that it could be anyone else's and I convinced myself that it was not really a lie as much as an omission, I suppose. But I told

Dolan and he said I couldn't prove it and got rather nasty about it."

Mary looked at Briana and smiled.

"He was the apple of his daddy's eye and was going to have quite a future in farming. And then, of course, the family history is impeccable!"

Briana understood. "When I was up at the farm with Tyler I was exposed to some of that impeccable family! I even walked around the area where Sabrina…."—she faltered momentarily—"where I lived those first four years. Nothing looked familiar, which convinced me for sure that I wasn't your child."

Mary was now sitting on the sofa with Briana next to her, gazing fondly at her newfound daughter.

"So did you tell Gladys then?" Tyler prompted. "How did the Roswalds find out?"

"Dolan got scared I'd tell, so just after the baby came, he confessed it all to his mother. She was very upset and came to see me immediately to see what claim I intended to make.

"Jack was so happy thinking the baby was his that I had never intended to have him know otherwise. In fact, I was very upset that Dolan had brought his mother into the picture."

Mary reached up and touched Briana's face. "You look like Dolan's sister, Melissa," she said. I can't believe the people up north didn't notice the resemblance."

"I was blonde then and of course, they weren't aware that I was part of the family." She glanced toward the men and said, "Oh no, Tyler—this makes Chad my brother!"

Tyler just laughed and explained to the Duncans a few things that had happened to cause Briana to lose respect for the teen. Mary laughed outright about Briana causing Chad's untimely fall in front of everyone at the dance.

"Dolan was cocky like that," Mary said. "But he sure was a ladies' man!"

"So Gladys was the only one in the family who knew about Sabrina being Dolan's child?" Tyler asked.

"Dolan's grandmother Lavida found out. One day when Sabrina was about two years old, we were invited to the manor for a barbecue, and I had dressed Bri in a pair of frilly overalls. It was a particularly warm day so I didn't put on a T-shirt underneath—all that covered her tummy was the bib front. Well, anyway, her birthmark was visible, and Lavida told me to take her home and dress her in clothes that covered that mark. I asked Gladys about it later, and she said Lavida had seen the Roswald stamp on my baby and suspected the girl was Dolan's. My, did that stir up a hornet's nest! Lavida's husband, Cyrus, had the same birthmark."

"Melissa's grandchild, Brenda, has one too," Briana informed her. "I didn't think about it being a family occurrence when I saw hers. Of course, I didn't know I was adopted at the time." Briana's voice faltered and she looked again at this stranger who was now her mother.

Jim spoke up. "How did you find out you were adopted? What caused the initial search for Jack Barton?"

Briana glanced over at Ty, and he smiled at her and winked. He was happy for her, and she was proud of him for all he had done to reunite her with her mother.

"I keep having these reoccurring feelings like I've been places before, yet there was no way I could have ever seen them. My folks had never taken my brothers and me too far out of California, so there was no logical reason why a big red courthouse in Marysville, Kansas, should send me into hysterics. Yet when I drove into that historic little town, I experienced terror like I had never felt before."

Mary gasped and Briana noticed tears rolling down her cheeks again. "Your castle! Heavenly Father, how ever-faithful You are!" Mary murmured her prayer. "You loved that big old red building, but one day while I was shopping, you ran away to see your castle by yourself. I was frantic! You never did things like that, and, of course, we had all heard about child snatchers. When I found you there on the sidewalk in front of the courthouse, you were almost as hysterical as I was because you were lost and couldn't find me. I couldn't spank you for running away. You had learned a good lesson, and I have thought of that many times as I raised my new family. Perhaps I was overly cautious with them so they wouldn't have to go through what you did."

Briana gave her new mother a loving look and continued, "I also remember a playground by the town of Frankfort, but I didn't feel threatened or afraid of it like I did the building."

"Yes, you would have no fear of that. Jack used to drive over to Frankfort to get parts, and he would drop you and me off at the park and pick us up on his return. He'd bring us treats, and we'd eat them at the little park. How upsetting it must be to feel these memories and not understand."

"It was like looking through a window that was fogged over. I would see images that weren't clear and I knew they meant something."

Mary exclaimed quickly, "First Corinthians 13: 11 and 12!"

"What?" Briana tried to recall the scripture, but couldn't.

A well-used Bible lay on the coffee table in front of them. Mary deftly thumbed through the pages and then turned the book toward her daughter, pointing to the scripture so Briana could read it aloud for all to hear. "When I was a child I spake as a child, I understood as a child, I thought as a child: but when I became a man, I put away childish things. For now we see through a glass, darkly...."

Briana smiled at Mary as she closed the Bible and replaced it on the table.

"Yes, that's it," he said. "But only God knew fully the fears and frustration I experienced. As a Christian I couldn't accept these psychic, déjà vu feelings, yet they were happening. I didn't tell anyone for quite a while, but when I did, Tyler thought possibly I had a twin somewhere who was experiencing these strange feelings. He then encouraged me to find my records, which of course were missing, and the search began."

Tyler added, "She kept insisting she had never been east of the Rockies, yet she had these reactions. There had to be a common denominator here of some kind. While she and her friend Shelly visited my farm over the Fourth of July, we took a tour of Stone Haven, which caused no problems. When we entered the manor, she looked up at the big staircase and began to shake. When we asked her what was wrong she kept saying, 'I'm waiting.'" Tyler reached over and took Briana's hand, giving her a feeling of reassurance. "She scared us all!"

Mary was nodding her head.

"You did wait there, Bri. I used to do housework for the Roswalds and when I'd go up to make beds you'd sit on the grand staircase and wait. Lavida caught you there one day and tried to make you leave. I heard voices and went to see what the problem was. She had you by the arm trying to pull you down the steps. You had a death grip on one of the ornate spindles of the rail and were very angry. Nothing to match the rage that came from me, however. No one was going to mistreat my child!"

Briana put her arms around her mother and gave her a hug.

"You were always a very good girl and never left the steps when I was working. I would have understood if you had been misbehaving or had broken something, but I had checked on you just seconds before Lavida got to you, and you were playing with your doll like a good little girl. Of course, after that I wasn't needed to do housework again. I didn't care." Mary smiled, remembering. "They were very glad to see me go after Jack was killed. I doubt if the rest of the family knew why I was disliked and I'm sure they didn't care. I had tried to persuade Jack to move away and find another job, but he liked it there. The pay was good and they treated him well."

Mary looked over at her husband and sighed. "You didn't know your wife had such a sordid past, did you? I'm sorry I didn't tell you about Dolan. It wasn't important, since his child was dead. Anyway I was a different person then and things of the past should be left in the past." She murmured, "My, the tangled webs we weave…."

Jim's voice was husky as he said, "Do you think I would ever love you less because of that?"

Bri smiled at that as Mary answered, "No. You're too understanding and kind to place blame."

Then she turned to Briana. "I hope some day you will meet someone as wonderful as my Jim. We've been so happy." With an audible sigh, Mary added, "I can't begin to tell you how I feel right now. I guess shock would come as close to describing it as anything. How brave you were to search for me!"

Tyler laughed and said, "You'll never believe how hard it was to keep her convinced she should continue that search. She was devastated when you said Sabrina was dead. Even more so, when you said you had seen the marker on the grave.

"The only thing that spurred us on was the fact that there was no death record. A few nights ago I was invited to her house for dinner. She had been saying for ages that she was going to let her hair go back to its original dark shade, but it came as a shock when she opened the door. You said she reminded you of Melissa, but in reality—she looked like my wife!"

Silence hung heavy for a second, then Tyler added, "I was married to Dolan's daughter Debby and the resemblance was staggering!"

"Oh Tyler, I'm sorry," Briana moaned. "I knew you were upset, but I couldn't imagine why!"

His eyes met hers in a steady, mesmerizing encounter and he went on to explain. "Halfway through dinner it dawned on me who you were. I didn't dare tell you my suspicions in case they were false."

He turned to the Duncans. "She's been on a roller-coaster ride all summer. First the strange 'happenings,' then the letter from her family saying she was adopted, and then the search began—only to get stopped at each turn."

"So how did you know who she was, if it was such a guarded secret?" Jim asked.

"A few years back, when Deb was first pregnant, her grandmother, Gladys, told her the story about Dolan's first child. She encouraged Deb to keep the secret, out of respect for her father, and I'm sure she did, except for me. Deb was so sickly in her pregnancy and so worried. We spent hours at home talking and planning. Our child was going to be perfect, brilliant, and beautiful."

Briana knew the Duncans were hearing the same expectations and dreams all parents have for their babies.

"One evening, after a visit from Gladys, Deb told me about a baby born to a farmhand's wife many years before and about Dolan being the father while the child was passed off as the worker's offspring."

"Then you have a child, Tyler?" Mary asked.

"My wife died before our child was born. I lost everything. My family, my dreams, and all of our plans. Then there was nothing." Tyler's voice was rough with emotion as he lowered his head to look at the notebook in his hands.

"Tyler and Deb were given a part of the Roswald farm as a wedding present," Briana interjected, hoping to give Tyler a moment to recover. "I went up there over the Fourth and it is lovely. It's a berm home with a huge in-ground pool. That was when I got to meet all of the family except for Bevin and Gladys."

"They're in Europe now, but they'll be home soon," Tyler explained. "And Briana's parents are coming from California for a visit in a few weeks." He looked at Briana. "How does it feel to have all these relatives when you've been used to just a few?"

"I'm having problems believing any of this," she said softly. "My parents are wonderful people, and I've had a very happy life with them. May I bring them over to meet you when they arrive? Or better yet, you can all come over to my house." Tears began to glisten in Briana's eyes.

"I guess I don't really know what to do now that I've found you," she said. "Will we be close, or will I be an infringement on your family? Will you be honest and tell me what you want or expect?" Briana stood up and the others rose, too.

Mary touched Briana's arm. "All I can promise is that I lost you once, and that won't happen again! I expect to be your friend for now, and only when you allow it will I be your mother. Is that okay?"

Mary took Briana's face in her hands and searched her face carefully. "You are very beautiful and I'm so happy you have found me. Can I introduce you again to my new family?"

Jim went out of the room and returned with their three children.

"Do you children remember me talking about the child I had before marrying your father and how she had died over twenty years ago? A crime was committed. She didn't die; she was stolen and adopted out to a family in California. Her name was Sabrina, but we called her Bri."

She took a deep breath and reached out for Briana's hand. "Briana Sheldon, who you met here a few weeks ago, is that lost child. My daughter Sabrina, all grown up!" Mary's voice cracked, and she blinked away the tears that flooded her eyes.

"You mean she's our sister?" Doug asked, looking at Briana with a frown.

"Not our real sister, silly. She'd be our half sister," Greg explained.

"Finally I'm going to get equal rights around here," Janet chimed in. "I've needed a sister to even up the odds for years. I suppose we're too old for slumber parties?"

Briana and the others laughed outright at their responses. What a delightful family. *Her* family!

CHAPTER 23

"What a horrendous thing to do to a young mother!" Briana wailed to Ty on the way home. "How could anyone possibly have done such a thing and lived with the guilt?"

"We'll find out, I promise," he assured her. "In fact, we'll know by the time your family gets here from California."

"Then you know! Who do you suspect? Oh Tyler, tell me, please?"

He ignored her question as he pulled into her driveway and shut off the engine.

"The Roswalds are having their annual masquerade party and a welcome home party for Bevin and Gladys on Halloween night. I want you to come with me and perhaps we can encourage Jim and Mary to come also. If my plan works, we'll have all the answers, and we'll know who did this and why."

He reached over and caught her hand in his and brought it up to his lips. "You've had quite an evening, haven't you? How does it feel to find a new mother and father all at one time?"

"I'm in a daze. Will I wake up and find I've dreamed all of this or, worse yet, what if Dolan won't admit it? Unless Melissa told them about the visit to her, they would have no way of knowing we were even searching."

"The day you and I went over to look at the area where the Bartons' cabin used to be, I mentioned to Dolan that you were doing some family history on the Barton family and that you thought there might be some connection. Our conversation was interrupted when I saw Chad talking to you." Tyler smiled and added, "Chad will come around once he finds out you're related." He laughed briefly when she moaned, then added, "You said once you had always wished you had a large family. Better be careful of such wishes, 'cause it looks like you got it!"

"Tyler, do I really look like Deb?"

"From a distance or at first glance, there is a striking resemblance, but in reality you're taller and resemble Mary quite a bit. When we go up to the farm I'll show you pictures of her."

"Mary—my mother—said I looked like Melissa. I guess I do in a way."

"You and Melissa are taller than Deb or Adrian, and I'm sure it's the dark hair that is runs in the family that makes people see the resemblance. You are more beautiful than any of the Roswald women there now, so you never need to feel inferior about that."

His hand stroked her face, then he caught her chin and pulled her toward him, brushing his lips over hers slowly, savoring them.

"You are going to be the belle of the ball come Halloween," he murmured.

She was trying to listen to his words but his lips were her only interest, and she purposely forgot what she had decided a few nights before. How could she ever resist this man? He must certainly be aware of her feelings, she thought, as his lips claimed hers.

Then she was free and he said, "You've had a big evening and I'm sure you want to place a phone call to California. I'll call you tomorrow and we'll do some planning about the party. You'll need to take Thursday and Friday off. Will that be a problem? Do you want to call the Duncans, or do you want me to?"

"Why don't you, since it's your invitation? You can tell them more about the party. All I know is that I'm going to be the main course."

She was laughing, but Tyler picked up on the fear underneath. "I'll be with you, so there will be nothing for you to worry about. Trust me!" What else could she do?

Briana called Shelly when she entered the house and told her the search was finally over, and that she was in fact Sabrina Barton. Then she told her friend about Dolan Roswald's involvement in it all and about Mary's joy in finding her lost child.

"I can't believe this, Bri. Has anyone called the Roswalds to let them know?"

"No, and just because Dolan's my biological father doesn't mean we'll have a lasting relationship. I have a feeling I won't be popular when we disclose all of this at the Roswald's big Halloween party." She explained as much as she knew about the masquerade plans.

"I'd be scared to death," Shelly admitted. "Isn't Mary afraid to go back there after all these years?"

"She has to know who abducted me and sent me to California. If Tyler's plan works, we'll know that night."

When Briana hung up the phone, it dawned on her that she should have first shared her news with her California family.

Her father answered and when Briana said she had an important story to tell, he had her mother pick up on the extension. There were many questions, and they cautioned her not to expect much in the line of support from the Roswalds. They didn't want her hurt, but were genuinely pleased the mystery was solved. Briana wondered after she hung up if they were concerned she would get involved with her new family and forget them. Never!

Mary called Briana the next evening, just after Tyler hung up from telling her about the party. "I don't know if Jim can get off work since it's such short notice, and you know they're predicting snow for Halloween. It never fails! Of course, a little snow never holds back the trick-or-treaters."

"I didn't have that problem in California. We don't have snow in Sacramento for Halloween," Briana answered. "My parents were very strict where we went, though, and we weren't allowed to eat anything that wasn't packaged. Isn't it a shame the way the world has changed?"

"Evil is always a part of life, but it's possible we don't pray enough. When prayers cease Satan sends in his demons. He causes things like stealing babies for money and sending a child to California never to see her mother again. How frightened you must have been!"

"I must have been affected by some of it because Mom said I had nightmares for a long time."

"The human mind is a very complex thing, you know. Why, I had even forgotten about your birthmark until Tyler mentioned it. Such an important thing my child had, yet I had forgotten it."

"But that was years ago and you have a new life now," Briana said.

"How do you feel about all of this by now? Have anger and bitterness crept in, and are you disappointed Jack wasn't your father? Do you wish I were different?" The last question from Mary was hesitant. Fearful.

Briana sensed the importance that would be placed on her answers, so she was thoughtful and careful in her reply. "I would love you no matter what you were like. You are, after all, my birth mother. But besides that, you are so brave. How could I ever want you to be different? Your children reflect what a good parent you are, and the love I see between you and Jim tells me you are a good wife. I'm not exactly angry about what happened, but confused. It was such a loathsome act that I'm appalled to think it could happen to everyday people like us and I'm reluctant to be introduced to Dolan as his daughter. I've been involved in a railroad spur line closure in Marshall County and therefore we've been at odds with the farmers up there. His son also caused me some problems."

At Mary's insistence, Briana told her about the phone calls and the motel incident.

"You're a real pistol-packin' mama!" Mary laughed, then sobered. "What if you had been killed in that room! I would never have known you or that you hadn't died as a child. Oh dear, do you think I'm going to be an overprotective mother now?"

Bri giggled. "That's okay, but you sure have a job in store for yourself!"

"Tell me what your parents said when you called them? Were they happy?"

"They both cried. My father was a product of foster homes but had never searched for his family. I don't think he even knew where to start. They were so pleased I learned the truth and are eager to meet you when they arrive. Mom will cry and Dad will do his reserved act to keep from crying, but they will just love you and your family.

"Meanwhile we need to do some planning about this party. Tyler said you would go if Jim could get off work."

"There is a good chance he can, especially if it snows. I should know by this evening. What costume are you going to wear?"

"I don't know—Tyler said he'd take care of that. I hope he knows what he's doing. I don't want to shock my new family in some weird costume. Let me know when you hear from Jim, because I am definitely going to need your moral support."

Briana had just hung up the phone when it rang once more. It was Tyler.

"How about meeting me for lunch tomorrow?" he asked. "We need to rent you a wig that looks like your blonde hair. Have you ever worn a wig before?"

"No, I haven't. Do you think all my hair will fit under a wig?"

"I don't know, but I'm sure someone can show us how to make it work."

"I suppose you still aren't going to tell me what you're planning?"

"That's right. I'll pick you up at twelve outside the Santa Fe building. Bye." Then he was gone.

The next day, Briana and Tyler found a wig at the costume shop that matched her blonde hair so perfectly she could hardly believe it.

"I'm not going to ride Abby and go to the party as Lady Godiva, am I?" she asked as they drove back to her building.

"Now why didn't I think of that?"

She gave him a questioning look and started to open her door.

"I'm glad your California family was pleased you found your birth mother," he said. "Are they getting excited about their trip?"

"Yes, but I hope they don't get caught in the big storm that's brewing out West. They should be here next week so maybe the storm will be gone by then. I think I'll have the Duncans over for a dinner when Mom and Dad are here. Will you come too?"

This will be his chance to say he'll be busy, she thought. She suspected that once their detective work was done, he would distance himself from her, especially since she looked so much like his late wife.

"Of course I'll come."

She looked up at him and smiled. Maybe she was wrong.

"Don't look at me like that," he growled unevenly. "You have no idea what effect you have on me." Then he reached out and touched her face. "We need to have time for us again. Commitments have kept us apart."

She couldn't think of anything to say, but she felt herself being pulled toward him for a gentle kiss. A kiss that was non-committal and quick. A kiss that perhaps would never have happened if she hadn't looked so lovingly at him. Did he consider her his orphan? His responsibility? The questions went unanswered as she quickly slipped out of the car and entered the office building.

Mary called that afternoon and told Briana that she and Jim would be able to go up north to the party. She had already been in touch with Tyler to discuss costumes and the arrangements for the weekend. Because of the storm coming in, Tyler would be driving rather than taking the plane.

"I hated to sound scared, but I told him the car sounded the best. I've never flown in a small plane. I wore a gypsy costume for another party last year, so I think I'll wear it for the Roswalds' party. Jim doesn't get into this costume stuff so he'll be a cowboy."

"I'm still relying on Tyler to choose my costume," Briana said. "We did get a blonde wig today, which he assures me looks just like my hair before I went back to being a brunette."

"I'm getting uneasy about this confrontation," Mary said, "but Ty said he would be introducing Jim and me as business associates, if anyone asks. He also said we'd come back Saturday if that's okay with everyone. With your folks coming he thought you might need a free day to do last-minute things. He's a very thoughtful man. Are you planning on keeping him, or do you have some other attraction somewhere?"

"He is someone else's attraction," Briana admitted sadly. But I'm going to enjoy my last weekend in his company and worry about the someone else later. She'll probably be at the party, too."

"Who is she? Will she go up with us?" Mary asked.

"She's part of my new family. Melissa's daughter, Adrian," Briana explained. Silently, she imagined future Roswald parties with the new daughter, Sabrina, being invited. Tyler and Adrian would be together and Briana with no one.

Later, Shelly popped in and asked if Briana would mind if she stopped by for a few minutes on her way home from work. Briana said that would be fine.

"Are you getting nervous about this party yet?" Shelly asked on her arrival that evening, pulling off her coat and draping it over the back of a big overstuffed chair. "I'd be worried sick, especially since Tyler won't tell you what he has planned. That alone would freak me out!"

"I trust him, but you're right. I am getting nervous. Let me light the gas log in the fireplace and we'll visit over a cup of hot chocolate. I love having a fire, but I wish it were fixed to burn wood so we could smell the scent of the logs as they burn. I'll bet that big stone fireplace at Ty's farm is cozy in the winter time."

"Oh yes, but then most any place with Tyler could be cozy! Imagine a white bear rug, a crackling fire, and no lights!" Shelly laughed at her friend's stricken expression. "I'm sorry. I didn't mean to shock you, but it sounds good to me!"

Briana tried to recover her poise. "Nothing you say or do shocks me, silly. I wonder if Ty and Deb enjoyed that scene?"

Shelly giggled and asked, "Are we talking bear rug scene or cozy fire?"

Briana should have let well enough alone and laughed it all off, but she was having a clear vision of Tyler and Deb loving one another the way she longed to be loved. Unrequited desire was something she was learning to live with.

"So what about you and Tom?" she asked, trying to change the subject.

"I said yes last night to his twenty-fifth proposal," Shelly admitted.

"Twenty-fifth proposal?" Briana nearly choked as she laughed. "Poor Tom! Congratulations, anyway."

"Maybe twenty-five was too many, but the more I said no the more he asked. When I was in Texas, my Dad and I had some good talks, and he told me he had been a poor excuse of a father and husband. He was so involved in building his business that he neglected his family. The fights they had were terrible, and we always felt it was our fault. Mom and Dad would hate the fact that we heard them, but I don't think they realized how guilty we felt."

Briana sipped her cocoa and thanked the Lord again for the parents she had. How miserable for Shelly to grow up in such an environment!

"Dad told me I'd be a fool if I let Tom get away and told me I couldn't judge all men by him. He was adamant about us communicating since not much of that went on in our home. If Tom and I are aware of my dysfunctional family, perhaps we can learn from their mistakes."

"So where's your mom, Shelly? Do you keep in touch with her?"

"Once in a while. She's remarried and has a new family, but I think I'll invite them to the wedding. They probably won't come, but the gesture will be there."

They sipped their drinks in silence for a second, then Shelly said, "I thought about announcing my engagement at work today, but since you are my best friend, I wanted to come over and tell you first. Will you be my bridesmaid? I'm going all out with a big traditional church wedding and all the trimmings. Tom is going to ask Tyler to be his best man. Maybe it will give Tyler some ideas!"

"I'm so happy for you. Of course, I'll be in your wedding—and I'll have a shower for you too. As for Tyler—well, his ideas, as you call them, don't include me. He is marrying Adrian. I really thought it would have already taken place by now—"

"Now where in the world did you get that crazy idea? Tyler isn't marrying that snob! How would you ever think that he could do that when he loves you?"

"He has never said he loves me," Briana said softly. "Anyway, Penny told me about it at the barbecue over the Fourth. She said she wished it were me he was marrying instead of Adrian."

Shelly was shaking her head in disbelief. "You can't possibly believe he could love Adrian and look at you with such intensity. The air just crackles when you two touch. No way is he in love with her. He loves you!"

Briana's voice dropped to a whisper, "I called him one night and Adrian answered the phone and said Tyler was in the shower. I'm not stupid. Naïve, perhaps, but not stupid. I feel guilty loving him when he loves her."

"He doesn't love her! He loves you. I think I'm going to have to sit him down and tell him some facts!"

"Oh Shelly, you wouldn't! Please don't say anything. Let all of this just coast until my folks leave, and then I promise I'll talk to him."

Shelly looked directly at Briana and warned, "You have two weeks, young lady, and then I'm going to take matters into my own hands."

Shelly picked up her cup and rose to place it in the kitchen sink. "Gotta go," she said. "Tom and I are going to the movies."

"Have you and Tom picked a date for the wedding yet?"

"Maybe April. How does that sound? I guess I should start collecting bridal magazines and books to get some ideas. And I'll need to let our pastor know so he can schedule it on his calendar. Well, I've got to hurry. See you later. Remember, you've got two weeks!"

Shelly shrugged into her coat, then turned and put her arms around Briana and gave her a sisterly hug. "I'm so happy," she sighed, then left Briana to her thoughts.

Briana was happy for her friend and had a light-hearted feeling about Shelly's belief in Tyler. Yet she was afraid to hope. As she climbed into bed, she tried not to think about the scheduled trip up north. When she said her prayers, she added a special one for Tyler's plans. Whatever they were! She also asked God to begin giving her the proper words to say to Tyler before her two weeks were up.

Tiffany was curled up in her little basket beside the bed, so Briana reached down and patted the furry pup, receiving licks from her warm, pink tongue. When the light was turned out her mind began to race over the scene at the Duncans' and she replayed it many times in her imagination. Then her thoughts moved on to her parents' upcoming visit and all the fun activities they would share. She was determined not to think about Tyler.

Oops! Too late. He was all ready invading her mind, body, and soul.

She turned over on her side and pulled the extra pillow down to hold in her arms. Was Shelly right? Did he love her instead of Adrian? Could she be that fortunate? But why hadn't he said something? He wasn't bashful about speaking out, no matter who was involved.

She finally relaxed and decided to add a P.S. onto her prayers. And then a peace came over her and a deep sleep claimed her.

The phone woke her, and she heard Tyler saying he loved her. When she became fully awake she found herself holding the receiver repeating "Tyler" over and over again. She shook her head to clear her thoughts and held the phone to her ear once more, but all she heard was the dial tone. Did the phone really ring? She looked at the clock radio on her bedside table; it said 1:40 a.m.

Tyler wouldn't have called at that hour. Tiffany was whining and wondering what was going on. Had Briana dreamed the call? She tried to remember exactly what was said—or what she thought was said!

"Hi," his low voice had greeted her. "I just called to tell you I love you." So simple. So clear.

"Did Shelly call you?" she remembered countering. Or had she? She had often sleepwalked as a child, waking up in her parent's room or elsewhere. She recalled how her brothers teased her about her night wanderings and wondered if this was the same thing.

Maybe this was just wishful thinking. She put her head down softly on the extra pillow, wondering how it would be to have her head on Tyler's muscular shoulder. With that thought she drifted off again into a peaceful sleep.

CHAPTER 24

Tyler had already picked up the Duncans when he pulled into Briana's driveway about 7 a.m. on Halloween day.

"Looks like snow," he said as he took her suitcase and cosmetic bag. "Mary suggested you two could sit in the back seat so you could visit. She's eager to meet Tiffany, too."

He was making small talk and Briana was glad. The touch of his hand when he took her case had caused her to catch her breath. She couldn't meet his eyes.

"I'll put Tiff's blanket on the floor so she doesn't sprinkle your velvet seats with her fur."

"She'll be okay on the seat. Poodles don't shed much and she'll want to be close to you." Then his voice dropped and he said, "Lucky pup!"

Mary welcomed Briana into the rear seat and greeted the excited pup.

"You get to go bye-bye," she cooed as she dodged the poodle's licking tongue. "She's adorable, Bri. Where did you get her?"

"Tyler gave her to me," Briana said, smiling at the dog. After stopping for a quick breakfast, Tyler pulled the Mercedes out onto I-70 heading west around the downtown part of Topeka.

"See the red church steeples?" Briana pointed out the old Catholic church on Fourth Street to her mother. "I think that looks like a castle, don't you? It was quite a test for me to discover it was just a building. No fears, no tears. But the Marysville building—well, that was another story. I thought I was losing my mind!"

They began sharing things from their lives and were so engrossed in their conversation they hardly realized they were leaving I-70 to turn north to Wamego.

Tyler met Briana's eyes a few times in his rearview mirror. She completely lost her train of thought each time that happened.

"How about a stop in Wamego?" Ty asked his passengers. "I need to fix Briana up in some western gear if she's going to be a cowgirl tonight."

"I'm going to be a cowgirl?" Briana asked

"Sure. I'm going to deck you out in some local clothes so you'll turn all the cowboys' heads at the party."

Briana felt a twinge of fear when she heard that. She had met some of the local boys and hadn't been impressed.

As they entered the main part of town, Briana peered out to read some of the dates at the very top of the old buildings. One said 1898 and was still very much in use. She saw Halloween decorations everywhere. Bales of hay, cornstalks, pumpkins, and scarecrows creatively decorated each business in the busy little town. She saw cloth ghosts flying from trees and flagpoles in the crisp October wind. Each business had done their part in celebrating the harvest and Halloween.

"A stop would be fine," Jim agreed. "We're in your hands!"

"First I want to drive over and show Briana the Dutch Mill. Have you and Mary been there?"

"We stopped here the time we went up to Marysville," Mary remembered, "but that was years ago. You're right, Briana needs to see the mill."

Turning east off the main street, Highway 99, they drove only a few blocks and came to a lovely park with a huge pond populated with geese honking and waddling about. Of course, the Dutch Mill was the focal point, standing high above the trees with its wooden top and vanes reaching high into the cloudy sky.

The rocky outer wall was in very good condition for being 120 years old, but Tyler explained that it had been moved from its original location twelve miles north of town and restored in 1988 to its normal function of grinding grain. It was now a tourist attraction and though it stood forty feet high, many adventuresome boys had climbed the outer wall, clinging to the rough stone surface.

"It's so wonderful that things like this can be saved for future generations," Briana said, turning to Mary. "Like Stone Haven. What a beautiful design, yet it's such a contrast to Tyler's berm home. It's like a history lesson."

"More like an architectural nightmare," Tyler laughed as they headed back to the main street.

"I'm looking forward to see your home, Tyler. I remember the area well, and if I'm right you have a good view of the valley," Mary said.

"Not the view Dolan has, but he and Irene built on the crest of Blue Point Hill."

"That's so funny you'd mention that, because he always talked about building up there." Mary turned to Bri. "He never wanted for anything, so he could afford to dream. Of course, Dolan was young and didn't realize that Jack and I couldn't even think about those luxuries. We were just glad we had a job and a roof over our heads."

Vanderbilt's Western Wear was on the west side of the main street, and the scent of leather permeated the air when they entered. Shelves of cowboy boots lined the walls while tables and racks of shirts, coats, and jackets crowded the floor. Briana saw big stacks of jeans and overalls and an ample selection of hats, belts, and ties.

"My goodness, what a big store!" Briana exclaimed.

"They get a lot of Topeka shoppers here, plus the college crowd from Manhattan and the local farm families too, " Tyler explained. "Now, let's see what we can find for you. You'll be a cowgirl for the first part of the party, so just pick out whatever you want. It's on me."

"I'll buy my own clothes!" Briana replied, only to be stopped by his hand on her shoulder.

"Not this time," he assured her. "And don't give me any backtalk! When we get to the farm I'll explain exactly how we will do this tonight, so you'll have to wait till then for the rest of the story."

"I don't know why you want me to wait a few more hours! You are scaring me half to death," Briana complained, looking up into his eyes.

"You don't need to be afraid," he promised. leaning down toward her lips as if he intended to kiss her right there in the crowded store.

"Did you call me last night?" she blurted out, halting his action with her question.

"No," was his quick response. "Did you have another prank call?"

"I think I dreamed it," she muttered almost to herself.

"Tell me about it."

The color on her face announced her embarrassment. Then with twinkling eyes he said, "Maybe you can tell me about it tonight when we're in the hot tub?"

The pit of her stomach became a whirlpool of emotion.

"Hot tub?" she squeaked.

Mary found them engrossed in each other when she approached, carrying a beautiful western print shirt to show Briana.

"Do you like this?" she asked hesitantly.

It was an Indian design of reds and black. "Beautiful!" Briana took it in her hands, then walked away with her mother to look at the rest on the bulging racks.

Tyler found Jim trying on a pair of boots. "My boots need to retire," he explained, "but we do quite a bit of Western dancing and my old ones know the steps! I might have to teach these new ones the two-step since the price is so reasonable."

Briana was nervous about her tight jeans, even though Mary insisted they would stretch, and Briana was aware of the open admiration on Ty's face when she stepped from the fitting room. He slowly inspected her, starting with her jeans and when he got to her Western shirt that pulled tightly across her breasts, his eyes stopped.

"Try on one of these," he said quickly, dropping his gaze to a couple of Stetsons he was holding. "This will help hold your wig in place."

"Black or white?" she asked, looking at her mother for advice.

"Are you going to be a good girl or a bad one?" Mary asked with a chuckle. "You remember how the Western movies always have the good guys in white?"

Tyler laughed out loud, then finished into a cough. Mary raised one eyebrow at the men and turned back to Briana.

"Never pay any attention to men when you're shopping for clothes," she advised, winking at Briana.

"I like the bad one," Tyler started and then laughed again.

"I'm getting the white one!"

"I think the white hat will look fine," Jim said seriously, then turned to Ty and whispered loudly, "I've seen bad ones with white hats, too!"

They all laughed at that, but Briana feigned anger only to be caught up in Tyler's arms in a bear hug.

"Come over here, and we'll see about a pair of boots for you," Tyler said, guiding her to a chair where she could sit down.

After asking her size, Tyler picked up two pairs of boots from a shelf close by.

She wiggled out of her shoes. "You'll need heavier socks," Tyler observed and from out of one boot pulled a pair of cotton socks.

"Are you a magician?" she laughed.

"No, I just know you women don't wear decent socks!"

"These work for me," she laughed, pulling up her pant leg to take off her knee-high nylon stockings.

Tyler's hand closed over hers on her calf. "I'll do that," he murmured.

The touch of his hand sent shivers along her spine. He lifted her foot briefly and pulled the thin material over her toes.

"Your foot is cold," he commented, massaging it with both strong hands.

That's the only part of me that's cold, she thought as she felt her blood heat at his touch. She clamped her mouth shut to avoid moaning out loud. She felt dismayed when he ceased the massage and began to pull on the white cotton sock.

"I can dress myself. I'm all grown up now."

His eyes slid over her body and up to her face. "I'm well aware of that, sweetheart," he murmured under his breath.

Briana settled on a pair of calfskin boots and twirled around to show off her full ensemble, to the approval of Mary and her husband as well as the admiring glances of Ty. Once she changed back into her own clothes, they were back on the road.

When they reached the farm, Bea was there to greet them and show them to their rooms. Briana had the same room as before and the Duncans had the room Tom had used.

Tyler and Jim went down to see the horses, so Briana showed Mary around and introduced her to Heidi and Spunky, explaining about the charming cat-dog relationship.

The pool was now covered, yet still dominant in front of the house. The inner patio was cool, but not frigid like the air outside, and even though the wind howled around the patio walls, back in the underground house it was quiet and warm.

Bea asked the women if they wanted a snack but they decided to wait for the men.

"Brr!" Tyler growled as he and Jim entered the kitchen from the utility room off the garage.

"There's a few flakes coming down out there," Jim added, brushing off his jacket.

Bea served them homemade vegetable soup, crackers, chips, and dip with crisp relishes. After the meal, Tyler explained what he had in mind for that evening.

"We'll go to the manor about 7:30, and Briana will be dressed in her Western wear. She'll have on her blonde wig and no one will notice any change in her at all. I have masks to cover our eyes," Tyler said as he reached to a sideboard and opened a small sack. "I wasn't sure about what colors you all would be wearing, so I just got us all black masks."

Jim tried his on, adjusting it slightly to fit his face. "This will work," he said. "I hate a full face mask."

"These parties at the manor usually go on until midnight, so I think we'll let Sabrina make her appearance about eleven o'clock. How does that sound?"

"Just how does she do this?" Mary asked.

"She comes walking down the big staircase, but she'll stop on the landing. I will arrange for the family members to be in the foyer at that time."

"Do you know who kidnapped Sabrina?" Jim asked.

"I think so. We'll know this evening, at any rate. When we're through here I want to have Bea help Briana with some things. She'll show you how to do your hair and she'll help you try on the clothes you'll wear when you descend the stairs, but first I want to show you all some pictures in my photo album. Come into my office."

Tyler led the way down the carpeted hall, past the sunken living room to the next room. They were all very curious, but Briana felt fear trying to encroach on her once more.

When Tyler opened the leather-bound photo album, Deborah Roswald Rainger stared back at them from the glossy prints.

"Oh my," Mary exclaimed as she looked from the pictures to her daughter.

Tyler smiled and agreed.

"The likeness is obvious, isn't it? I also rented an English riding habit like the one Deb used to wear when she was in competition. I have the crop that Dolan gave her and a scarf she wore around her neck."

He looked closely at Briana, who sat quietly, paling at the thought of all this.

"I hope the clothes will fit. I had to guess." His eyes ran slowly over her. "Bea will help you with your hair. See how she caught the top back and fastened it with a clasp, high on her head?"

Briana looked closely at the pictures and felt tears burning her eyes. "Oh, Tyler, she was so young!"

"Yes, she was," Tyler agreed, "Her death was so sudden but I've recently realized that life does go on. I know she would have wanted me to find happiness again; I would have wished the same for her." With Tyler's permission, Briana took the album with her to reference while Bea helped her get ready.

They drove over to the manor about 7:30 and were greeted at the door by Gladys and Bevin. Tyler introduced Briana and the Duncans. The latter, he explained, were business friends from Topeka.

Tyler looked fantastic in his pirate costume. His white blouse shirt open to his waist made Briana's eyes stray in his direction more than was necessary. His tight black pants weren't overlooked, either.

Briana had shared with Mary her fears about seeing the staircase again, but Mary said now that Briana was aware of what had transpired it was possible she wouldn't be affected at all. They had prayed about it anyway. There it was, winding its way down to the foyer, and, praise the Lord, no terror gripped her. She turned to meet her birth mother's questioning eyes and smiled. Now she could relax and get to know her new set of grandparents.

The party was wonderful, but Briana would have enjoyed it more if she could have omitted her eleven o'clock trip down the stairs.

Mary whispered to Briana her own feelings of anxiety after they were introduced to Irene and Dolan.

"He's still very handsome, isn't he?" Mary began. I'll be surprised if any of this even rattles him!"

"We'll see," Briana answered. "I'm not sure Tyler's idea is going to work. What if—?"

"You'll do fine," Mary assured her as they made the rounds meeting the rest of the family and friends.

CHAPTER 25

The time was drawing near and Briana couldn't keep her eyes off the big grandfather clock in the foyer. She was due to meet Bea upstairs at 10:30 for the change of costumes.

Many of the people with small children had left already, since Friday was another school day. Some of the farm families had also gone home so they could get up at dawn for chores.

Mary accompanied Briana to the bedroom where the transformation was to take place. "You know, I would rather stay anonymous than walk down those stairs right now," Briana said. "I'm only doing this for you," she said, then hesitantly added, "my mother." Mary began to cry and put her arms around her daughter.

"I wouldn't encourage you to do this either if there were another way. But Bri, even now, at this last minute, if you want to say, no, it won't matter to me.

The main thing is that I've found you. It's your choice, Sabrina."

Bea stood by quietly, holding the crop and black hat that would finish off the costume. Tyler had shared with Cecil and Bea the details about Briana's abduction and explained her parentage. The Millers were appalled and were eager to see the person exposed who could take a child from her mother. Briana took a deep breath and resolved to go through with it.

The grandfather clock was chiming exactly eleven o'clock when Bea opened the bedroom door for Briana, then watched as the young woman walked slowly to the staircase.

When Briana reached the top step she could not see below, but could hear the merriment of the party. As she descended a few steps, she began to see the foyer floor and could tell that people had gathered there.

Heavenly Father, please work in this and protect us all. Let only the truth come out in such a way that all will be done for Your Glory, she prayed as she descended another step. *P.S. Lord, please keep my knees from giving out!*

Then she heard a scream and she stopped, realizing she was on the landing.

"It's Deborah," she heard Irene scream.

It wasn't fair to the innocent ones, Briana thought, and wondered if Tyler was right in doing this.

"What's going on here?" she heard Dolan bellow as he started for the staircase, only to be stopped by Tyler.

Everyone was talking and Briana couldn't hear what Tyler told Dolan, but her father went away from the stairs and resumed his place beside his wife.

Out of the crowd came Lavida, slightly unsteady on her feet but determined to get a closer view. "Satan allows the undead to walk!" she yelled as she pointed a crooked, arthritic finger toward Briana.

"Satan has been very busy," Tyler agreed, as he climbed a few steps toward Briana. "I want you all to know that this is Briana Sheldon, whom most of you have met."

There was a ripple of conversation before he continued.

"Briana had some frightening experiences here in our county when she came from California.

"Irene, you remember what happened here when she saw this staircase a few months ago. That was because she had been here before."

He waited for that to sink in and for the murmurs to cease. Then, as his arm circled Briana's waist, he said, "Doesn't she resemble Deb? But then she also bears a striking resemblance to Melissa."

Everyone turned toward Melissa, who by this time had her mask off, as did many others. "With the dark hair, Briana also looks like Adrian," Tyler continued.

Adrian glared at him from below, then turned her back and disappeared into the puzzled crowd.

Dolan found his voice once more and lashed out at Tyler.

"What kind of game are you playing here, Tyler? This is not the proper time to flaunt one of your bimbos for our inspection, even if she does look like Deb."

Briana cringed at his tone and shut her eyes to block out the view of everyone hearing her own father calling her a bimbo.

Before Tyler could respond, Mary stepped out of the group, climbed three steps, turned around with her mask in hand and did some lashing out of her own. "Don't you dare call our daughter a...a bimbo!" Trembling, she caught hold of the rail and drew herself up to her full height.

"My God!" Dolan moaned as he recognized Mary.

Gladys stepped forward to Dolan and said in an almost hysterical voice, "This is ridiculous! This is all in the past and I will not allow it to be discussed this way. Mary, you can meet with us later if you feel you have some claim to make, but for now, as far as I'm concerned...."

It was there that Tyler broke in.

"I realize this has been a shock, but if you all will bear with me one minute, I'm sure we can come to a settlement."

Briana looked sharply at Tyler only to have him wink at her. What game was he playing? No one wanted a settlement!

"This cannot be our child," Dolan insisted as he looked from Mary to Briana. "She's dead. They said she died!"

"Who said she died?" Tyler asked as he and Briana slowly descended the steps to Mary. Briana's hand searched and found her mother's icy fingers and grasped them.

"Who told you my child was dead?" Mary asked in a voice not her own.

"Grandma told us." Dolan turned and looked inquiringly at Lavida.

"They moved to Topeka and that's all I know," the elderly lady said with bravado. Then she added, "The child died, and good riddance. A bastard child of Satan!" Lavida's voice became shrill, and the others turned to look at her.

Irene finally found her voice, and turned to Gladys.

"What's this all about? Is this girl Dolan's child?"

Gladys leaned heavily on Bevin and lowered her head. "None of this needs to come out in front of everyone," she began.

Bevin looked down at his wife and asked incredulously, "You mean you knew about this? You knew our son had fathered a child and you didn't tell me? Why?"

"No one needed to know. Mary's husband was so proud of his child that we...Mary didn't want it told either," she finished lamely.

"I want no settlement for something that happened over twenty years ago," Mary said as her eyes searched the small crowd. "What I do want is to know is who stole my child and sent her off to California as an orphan!" Mary's voice was steady and articulate, but she was clearly angry, and Briana shared her mother's anger to the core.

Bevin and Dolan stepped forward at the same time, with confusion and disbelief on their faces. For one joyous second, Briana realized that her biological father had no part in the crime, and it was obvious that her grandfather didn't either.

"What are you talking about?" Bevin bellowed in a deep, angry voice. "Your child was stolen?" He looked behind him at his family and searched each face. "I thought Dolan said she was dead just now. Who, here in this hall, knows what you're talking about?"

It wasn't just a question—it was an order from the head of the Roswald dynasty. Silence hung heavy over the group.

"Who can explain what happened to this child?"

This time his eyes rested on his wife and they all witnessed her determination crumple, and tears began to stream down her cheeks. "Dolan was so young," she began. "And Mary flaunted herself at him…."

"That's not true, mother!" Dolan interrupted. "He looked at Mary, then to Briana. "She drove me crazy, but she never flaunted herself or was anything but a lady."

Mary's hand tightened on Briana's.

"I was out of line," he continued. "I wanted her so badly I practically raped her."

His hands came up to his face as if to erase the memory of the scene in the barn. Everyone was shocked into silence.

"She hadn't planned to tell anyone about it being my child. But one day when we were talking, she said it was only fair that I knew, even though her husband had claimed it and was delighted. I couldn't believe this was happening to me. I was only sixteen years old with my whole future ahead of me. That was when I broke down and told Mom."

Bevin turned and looked at Gladys. "I can't believe you didn't tell me," he stammered.

Gladys stared down at her hands, refusing to look at him, "Mary said there would be no trouble, so the fewer people that knew, the better things would be. Then after Jack was killed...."

"Tyler, just what went on after Mary and her child left the farm?" Bevin was impatient now that it was evident a crime had been committed.

"Mary can explain," Tyler suggested as he turned to her and gave her a confident look. Mary told her story to a captivated audience who received it in disbelief.

"Surely you checked on your child's death," Bevin insisted.

"I saw her grave marker and that was all I needed to know. If I hadn't been a Christian, I would have killed myself," she whispered.

Briana put her arm around Mary and began to weep.

"I had lost everything," Mary continued. "My husband, my baby...."

Tyler spoke up. "Dolan, you said your grandmother told you Sabrina died. How did she know? How could she know about Sabrina if it were such a well-kept secret?"

"Grandma Roswald saw a birthmark on the child and asked me about it," Gladys admitted. "It's a family mark. Grandpa had one also."

"Brenda has one, too," Briana added. "We talked about them one day by the pool, but of course, I didn't even know at that time I was adopted and I had no idea I had already met my real father."

Chad chose this time to stroll forward from the crowd and stopped beside his father to look up the stairs at Briana.

"She's my sister?" He was incredulous. "The Devil must really be having a blast with our family!"

"We'll survive," Briana replied. "At least you have an older sister who can make you mind!" She watched this sink in as he smiled sheepishly and shook his head in disbelief.

"Gladys, did you know that Mary's child had been taken?" This was Tyler again, all lawyer now.

"No," she answered. "I knew she had died...I was told she was dead...." She turned and looked at Lavida, whose face was distorted.

Suddenly the old matriarch staggered as people close by steadied her. She passed her hand over her eyes and opened her mouth to speak. "Evil," she breathed. "She is evil!" she cried out, then slumped to the floor.

The next day, Bevin called the farm and asked Mary and Briana to come to Stone Haven to talk to Lavida. Tyler and Jim drove the women to the old rock house through three inches of new snow.

"The country looks so clean and pristine," Mary said. "Maybe it will mean a clean beginning for everyone. I hope the old lady isn't seriously ill, because I wouldn't want harm to come to anyone else."

Gladys met them at the door and took the women upstairs. Lavida was in bed, but Gladys assured them she was fine. "The doctor's been here and said Lavida was ornery as usual, and fit as a fiddle!"

Briana looked down at the sad face of her great-grandmother and wondered how Lavida could have ever misunderstood what the Lord had told her about little Sabrina. How could an innocent baby be deemed evil, then banished and forgotten? Perhaps the Lord was not consulted? Or if He were, it was possible that Lavida didn't listen.

"You say you know Jesus," Lavida cackled hesitantly, not meeting the eyes of either Mary or Briana.

"We know Jesus," Briana answered, including her mother.

"I've been a Christian for a long time. Longer than you both have been alive," the old woman said. Mary and Briana did not respond.

"You were my first great-grandchild," she murmured from the bed. "It should have been a joyous occasion, except it was in sin. The sin was Satan!" the old lady blared with vigor that shocked the two at her bedside. "That's where the problem lies," she continued. "He's a liar and a cheat. He destroys and kills and because he hates us Christians, he tricks us."

"How were you tricked?" Briana asked.

After a long pause Lavida looked up and searched the faces of the two women.

"I saw the mark on your body, and it was just like the one on my Cyrus. In Martha's journals, I found that the mark appeared from time to time, which meant you were a Roswald. Blood never lies!"

She reached into the neck of her lavender flannel nightgown and fingered a chain of gold, then extracted the small cross that hung from it.

"When I asked Gladys, she thought I was accusing Bevin of this sexual act. Perhaps I was. All I knew was that the farmhand's child was a Roswald!" Lavida closed her eyes and seemed to be reviewing that scene in her mind.

"Gladys said the child was Dolan's. How could that be? He was a little boy, but he had grown up and I didn't notice. He was one of my favorites, because he was so like my Cyrus."

Her lips quivered slightly. "I miss Cyrus so much. What a wonderful husband he was. So good and caring and such a good father and farmer." She was radiant as she spoke and neither of the onlookers would ever doubt the love they had shared over the years.

"But Dolan was grown up," Mary pointed out. "He was sixteen and was very handsome."

"Satan was a beautiful angel also before he was cast out of Heaven," the old woman answered, then shut her eyes again.

"She was such a cute little girl," she remembered. "Those dark curls should have alerted folks that she was a Roswald, but if anyone suspected, they didn't say. Her parents brought her to a picnic or something at the manor and her Roswald mark was visible for the whole world to see."

"You made me take her home and change her clothes," Mary said defiantly. "That was when I became aware that you knew our secret."

"It would ruin Dolan's reputation and your marriage to have the child running around the place," Lavida said. "You young people just don't realize how immoral you've become. God will deal with your vile conduct."

"But God doesn't steal and destroy!" Briana said angrily. "He didn't take me away from my mother and send me off to California to be with strangers."

A deep sigh came from the bed and the sad old woman raised the tiny cross to her lips. "The child's mother was dying and the lady who was caring for the girl called me as a last resort, saying she could not afford to keep her. I got the impression she was wanting money from us, so I dealt with it myself and I didn't tell anyone."

"Did you ever send Connie money?" Mary asked.

"No, I was wrong. The woman just wanted to get rid of the child, because she had to go somewhere up north and couldn't take the child with her. Mary was terminal and lingering. It would only be days before she would die."

Briana heard her mother sniff and turned to see tears streaming down her cheeks.

"I had to quietly find another solution to this disgrace. Since I was on a committee here in town that dealt with foundlings and adoption services, I did some checking and found a service out of Kansas City who would take the child and place her with a respectable family. I was not told where this family would be, or when the child would be taken. They were going to pay me for her, but I explained that it wasn't necessary. They said they would deduct the amount on the other end. I hope they did."

Briana couldn't imagine anyone treating life so carelessly. She wished she could stay angry at this old tyrant, but she mainly felt pity.

"Did you know later that I hadn't died?" Mary asked.

"Not for years. Gladys saw you on the street in Topeka at one time and she mentioned it. She didn't talk to you, of course, but was very shocked to see you alive. Not half as shocked as I was!"

"So why didn't you try to find me and tell me where my child was?"

"I didn't know and it was too late," Lavida whispered sadly. "The people who took your daughter weren't with a legal adoptive agency. I had no way of knowing where the child was or what her new name would be. I only knew that the babysitter had concocted a story for the other tenants of the apartment house explaining that the child had died."

Lavida looked up at Mary and asked, "Is that what you were told?"

Mary was wiping her tears with a tissue as she remembered the words. The horrible, heart-wrenching words that pneumonia had claimed Sabrina's life.

"Yes," Mary whispered, realizing the woman had probably missed a good portion of her discourse the night before.

"I was very upset about this turn of events," Lavida went on. "If the mother of the child were still alive, she would want to see where her daughter was buried. She might even visit her husband's grave, so what better place to sprinkle the ashes of her child? It was easy to get a marker and place it on the grave."

"There was definitely a lot of evil going on," Mary said accusingly. "I believe people have choices in life. They can do what is right and live godly lives in Jesus, or they can ignore his teachings like you did, causing pain and suffering to the innocent."

Had her old great-grandma not looked so defeated, Briana would have cheered her mother's words.

"You are right, of course, and I have been punished all these years for my interference," Lavida said. "Cyrus was taken from me, though I asked God to spare him and take me, but that would have been too easy. I was left to suffer, and I knew why, but of course I couldn't tell a soul." Tears trickled down the wrinkled, parchment-textured cheeks. "I am so sorry," she whispered.

There was silence in the room for a long time, then Briana said, "I've had a very good life. The people who adopted me are the best parents a child could want. They had a secret also, that was kept hidden for over twenty years. They adopted me illegally, but never told me until I moved to Kansas and stumbled onto familiar places.

"My family is happy I have found my birth parents, but I'm not sure I will tell them my own great-grandmother was the one who sent me away."

Anger tinged Briana's words and she would have left the room if Mary had not caught her arm and stayed her. Lavida was crying, so Mary sat down on the edge of the bed and took the frail, blue-veined hand in hers.

"I have found my child, Lavida. She has been brought up well, and I'm proud of her, so I forgive you, before God and Sabrina, for what you did. You should not have to live the rest of your days with my anger and condemnation eating at all three of us.

"You have claimed to us that you are a Christian and I don't doubt that. I also do not doubt the fact that God has reunited my daughter and me for a particular reason. That reason, I believe, is to give us an opportunity to tell you we forgive you. To let your life be free of the guilt and the burden you have had to bear all these years."

Briana saw her mother's face almost glowing with love as Mary rose from the bed.

"I'm so sorry," Lavida cried. "I was the evil one. I was wrong!"

Briana looked at her misery and stepped closer to the bed.

"I have listened to all of this with anger in my heart," Briana began. "I was rejected—not because of myself, but because of an error my parents made. Yet I was a secret that couldn't be silenced, not even over the years.

"Whether I'm called Sabrina or Briana, I am me, not just Mary's indiscretion or Dolan's lust. I'm me! I have parents, and I have a career, so I will not be a burden to anyone, especially not the Roswald family.

"What I have heard here today has not been about someone trying to get rid of a child to hurt the mother, but about someone who was protecting a grandson who was loved and cherished in spite of his youthful mistake. You are a very strong woman, Great-Grandma Roswald. You're made of pioneer stock that is badly needed in our society today.

"You made an error that affected many lives, but if my mother can forgive you for the years of pain she has endured, then I certainly shall also. God will be the judge when it's all said and done. We are mere mortals who try not to judge lest we be judged!"

Lavida reached out with her wizened hands and caught both of their hands in hers, but could not speak.

CHAPTER 26

The ride back to Tyler's farm was a silent one and neither of the men asked what had taken place upstairs. One look at the emotional expressions on the women's faces told them they wouldn't want to discuss it right now.

When they entered the house Bea told Mary and Jim that they had a phone message from home and needed to return the call immediately. Fortunately, it wasn't a major emergency. Janet had fallen in the snow while trick-or-treating with Doug and had broken her left wrist. Greg had taken care of everything and she now sported a cast.

Mary asked all the usual questions and was finally satisfied that Janet was all right, but somehow the exuberance and intensity of the whole weekend had diminished. Tyler suggested going home early and Briana was glad when Mary and Jim agreed.

On the way back to Topeka, Mary and Briana told the men about their confrontation with Lavida. They shared the emotions everyone felt, the guilt that was exposed, and how their anger was put to rest.

"Are you satisfied with the end results, Mary?" Tyler asked when the whole story was told.

"I'm just so happy to have Sabrina...Briana...." she laughed, "...my daughter back, that I really can't even think about the crime. I feel that Lavida has suffered enough for her part in this. She's old and very sad."

"I'm going to send her a card when we get home," Briana decided. "She might tear it up, since I'm so evil, but at least I'll know I reached out."

"You aren't evil!" Tyler growled, looking at her in the mirror.

"Good luck convincing her!" Briana quickly answered.

The smile Briana got made her shiver as if he had touched her, and she remembered about the hot tub. It hadn't been mentioned, but of course the evening had been rough on everyone. There would not be another opportunity to share it, because she would not be coming back up north, nor would she have another occasion to go to Tyler's farm. She felt sad about that, but she would have to bury herself in her work and put him out of her mind.

Tyler delivered the Duncans to their home first, and Janet came out to show them her cast and to collect their autographs on it. Briana wrote, "Your Sis, Bri," which delighted the girl immensely.

When Briana and Tyler reached her driveway she asked him if he wanted to come in for coffee. He seemed to realize that she was exhausted and preoccupied, so he declined. He did walk her to the door, carrying her suitcase. After setting it in the doorway, he gathered her into his arms and just held her.

She tensed at first, then began to respond to his touch. Tears seemed to flood her eyes so she squeezed them tightly, hiding her face in his neck. She knew that she sensed her reluctance to talk and respected that. Briana's heart was so full of love she thought she would explode.

Finally he grasped her shoulders and stepped away. "I need to let you go so you don't catch cold." While his mouth was saying that, his eyes were saying something else.

Her lips parted to reply, but no words came forth.

"Briana..." he began, but at the same moment Tiffany began to bark, wondering why they weren't coming into the house. The moment was lost. The spell was broken, and with a quick kiss Tyler was gone.

As Briana put her things away, she reflected on the whole trip. She had enjoyed her mother's company very much. She was wonderful to be with, and so was Jim. The party had been enjoyable until the announcement on the steps. Even that went well, in spite of the emotional scene that followed. The disclosure was behind her, and she had come away unscathed. She was so glad her mother Mary had been with her giving her support.

The fear and recrimination were at an end, and the anger she and Mary had felt was gone. An old woman would spend a few happy years knowing that mother and child had been reunited.

Once more, Briana let Tyler invade her memory. She had almost whispered that she loved him when he embraced her on the porch, and she wondered how he would have reacted if she had done so.

Tyler had not mentioned Adrian lately, and he had not been seen with her at the party. Briana hoped Shelly was right. But if she was, why didn't he talk about his future plans? Why, when everything else was working out so well, did she and Tyler feel closer in some ways—yet farther apart than ever?

When her parents and brothers arrived that Sunday, Briana could hardly wait to pull open the door and be thronged by them. The boys teased her about her dark hair, then got introduced to Tiffany, who immediately went in search of her ball so the boys could throw it for her.

The big family dinner was set for Tuesday evening and Briana had been in touch with the Duncans about her plans. Tyler, Tom, and Shelly were invited too, so her little home was going to be packed.

Briana had confided some of her anxieties about such a big party to Mary on their Marysville excursion and Mary had suggested that she could come early and help. Mary would bring food, even though Briana insisted she had enough. Shelly had received the same instructions and was still bringing a cake.

Briana decided that God had timed this very well, because this way her two mothers could meet before the rest of the crowd arrived.

When the doorbell rang, her brother Richard answered it and seemed pleased that Mary had brought Janet with her. Briana came out of the kitchen, wiping her hands on a tea towel, and greeted the new arrivals.

"I'm so glad you came early. Mom and I aren't making much headway."

"I thought perhaps an extra set of hands might be needed, so I asked Janet to tag along. Although with Janet, we'll just get one extra hand! The men will come later."

Briana turned to welcome Janet but she was talking to Richard, who was signing her cast. Janice came out of the kitchen about the same time that Mark and Wade entered from the garage.

"Well," Briana began, fidgeting and twisting her towel. "Mom, this is Mom!" Everyone laughed at her self-conscious introduction.

Janice looked at Mary for only a second, then put her arms around the stranger and said, "Thank you for such a lovely daughter. I'm so sorry she was taken from you in such a way, but we have kept her safe and brought her up to be a good Christian woman."

Mary hugged Janice and together they wept, and so did everyone else. Then the sharing began as the story was told from the Sheldons' side while the women prepared the meal.

Mary told Janice about Briana's childhood, then turned to Briana to add, "By the way, I was up in the attic the other day and found a box with some of your clothes in it. Your doll was there and I meant to bring it, but I'll call and see if Jim will. It really looks bad compared to the modern dolls, and it was well used. Of course, you took it everywhere when you were little."

"My, how she mourned for her baby when she came to us," Janet said. "Poor little one, taken from her mommy and her baby all at once. How could a Christian person do such a thing?"

Mary smiled and shook her head. "Lavida was wrong," she said, "and she has been eaten alive with guilt over the years, but she's eighty-five now, so I'm glad we found out the truth before she died. I'm sure she asked God's forgiveness when she became aware that I was still alive, but this whole episode needed to come out to clear the air."

They went over the search for Briana's real parents and Janice was made aware of the courage it took for Briana to keep going.

"But it was worth it, Mom. Look what a lovely new mother I have and sisters, brothers, grandmas, and grandpas. A great-grandma, aunts, and uncles!" She cast a glance at Mary. "I wonder just how popular I'll be with the Roswalds after my coming out?"

"That will be the real test," Mary said.

Later her family and friends gathered around the big table and everyone devoured the food after a heartfelt grace was said. The laughter flowed and it felt like they were already family. After complimenting the women on the fine meal, the men offered to do the dishes and were quickly taken up on their offer, giving the women time to bring out the photo albums. Viewing pictures of a baby born to a farmhand and his wife brought new tears to Janice's eyes. Mary gazed intently at her child growing up before her eyes in school pictures from kindergartener to college graduate.

The laughter and camaraderie in the kitchen announced that the men were enjoying their work also. Greg had brought his guitar and was playing some tunes in the front room. Before long, they were all singing. Tyler had an excellent voice. He glanced over at Briana a couple of times and smiled.

Her mother from California watched the exchange and smiled. "He's a wonderful man," she whispered, causing Briana to look at Tyler, only to find him taking in this whole scene. Briana blushed and turned slightly to hide from his gaze.

"He's more than wonderful, Mom. He's the love of my life!"

Her mom beamed and glanced back at Tyler. Briana of course, had to sneak a peek just to see if he was still looking her way. He was. She felt like a teenager when he laughed outright

"You need to tell me more about this affair," her mother prodded.

"Mom, it isn't an affair! I'm still not willing to lose my virginity for just anyone. It has to be my husband, Mom, just as you taught me."

"You're still my smart daughter," Janice complimented, patting her hand lovingly.

The evening was a great success, and so was the rest of her family's visit. Richard called Janet to see if she could go out with him, but Mary and Jim explained that she was too young. They suggested that all of them might go to the movies together, which they did. Janice, Wade, and the boys visited the museum and malls while Briana was at work; when she got home, they filled her in on their day. Then on Thursday morning, after a teary farewell, the Sheldons headed west again, retracing their way home to California.

Briana felt the time had gone too fast, though she enjoyed the quiet in her house and the chance to focus more closely on her job. Kyle updated her later that day about a tentative settlement on the spur line problem in Marshall County.

"Tomorrow there's a final meeting in Marysville, and I'd like you to go with me. It's set for two o'clock, so I think we'd better plan on staying over. I still can't afford to get tired even though the doctor says I'm recovering faster then he expected. I'll make reservations, if that's okay?"

She agreed and remembered her last stay up there in a motel. What a strange turn of events—now one of those culprits was her own brother.

Kyle picked her up at her home the next morning, and they followed the same route out of town that Tyler had taken when they went to the Roswalds' party. When they reached Wamego, Briana recalled the scene at the boot store and wondered if Tyler would be at this meeting. She should have called. Maybe not. If he were going, he should have informed her.

"Am I really necessary at this meeting?" she asked Kyle.

"Now is not the time to decline," he laughed. "You were asked to attend by the Roswalds. I think they were satisfied with the way you handled the groundwork on this."

"It could be they are trying to be nice to me since we're now related!"

"Well, I don't know their motives, but I'm pleased with the way it worked out. You did an excellent job on this case, which was not an easy task with me on sick leave. Everyone has profited, and at least the Blue Line spur will be secure under a small shortline from Nebraska. It will be in their best interests to expand into Kansas even though it's only a spur. The line could have been bought for salvage, so I'd say the Roswald group should feel pretty good about the transaction."

The meeting was held in the same building as before, in the same conference room. Briana scanned the room for Tyler, looking at the small clusters of men chatting prior to the start of the meeting. She was disappointed not to find him, but she did see Dolan, who broke away quickly and came toward her.

"I've started to call you so many times, but to tell you the truth, I always lost my nerve."

Briana looked at her father in bewilderment. "You lost your nerve?" She was amazed. "But why?"

"I'm not proud of my part in this disaster of parenthood, but I want you to know how pleased I am that this has all come out. What a horrible thing it is to have to go through life holding secrets.

"In the Sixties these things were not uncommon anywhere in the country. Hippies were pollinating the flower children and no one thought a thing about it, but this just wasn't done in the Roswald family!

"I really thought you and Mary had died. I even went over to Jack's grave one year when we were putting flowers out for Memorial Day and there was a marker with your name on it." Dolan's eyes filled unexpectedly with tears and he turned away.

Briana caught hold of his arm and said softly, "I've had a happy, good life in spite of what happened to me. I was blessed by God when I was placed with my folks in California, because they were the best parents a child could ask for."

She bit her trembling lip before adding, "Mary and I have forgiven all of you for any wrongdoing, and nothing can be changed. We are who we are, and you don't need to worry that I will interrupt your life or that of your family. I'm delighted to be reunited with my real mother, and she has a lovely new family I enjoy very much.

"I passed the Kansas bar exam in September, so now I can practice law here in this state. The Santa Fe has been good to me, so I'll probably stay employed with them, but I'll make that decision when the time comes."

Briana glanced past Dolan to watch a familiar figure enter the room. Tyler's eyes also swept the room until they met hers. "Hi," they said across the fifteen-foot expanse.

Dolan turned to see who had caught her attention and greeted the young lawyer as he drew near.

"Glad you could make it," Dolan said, shaking Ty's hand. Before they could say any more the meeting was called to order and people took their seats.

Briana's briefcase was in the chair beside Kyle, so she was obligated to sit there, but she was hoping Tyler would sit nearby. As it turned out he took a seat four chairs to her right and she couldn't see him at all. Maybe it was just as well, since she didn't want to make a fool of herself in front of all these businessmen.

Just before the speaker began, the outer door opened and Irene and Chad entered, taking seats by the door. Briana turned and met Chad's stony stare. Irene smiled, then gave her attention to the speaker.

The meeting went into great detail, explaining the plans for repair as well as reinforcing some bridges and trestles. The short line railroad intended to update the spur and hopefully draw in other business in addition to the farms. It would also increase their ability to connect with another short line they hoped to acquire next year. Eventually, this might even reduce the shipping costs of cattle and grain for the Marshall County businesses.

There was an abundance of dry discussion and Briana really did try to keep her mind in check, but in the end she gave up. Tyler was there and she wanted to be close to him. She hoped he felt the same.

CHAPTER 27

The crisp winter air caught at Briana's long, dark hair as she and Kyle emerged from the courthouse and walked across the parking lot to his car.

"Well," he began, "I guess that will be the end of our work up here."

Briana turned to reply, but was stopped by two strong hands that grasped her shoulders from behind.

"I'm going to borrow your assistant, Kyle," Tyler said. Without waiting for an answer, he began guiding her toward his pickup.

"How long are you planning to detain me?" she asked breathlessly.

"Forever," he whispered.

"I have a suitcase in Kyle's car...." she began.

"Aha, you came prepared!"

He was teasing her and she tried to take it lightly, but longing was pulsing through her entire body.

"No...er...Kyle and I were staying the night."

"Are you two-timing me?" Tyler asked.

Kyle entered in with a light-hearted rebuttal. "She has a reservation at the Best Western...." he began, then chuckled. "Actually, we both have a reservation!"

"So what you're saying is...."

Tyler would have continued jesting, but stopped mid-sentence as Briana's raised voice accused, "Sexual harassment! I will not be subjected to such goings-on in the courthouse parking lot!"

Hard-pressed to keep from laughing, Tyler suggested, "Then let's go to the farm where we can continue this."

Bri looked at him for a second, thinking he was inviting both Kyle and her, but Tyler quickly said, "We'll get your things first and then you can spend the night with me."

Her brain wouldn't function. What in the world was Tyler trying to do to her reputation? She had only a second to glance at Kyle before Tyler urged her toward Kyle's car. Then Dolan and Irene approached them.

"I'm glad we caught you before you left, Briana," Dolan began. "We would like you and Tyler to come for dinner this evening, if you can. Nothing fancy, you understand."

Irene smiled and said, "Please say you will." Then she looked closely at Briana and added, "You'll have to excuse all of us for staring at you, but you look so much like our Deb. Especially at a distance." Tears welled up in the woman's eyes and Briana felt compassion.

"I'm sorry to bring back your loss each time we are together. I wish I had known her, but maybe you can tell me more about her this evening?"

"Then you'll come? Great. Come around six or earlier. I'll plan dinner for 6:30."

Irene was clearly pleased the invitation had been accepted, but Briana looked past the couple and saw Chad watching the group from his father's truck.

"We'll see you tonight, then," Dolan's voice boomed as they turned to join their son.

Before Briana could take it all in, she was sitting next to Tyler as he wheeled his truck out onto the red-bricked street and headed south to his farm. He kept up a steady conversation about the spur line and went into details about the new railroad taking it over.

As they talked, Briana remembered why she loved this man. He was so easy to be with—comfortable and interesting, too. He had a great sense of humor and she loved him to distraction.

Bea met them at the door and asked Tyler what time they would want dinner. Tyler explained their plans.

"So where's our little Tiffany?" Bea asked.

"Mary's daughter Janet is babysitting her at their house, and the whole family adores her. I hope she'll behave, but I'm afraid I've spoiled her miserably."

Tyler took Briana's suitcase to her usual room and after setting it beside the bed, turned and caught her in his arms. "I have missed you so much," he murmured as his lips sought and claimed hers.

Helpless to stop herself, Briana's hands went up to the back of his head and she surrendered to the desires she was experiencing.

A discreet coughing sound interrupted them. Briana opened her eyes and saw Bea in the doorway.

"I'm sorry, Tyler, but Cecil is on the phone. He's at the stable." Tyler released Briana and left the room. Bea started to follow but Briana called out to her.

"Bea, I hope you don't mind that I'm spending the night here. I don't want you to think...." She hesitated, wishing she had never brought up the subject.

Bea smiled and took Briana's hand in hers.

"You don't have to worry about offending Cecil and I, my dear. You can consider us chaperones if anyone else gets nosy!"

Bea lowered her voice and looked down the hall. "Tyler had a long talk with us one evening in answer to some questions we raised about you. He said for a modern California girl you had very strict moral values. He was letting us know you were...are...That you didn't...well, he respects you and wouldn't do anything to jeopardize that."

Briana was thinking about that conversation as she and Tyler drove up the hill to Dolan and Irene's home that evening. This seesaw relationship could not endure much longer, and if need be, she would end it this very night.

The Roswalds were excellent hosts, and the meal was delicious. The steak was "the best," of course.

Briana began to smile when she realized their favorite term now included her. If everything the Roswalds had was the best, then she was half best. Wasn't she?

Chad, Mark, and Penny were very talkative and Chad even asked if he could watch when Briana showed Penny some self-defense holds.

"You are one mean lady when you're riled," he admitted. "Do I have to call you Sis?"

Briana laughed. "You can call me anything you want as long as it isn't offensive. You can be sure I'll let you know if it is!"

Mark explained that Grandma Lavida had told them Briana was an evil spirit, and that she was there to haunt the Roswald family.

"That's when Chad decided we'd call you and scare you off. Boy did Tyler chew our butts out over that!"

"Mark, you can't say 'butts,'" Penny reminded him in a lecturing tone.

"So what? Does 'rears' make it sound any better?" he sneered.

"There is a code of decency, Mark," Briana said. "You didn't have to explain what Tyler chewed on. I got the point." She continued, "I'm sorry you have all been dragged into this situation, but I'm very glad to have found my birth mother and father. Now I have three sets of parents!"

"You don't look much like Deb," Chad informed her bluntly. "Deb was the greatest sister in the world."

"I'm sure she was, Chad, and I am not in any way going to try to take her place. My life is in Topeka, so there is no way I will interfere with your family. Your mother showed me the albums with Deb's pictures in them. She was so young to die! Tyler says she's with God now, and she is much better off than any of us here on earth. It is such a comfort to know a loved one is saved."

The children looked at her in amazement as tears trickled down her cheeks over the sister she had never met. Chad cleared his throat and walked away, but Mark and Penny wept with her.

It was late when Tyler brought Briana back to his lovely berm home nestled into the base of Blue Hill. Bea and Cecil had stoked up the fire in the magnificent stone fireplace in the sunken living room. The lights were low, causing the flames to cast shadows out into the room. *This is all so beautiful,* Briana thought as she hesitated at the arched doorway. The firewood snapped and crackled as it burned and she breathed in the sweet aroma it created.

"Let's go out to the hot tub before we retire," Tyler suggested. "If Bea followed my instructions, there's a swimsuit on your bed. Of course, skinny dipping is also allowed!" He watched her face turn sober at his teasing, yet suggestive remark. He quickly assured her, "Maybe not tonight...our relationship still isn't defined. I didn't mean to make you uncomfortable."

The swimsuit was there, but Briana had almost lost her nerve. She had swum with him in the pool, of course, but this was more intimate. She knew her feelings for him were passionate and she recognized a similar fervor in him. How she yearned to know what his true intentions were! A long white terrycloth robe was lying next to the swimsuit, so she decided that would cover her well enough until she could quickly step down into the tub.

The enclosed patio was cool when she walked out of the front door, but her robe kept her toasty.

"You would have taken less time if you'd opted for the skinny dip plan," Tyler joked as she quickly lowered herself into the warm water.

He reached out and took her forearms, guiding her to a molded seat next to him and put his arm around her shoulders. Briana tensed at his tender touch and started to pull away.

"You are safe with me, my darling," he whispered in her ear, then claimed her lips.

"Oh Tyler, please...."

"I love you, Briana. I can't get you out of my mind—and believe me, I've tried. You just walked into my life and stole my heart."

He was kissing her again and Briana tried to digest his words, but her mind was still on his "I love you."

He turned her around to face him and then murmured, "Marry me, Briana. Put me out of my misery and say yes, sweetheart."

"I can't believe this is happening. Tell me I'm not dreaming. Of course, I'll marry you. I love you so very much. But...."

"No buts, just kisses," he growled, claiming her lips once more as he hugged her tightly. Briana knew it wasn't the warmth of the hot tub that was making her light-headed.

Later they curled up on a quilt in front of the warm fireplace, wrapped in their terrycloth robes. The throw pillows from the sofa made a cushion for Tyler's head and his arm made one for Briana's. When would she wake up? Was this real?

He dropped kisses on her head and sighed, "You're the loveliest fiancée a man could ask for."

"Tyler, you won't compare me with Deb, will you?"

"As a wife or lover?"

Briana blushed and buried her face against his neck.

"Either," she answered breathlessly.

"Since you have no experience in either, I'll make sure you learn it all. It takes a lot of practice," he assured her. "Somehow I'm sure you'll excel in both categories." Briana smiled at his confidence and prayed she would be able to bring happiness to Ty. But there was one more issue she had to resolve.

"I thought you were going to marry Adrian," she blurted out.

"You *what?* Why would you think that?"

She told him about Penny's report, and he assured her it was a figment of the child's imagination.

"I've never been serious about Adrian," Tyler assured her, astonished that she could think such a thing.

"But I called your apartment one night and she answered, saying you were in the shower. What else could I think?"

317

"I have never showered with Adrian in my apartment. She would probably have jumped in to share it with me!"

"Exactly what I thought," Briana agreed.

"She and Brenda stayed at my place the weekend the colt was born, since they were having new carpet laid at their place. Was that when you called?"

"Maybe." she snuggled closer to him. "I was so jealous I vowed never to let you touch me again. In fact, I was through with you forever!" Her voice softened. "Until I saw you again, that is. You don't know the anguish you've caused me."

"Poor baby," he murmured as he kissed her softly. "Any other questions you need answered?" he asked, pulling his arm free from her head and leaning over her.

"That lady at the courthouse—Dorothy, I think. She asked you if 'she' had set the date yet. I assumed that meant the wedding date."

"Briana, you poor darling. No wonder you are such a good lawyer—you don't miss a thing! Dorothy asked me if Gladys had set the date for their return to the States."

Briana reached up and pulled his head down to her waiting lips, then murmured, "Even believing you were committed to someone else, I still couldn't keep away from you. Oh Tyler, I do love you so much!"

After a while, Tyler asked, "When will we get married? It has to be soon. I don't play this monk role well."

Briana laughed, visualizing him in a brown robe with a hood. "I agree, sweetheart. How about a New Year's Eve ceremony?"

He groaned. "How about tomorrow?"

"What kind of wedding? It has to be performed by a pastor," she mused. "Do you want a big church wedding?"

"We're going to have to if we are going to accommodate the whole United States trucking fleet! Are you ever going to explain about them?"

"I might," she said playfully. "Does it worry you?"

"The only thing that had me worried was that you might say no. I talked to your parents before they left and your father gave me his blessing. I also told Dolan tonight that I hoped to marry you. He offered to give us a large formal wedding; as your father he felt it was the least he could do to make up for the lost years. What about that?"

"Oh my, should I accept all that? He's like a stranger. None of my family are wealthy enough to spend big money on weddings."

"He offered, Bri."

"But would it be proper?"

"He's your father. But, it's your choice. I think we should send your California family airline tickets for the occasion. Will they be surprised?"

"Probably. I told Mom you were marrying someone else."

"I think she and your father realized that wasn't true when I found a chance to talk to Wade while they were visiting. I made them promise not to breathe a word to you until I had a chance to propose so I see they kept the ruse up. I'm so glad I was able to meet the wonderful family that helped you become the woman I love."

He chuckled. "Will I be marrying Sabrina or Briana? I guess we'd better get your records in order before the wedding. What else do we need to do before the big day?"

"Do you have a bear rug?" she asked softly in his ear.

"Bear rug?" he looked down at her flushed face and frowned for a second.

"It would look lovely here before the fire for our wedding night," she whispered shyly.

"I'll order one tomorrow, my love," Tyler promised, and he began kissing her once more.

ABOUT THE AUTHOR

Peggy Merritt was born in Spokane, Washington, to a very interesting group of relatives. Her great-grandmother was first cousin to Mark Twain. Of course, she didn't know who he was back then.

Peggy's grade school teachers encouraged her interest in writing and asked her to write the school play, which she did. Her first published novel was *Snow Cap*. Poems have always come easily to her, so her notebook is full of them from over the years. She has lived near Topeka, Kansas, for over forty years.